more
Pongwiffy
stories

This omnibus edition published in Great Britain in 2018 by Simon & Schuster UK Ltd
A CBS COMPANY

Pongwiffy: The Spell of The Year first published by Viking 1992
Pongwiffy: The Holiday of Doom first published by Viking 1995

1 3 5 7 9 10 8 6 4 2

Simon & Schuster UK Ltd
1st Floor, 222 Gray's Inn Road
London
WC1X 8HB

www.simonandschuster.co.uk

Simon & Schuster Australia, Sydney
Simon & Schuster India, New Delhi

A CIP catalogue record for this book is available from the British Library.

PB ISBN 978-1-4711-6740-9
eBook ISBN 978-1-4711-6741-6

Printed and bound by CPI Group (UK) Ltd, Croydon, CR0 4YY

Simon & Schuster UK Ltd are committed to sourcing paper
that is made from wood grown in sustainable forests and support the Forest
Stewardship Council, the leading international forest certification organisation.
Our books displaying the FSC logo are printed on FSC certified paper.

CONTENTS

WITCHES AND FAMILIARS

more

Pongwiffy
stories

The spell of the year

CHAPTER ONE
An Interesting Find

'Well now, just look at this! Hey, Hugo, look what I've found!' called Witch Pongwiffy from the murky depths of an ancient chest.

At the time, they were in the middle of spring-cleaning – yes, *spring-cleaning* – Number One, Dump Edge, which is the name of Pongwiffy's hovel. Well, if you want to be strictly accurate, Hugo and the Broom were spring-cleaning and Pongwiffy was getting in the way.

'Oh my. Now vat she got? Old bird's nest? Anuzzer overdue library book?' sighed Hugo to the

1

Broom, who was wildly rooting about under the kitchen table.

The Broom gave a disinterested shrug. It had never been allowed to sweep up before, and was terribly over-excited. It had just built its first ever pile of dirt, and right now all it could think about was adding to it.

'No, really!' insisted Pongwiffy. 'This is interesting! Come on down and see for yourself.'

'No. I spring-cleanink,' said Hugo firmly.

He was standing on the top step of a rickety stepladder, swiping at cobwebs with a feather duster. He had declared war on the Spiders, and nothing was going to stop him.

'Spring-cleaning, my foot! I'm talking *Magic* here. Look at this! It might well be the discovery of the century!'

Pongwiffy emerged red-faced from the chest and scuttled across the hovel, scattering the Broom's beautiful dirt-pile in all directions. In her hand, she held a large, mouldering book.

'Look! Granny Malodour's old Spell Book! I've often wondered where it got to. She gave it to me for my eighty-first birthday. Of course, I was just a youngster then. Thought it was old-fashioned sort

2

of stuff, never really bothered to look at it. And it's been at the bottom of the chest all these years. Oh, stop it, Broom!'

The Broom was enthusiastically trying to sweep her out of the door. Being so new to this spring-cleaning business, it hadn't quite got the hang of things yet. Pongwiffy gave it a brisk kick which sent it zooming off into a sordid corner, where it worked away humming to itself, not being the type to bear a grudge.

'Well, well, well. Just fancy. Old Granny Malodour. It's ages since I thought of her.'

'Who Granny Malodour?' asked Hugo.

'You've never heard me talk of Granny Malodour? If you think *I'm* smelly, you should have got a whiff of Granny. Lived by herself in an underground cave. Shared it with a skunk for a while, but even he had to come up for air eventually. She was an expert on cave fungus, you know. There were at least six varieties growing on her sofa. And as for Magic! There was no one to touch her. She kept at it, you see, down in that old cave of hers. She only came up for important family gatherings. When there was cake. She was a Serious Witch. You wouldn't catch her wasting time doing stupid *spring-cleaning*!'

3

Pongwiffy glared scornfully at Hugo, who shrugged and continued with his dusting.

'I'll never forget her famous Wishing Water,' went on Pongwiffy nostalgically. 'Wonderful stuff, that was. She used to send up a bottle every Hallowe'en, I remember, and we'd all get a sip, even us little kids. Tasted disgusting, but it was worth it.'

'Vy? Vat 'appen?'

'Why, we'd all get a wish, of course. And it always came true. Granny's potions were like that. Very reliable.'

'Vat you vish for?' asked Hugo.

'A little Sweet House all of my own,' said Pongwiffy dreamily.

'Vat 'appen to it?'

'It melted in the heat and flies got stuck to it. In the end I had to throw it away. But it was lovely when it was new. I can taste that chocolate guttering now.'

'Vishing Vater sound good stuff,' said Hugo. 'Vy ve not make some?'

'I wish we could,' said Pongwiffy regretfully. 'Granny Malodour always kept the recipe a secret. Probably thought it wasn't good for us to get too much of a good thing. Oh, do stop flicking that

4

duster about, Hugo, you're driving me mad. Leave the stupid old spring-cleaning. So what if there's a crumb or two on the floor? I couldn't care less.'

'That because you not 'Amster,' Hugo pointed out. 'Me, I live close to ze ground. It awful down zere.'

It was true. For anyone hamster-sized, the hovel floor was a minefield. If the toast crumbs didn't get you, the smelly socks would. If by some miracle you avoided both, the chances were you'd slip and drown in a puddle of skunk stew.

But if it was bad at ground level, it was even worse higher up – because higher up were the Spiders.

Ooh, those cocky Spiders. They were really getting above themselves these days, acting as though the place belonged to them. Just recently they'd taken to practising daredevil trapeze acts on the trailing cobwebs looping from the ceiling.

'Hoop-la!' they yelled to each other in Spider language. 'OK, Stan, now the triple roll, after three! Don't worry, I'll catch yer!'

Hugo had put up with it all for as long as he could. But when high-diving into his bedside glass of water became the latest Spider craze, he had dug his paws in and declared that Pongwiffy must choose between him and the dirt, for one of them had to go.

After careful thought, Pongwiffy had decided to part with the dirt. After all, dirt could be replaced, whereas a good Familiar was hard to find. Besides, he owed her eleven pence.

'You're supposed to be my Familiar, remember?' Pongwiffy reminded him, picking bits of cobweb from her mouth. 'I do think you could show a bit more interest. After all, it is a family heirloom.'

Crossly, she opened the ancient book and gave a wail of disappointment.

'Oh no! The bookworms have been at it. Look, they've chewed up nearly every page!'

'Typical,' said Hugo. 'All zat fuss about nussink. Typical.'

'Oh, wait a minute! There's something written on the inside of the cover. It looks like Granny Malodour's writing. It's faded, but I think I can make it out. Where are my reading glasses?'

'Zem I sling out.'

'You threw out my *reading glasses*? How dare you!' Pongwiffy was outraged.

'Zey got no glass. Zey not glasses, zey frameses.'

'I know, but that's beside the point. I always saw

better with them.'

Huffily, Pongwiffy carried the disintegrating book to a window so that she could see better. Hugo was still concentrating on cobwebs and hadn't got to the window-cleaning stage yet. The cracked pane was so encrusted with dirt that it let in marginally less light than the wall. Pongwiffy briefly considered cleaning it, then smashed it with a poker to save time.

The Broom did a double take at the sound of falling glass and came rushing up, keen as mustard. The sun, long a stranger to the inside of Pongwiffy's hovel, burst in curiously, lighting first on the opened book with Granny Malodour's spidery writing scrawled mysteriously all over the inside cover.

'Well, I never did! Would you believe it! Just fancy that. Hugo, guess what Granny's written inside the cover?'

''Ow I know?' said Hugo with a shrug. 'Vat?'

'The recipe! The *recipe*, Hugo! For Wishing Water! Oh, this is the most amazing piece of luck! Just think, Hugo, Granny's secret recipe, and it's been passed down to me! Ooh, I simply can't wait to try it out. You don't get spells like this nowadays. There are some very interesting ingredients. It'll be quite a challenge getting hold of some of these, I can tell

7

you. Hey! I've just had a thought! I could enter it for the Spell of the Year Competition!'

'Ze vat?' asked Hugo.

'Spell of the Year Competition. As advertised in *The Daily Miracle*. The winner gets a big silver cup, and all sorts of brilliant prizes. Where's yesterday's paper?'

'I sling out. I sling out all ze papers.'

'You threw it *out*? Idiot!'

Furiously, Pongwiffy ran out of the hovel. There was a scrabbling noise, followed by the sort of slithering crash that might be made by a very tall pile of old newspapers falling from a very great height. Then she was back.

'Found it. Look!'

Eagerly, she waved *The Daily Miracle* under Hugo's nose. Hugo looked. Sure enough, the Spell of the Year Competition took up most of the front page.

'Vat make you sink ve vin?' said Hugo.

'Win? Of course we'll win. What chance has a common old Cure For Warts or a stupid old Frog Transformation Spell against a bottle of Granny Malodour's Wishing Water? I tell you, Hugo, with a superior potion like this, we can't fail. Anyway, it's time a Witch won for a change. Last year it was won by some daft conjuror with pigeons up his jumper. Batty Bob and his Boring Birds or something. We'll have to keep it terribly secret, of course. I don't want the other Witches knowing. If they know I've got Granny's recipe, they'll all want it. We'll have to work undercover. Ooh, I simply can't *wait* to get started, can you?'

'Ya,' said Hugo firmly. 'I can. Right now, I do spring-cleanink. You vanna do Magic? Get your Vand and mend zat broken vindow.'

'I shall do no such thing,' said Pongwiffy. She snatched up her Wand, threw it on a chair and sat on it, sulking. Hugo and the Broom ignored her, and quite right too.

CHAPTER TWO
The Spell

Late that night, sitting in her rocking chair in a spanking-clean hovel, nose buried in a hanky, Pongwiffy brooded over Granny Malodour's spell.

All was quiet. Hugo had flaked out on top of a pile of ironing. His cheek pouches sagged with exhaustion and he was snoring loudly.

Outside the hovel, the Broom was soaking its sore bristles in a bucket of water. On the doorstep, a multitude of evicted Spiders were preparing to leave with bitter little cries of 'Come on, boys, we know when we're not wanted', 'Don't forget the flies, Gerald, we'll be peckish later', and things like that.

Pongwiffy peered at the ancient writing by the light of a single candle. She couldn't stand it any brighter in the hovel, because everywhere was so blindingly clean it hurt her eyes.

She hated it. She loathed the way the pots and pans glittered and the way the floor winked at her, daring her to walk on it in muddy boots. She liked her cardigans how they were before, all comfortably matted up and dirty brown with those special holes for her elbows. Pink and blue they were now, with a sissy smell that came from something that Hugo had poured in the water.

In fact, everything smelt all wrong, even the air, which Hugo had sprayed with something out of a can called *Reeka Reeka Roses*. The only way she could breathe was with a hanky over her nose. The hovel just didn't feel like home any more. Pongwiffy hardly dared move without the Broom following her about in case she dropped a crumb. And the fuss Hugo had made when she attempted to climb into bed without washing her feet!

'Oi! Vat zis you do?'

'I'm going to bed, if you must know.'

11

'Not vizzout vashink ze foots.'

'Wash my *feet*? *Me*? Have you gone *mad*? Why?'

'Cos zose is clean sheets.'

'Uggh! So they are!'

Pongwiffy jumped away from the bed as if scalded. 'You don't expect me to sleep in *those*, do you? They're – they're *white*! Yuck, I nearly touched one. Where are my old grey ones?'

'Zem I sling out.'

'*You threw out my sheets?*'

'Ya. Zey not nice. Zey got 'oles. Zey got crumbs. Zey like bottom of ze birdcage.'

'I know. It took years to get them like that, you interfering Hamster. Well, if you think I'm getting in between *those*, you can think again. I'd sooner stay up all night.'

'OK,' said Hugo, yawning. 'Me, I go sleep.'

So that's why we find Pongwiffy in her rocking chair in the small hours of the morning, brooding over Granny Malodour's spell.

And this is what it said.

Wishing Water

(YE RECIPE)

1 x Whisker of Wilde Cat ↑

½ x Bucket of Beste Quicksande

1 x Feathere of Vulture

Fresh Locke of Goldene Hayre from Ye Hede of a Pryncess (Best Cut at Midnight Under Fulle Moone)

1 x Bobble off Ye Hat of A. Gobline

Seven Stolen Stars from a Wizard's Cloake of Darknesse

½ x Jug of Skunke Stocke

1 Teaspoone of Beetle Doos

Frog Spawn & Fly Droppings to Taste

METHOD

On ye night of ye fulle moone, place ye quicksande to simmere in cauldron over a low fyre. Using thy left hand only, take thou a sharpe knyfe and finely chop dry ingredients (hayre, whisker, bobble, feathere and stars). Mix. Add gradually to ye hot quicksande, stirring all ye time. Pour in skunke stocke. Add beetle doos. Season to taste. Bring to boyle. Sit with thy nose pointing due north and thy boots on ye wrong feet. Recite thou ye following chant:

> Snap and crackle, scream and cackle.
> Can't catch cows with fishing tackle.
> Bubble, brew, the way thou oughter.
> Then turn into Wishing Water!

Continue chanting until thou hearest ye cockerel crowe five times. Remove cauldron from heat and allow to cool. Then say ye Magick Words (Bottoms Up!), drink thou of the potion and make thy wish. Best with a side salade.

'Hmm. Sounds easy enough,' muttered Pongwiffy. 'Mind you, some of these ingredients could be a bit tricky. Best have a look to see what I've got.'

Candle in hand, she marched to her Magic cupboard. Now, usually her Magic cupboard was stuffed so full that the doors exploded outwards the moment they were touched. Jars of frogs' legs, packets of beetle eggs, old Wands, cracked crystal balls and paper bags of mysterious powders marked DONT NO WOT THIS IS would all come tumbling out in a huge, satisfying jumble.

Not now, though. Now it was empty. Hugo was nothing if not thorough.

'Right,' said Pongwiffy grimly, surveying the bare shelves. 'Time to make a list and go shopping, I think.'

The next half an hour involved the back of an old envelope, the stub of a pencil, a great deal of head-scratching and a fair amount of scribbling. As soon as the list was finished, she seized her basket and rammed on her hat.

'I'M OFF, THEN,' she announced in an unnecessarily loud voice. 'OFF TO THE SHOPS. STOCKING UP.'

She needn't have bothered. Hugo merely snored even louder. Scowling, she kicked the door open with an almighty crash and stomped out into the moonlit night.

Outside the hovel, the Broom slept in its bucket. All around the front garden, tall piles of beloved junk teetered under the moon, doomed to be returned to the rubbish dump the following morning.

There was her favourite battered old sofa, the one that had nearly got stolen by two Mummies last Hallowe'en. And there was her photograph album with those irreplaceable snaps of Witch Gaga running amok at last year's Coven outing to the Haunted Show House!

Ah! There was her framed letter from Scott Sinister, the famous film star! And there, scattered about all over the place, lay her collection of rude notes to the milkman, which went back seven years. And there were her oldest, smelliest, comfiest cardigans, the ones which Hugo considered a health hazard and refused to wash. There was her first tall hat, a bit battered to be sure but bringing back fond memories. And there was her box of old Wands and her first chemistry set and a pile of crumbling books with titles like *Know Your Omens and Portents* and *My First Little Book of Curses*. And there was her favourite hot-water bottle, and her dead poison plant and her second worst cauldron . . .

Pongwiffy's eyes misted over. But not before she became aware of the accusing stares of a hundred or more exiled Spiders, who muttered and pointed resentfully.

'Huh. Some landlady.'

'After all we done for her.'

'Never got behind with the rent, did we, Mother?'

'Oh Dad! Never to dangle from me own little rafter again. Webless, at my age.'

'Never you mind, Ma, we'll look after you. We'll find you a little nook where you'll be made welcome, see if we don't. Right, boys?'

'I don't think me poor old legs'll get me there. I got terrible rheumatism in all eight knees. Anyway, it won't be home. I'll die of a broken heart, I know I will. If somebody don't step on me first. Or a bird don't get me.'

All of this made Pongwiffy feel even worse. With a guilty flush and a heavy heart she slunk away, heading for the Magic shop. A shopping trip might take her mind off things.

CHAPTER THREE
Dunfer Malpractiss

'Ear yer bin spring-cleanin' dahn your place,' remarked the man behind the counter with an unpleasant leer. His name was Dunfer Malpractiss and he was the owner of Malpractiss Magic Ltd, where all the Witches went to buy ingredients for their spells.

Malpractiss Magic Ltd was, as is usually the case with these sorts of places, a wandering shop which came and went as it pleased. You could never be absolutely sure, if you ran out of eye of newt on a Saturday night, that the shop would even be there to sell you any, let alone have it in stock.

However, Dunfer Malpractiss wasn't stupid. He had a lot of regular customers in Witchway Wood, and the likelihood was that Malpractiss Magic Ltd would be found in the usual place (by the stream under the old oak tree) most nights between the traditional opening hours of midnight and dawn.

'None of your business what I've been doing,' snarled Pongwiffy.

'Yer. Not before time, eh? I'm told it's a bit of a tip, your place,' mused Dunfer, sucking his moustache. It was one of those unpleasant wet ones which droop into cups of coffee and always get covered in froth.

'So? I like it like that. Are you serving or what?'

'Keep yer 'air on. Only sayin'. What were it you wanted again?'

'I've told you!' Irritably, Pongwiffy waved her shopping list under his nose. 'I need a Wilde Cat's Whisker, some Beste Quicksande, a Vulture's Feathere, a . . .'

''Old on, 'old on. One fing at a time. Wilde Cat's Whisker, were it?'

'Yes.'

Dunfer Malpractiss pulled at his nose with

19

dirty fingers.

'Nah. Fresh out. What were the next?'

'Quicksande.'

'Nah. No call fer it these days. There's a pool of it in the Wood somewhere – go an' 'elp yerself.'

'What about Seven Stolen Stars from a Wizard's Cloake of Darknesse?'

'Nah.'

'A Bobble off ye Hat of a Gobline?'

'Nah. Old fashioned sort o' ingredients, ain't they? What sorta spell you doin', anyway?'

'Never you mind. What about Beetle Doos?'

'Nah. No call.'

'Skunke Stocke Cubes?'

'Nah.'

'Frogspawne and Fly Droppings?'

'Nah.'

'Well, you're not much help, I must say,' grumbled Pongwiffy. 'I suppose you haven't got a Vulture's Feathere either?'

'Nah. Gorra coupla budgie ones goin' cheap.'

'Certainly not. It says Vulture, very definitely. I don't know, I thought this was supposed to be a Magic shop. What *do* you sell here?'

She glared around crossly. The shop was

full of shelves, and the shelves were full of jars, bottles, cans and boxes. Several sullen-looking used Broomsticks slunk around behind the counter. That was funny. Why weren't they in their usual place? Pongwiffy suddenly noticed that the Used-Broom rack was stacked with brand new, bright yellow squeezy mops with white plastic handles.

'Cleanin' stuff, mostly. Spring-cleanin' time o' year, ain't it? Yer, I got soap 'n' mop-'eads 'n' tins o' beeswax 'n' air-freshener in cans. Want some? *Reeka Reeka Roses*, this year's smell, very popular, on special offer, I'll do you a squirt . . .'

'Don't you dare!' cried Pongwiffy in alarm. 'Now look, Malpractiss, I'm not *interested* in your cleaning stuff. I'm a Witch, remember, and what I'm interested in is Magic. Got that? So what I want is quicksand and a bobble and a whisker and a feather and a fresh lock of hair from the head of a Princess, and if you can't help me, I'll just have to . . .'

''Ang abaht, 'ang abaht. A lock o' golden 'air orf a Princess's 'ead, did yer say?'

'Yes. Why, have you got one? Strictly speaking, it should have been cut at full moon.'

'Fink I can 'elp you there, matter o' fact. Now, where were it again . . . ?'

21

Slurping into his moustache, Dunfer Malpractiss disappeared into the gloomy shadows at the back of the shop. Moments later, he returned.

'There yer go!' he announced triumphantly, slapping down a dusty old shoebox on the counter. 'One lock o' golden 'air, guaranteed orf a genuine Princess's noddle. That'll be twelve pahnd . . .'

'Just a moment,' interrupted Pongwiffy, taking the lid off the box and peering suspiciously within. 'Is this fresh? The recipe distinctly calls for fresh.'

'Eh? Oh yer, fresh as anythin', that,' said Dunfer, looking shifty.

'Then how come it's grey? This is *grey* golden hair.'

'Eh? Nah, trick o' the light . . .'

'Trick of the light, my foot. Look at the sell-by date on this box, you old fraud. See? BEST USED BEFORE THE STONE AGE.'

'Yer? No kiddin'? 'Ang on, less 'ave a look . . .'

'Never mind. I shall take my custom elsewhere in future,' said Pongwiffy grimly, and strode out with her empty basket.

'Sure yer don't want no bin liners?' came the sad cry.

'Only to stick your head in,' retorted Pongwiffy

rudely, and set off through the trees. Disappointment had made her all the more determined. All right, so Malpractiss Magic Ltd had been a complete waste of time – but the night was yet young, and there was more than one way to skin a cat.

Thinking of cats reminded her of the first ingredient of Granny Malodour's spell. A Wilde Cat's Whisker.

The nearest thing Pongwiffy knew to a wild cat was Dead Eye Dudley, the battered, one-eyed tomcat who belonged to Witch Sharkadder (Pongwiffy's best friend. Sometimes). In fact, they didn't come any wilder than Dudley, who had spent one of his nine lives as ship's cat on a pirate ship. Or so he said.

'I'll go and ask Sharkadder right now,' declared Pongwiffy, setting off through the trees. 'The direct approach usually works. After all, she is my best friend.'

But first, she decided to pop home and collect a few of those rock cakes she had made last month. Just as a little gift.

She hoped Hugo hadn't slung them out.

CHAPTER FOUR
Ye Wilde Cat's Whisker

'Oh, it's you,' said Sharkadder, opening the door a grudging crack. 'What do you want, Pong? I'm terribly busy. I've just finished washing my floor. I don't want your dirty great boots all over it.'

Pongwiffy was shocked. 'Washing the *floor*? What, *now*? But it's the witching hour! Why aren't you cackling over a brew?'

'Because I'm spring-cleaning. It was lovely to see you, Pong. Now go away. Come back in the morning.'

'But I've brought you some rock cakes. Fresh

baked this afternoon,' lied Pongwiffy, trying to force her basket of month-old cakes through the crack.

'Oh, really?' said Sharkadder, immediately suspicious. 'What for? What d'you want?'

'Nothing. Why are you so suspicious all the time? Oh, come on, open up, Sharky. I thought we were best friends. I've had an awful evening. I've just been to the Magic shop and couldn't get a thing I wanted. I just want to put my feet up for two minutes and have a glance at your catalogue. Let me in, do.'

'Oh, very well,' sighed Sharkadder, suddenly taking her shoulder away from the door. Pongwiffy fell past her into the cottage. 'But you're not to stay long. I haven't started the polishing yet.'

Sharkadder waved a tin of beeswax at Pongwiffy and tapped her foot impatiently. She wore a frilly apron with little green frogs embroidered on the pocket. A matching green scarf was twined around her head. Her precious talons were protected by rubber gloves.

Pongwiffy stared around in disapproval. Everything twinkled and gleamed back at her.

'Looks nice, doesn't it?' said Sharkadder.

'No,' said Pongwiffy. 'What's that awful smell?

25

Wait, don't tell me. *Reeka Reeka Roses*. This year's smell. On special offer.'

'How did you know?' said Sharkadder, impressed.

'Never mind. By the way, what are you doing for this year's Spell of the Year Competition?'

'Oh, I don't know. I'll probably enter the formula for my new spot cream. Why?'

'Oh, nothing. Here are your rock cakes,' continued Pongwiffy, holding out the basket. 'I tried out a new recipe. Same as the old one, but you add the granite chippings *after* the egg. That's why they might be a teensy bit harder than usual.'

'Oh, lovely. Very kind. I'll get the hammer,' said Sharkadder, who knew Pongwiffy's rock cakes of old.

'Oh, don't bother now. I should save them until after I've gone,' said Pongwiffy hastily. 'Otherwise you might get chippings all over your nice clean floor.'

'As if you cared about that!' cried Sharkadder. 'Although,' she added curiously, 'correct me if I'm wrong, a little bat told me you've been doing a bit of spring-cleaning yourself!'

'Not me,' denied Pongwiffy stoutly. '*They* are. Hugo and the Broom. Not me. I don't approve.

27

I like my dirt.'

'Nobody else does, though, do they?' Sharkadder pointed out. 'I bet I'm the only visitor you ever get to your hovel.'

'No, you're not,' protested Pongwiffy. 'Loads of visitors come to Dump Edge.'

'Don't shout, Dudley's asleep. Anyway, they don't. Nobody ever goes there because it's so disgustingly dirty and smelly. Even Sludgegooey said she thought you ought to clear up a bit more, and you know what *her* place is like. Actually, talking about visitors and you being so dirty and smelly and everything reminds me: whatever happens, *do not* come to tea next Sunday.'

'Oh. Why not?' asked Pongwiffy, crestfallen. She enjoyed going to Sunday tea with Sharkadder. There were snail and cucumber sandwiches and sometimes little bat-shaped biscuits with currant eyes, as well as one of Sharkadder's delicious fungus sponges.

'Because my nephew Ronald is coming, that's why.'

'Oh,' said Pongwiffy. 'I'm not good enough for your relations, then?'

'Exactly. He's just passed his Wizard exams, you know. With honours.'

28

'I know,' said Pongwiffy. 'You told me.' She had little time for Wizards in general. For Ronald she had no time at all.

'Did I? He's done awfully well, you know. He's a member of the Wizards' Club now. It's very exclusive. There's a secret password and everything. All terribly hush-hush. Well, it would have to be, wouldn't it? I mean, you don't want any old riff-raff wandering in. Ronald's going to have his own chair and everything. They're going to give him his very own locker to keep his Wand and sandwiches in. And his own peg in the cloakroom. Did I tell you?'

'Yes,' said Pongwiffy. 'Several times.'

'Oh yes, he's done quite brilliantly,' boasted Sharkadder. 'Top of his year, he tells me. He's rather hoping to become a Royal Wizard, you know. Straight in at the top.'

'He would,' said Pongwiffy.

'Yes, he's got an interview with King Futtout over at the palace the day after tomorrow. I've bought him a lovely Good Luck card with horseshoes on it. Do you want to sign it?'

'No,' said Pongwiffy.

'I'm sending him some of my new skin cream to try and do something about his spots. Oh yes, he's got my brains all right. A pity he hasn't got my complexion. Anyway, he's coming to tea on Sunday, and I don't want you here letting me down.'

'Oh, but . . .'

'No. That's final. I want everything to be nice. Ronald's used to nice things. At the Wizards' Clubhouse they eat off matching plates, you know. With paper serviettes and everything. He told me. I'm not having you here smelling the place up and putting your boots on the table and making rude remarks. Understand?'

'I suppose so,' sulked Pongwiffy.

'Good. That's settled, then. Here – you can take the catalogue home to look at if you like. If there's nothing else, goodbye.'

'Actually,' said Pongwiffy, 'there *is* something. I wanted to ask you a small favour.'

'Oh, you did, did you? Now we're getting somewhere. What?'

'I was just wondering if you could spare me one of Dudley's whiskers, actually.'

'Oh, you were, were you? Why?'

'Oh, you know, no special reason.'

'I suppose you need it for some stupid spell. Well, even if he agreed, which he won't, how do you

30

propose pulling it out without hurting him? He's got feelings, you know. He's not a machine. You can't stick a coin in and wait for a whisker to drop out.'

Pongwiffy hadn't thought of that. She peered into Dudley's basket. He was spitting and hissing and flexing his claws in his sleep, heavily involved in one of those fierce, piratical dreams of his.

'Well, I suppose the easiest thing would be to give him a little tap on the head with a mallet or something. That way he wouldn't feel a thing.' Pongwiffy didn't feel too hopeful as she said it.

'How dare you,' said Sharkadder coldly. 'I'll tell him you said that when he wakes up. He'll probably scratch you.'

'No, he won't. He's too scared of Hugo. Oh, come on, Sharky, it's only a *little* favour . . .'

'Yes, that's all you ever want, little favours! Well, I'm tired of doing you favours. Go and pull out a whisker from that pint-sized Hamster of yours. You think he's so wonderful, don't you? Just because he beat up my Dudley once. Well, let me tell you, Dudley had a bad back at the time. He's still got it, as a matter of fact. If he was in good health he could make Hamsterburger of your Hugo, so there.'

'Oh no, he couldn't,' said Pongwiffy stoutly.

31

'Oh yes, he could,' insisted Sharkadder, hands on hips.

'No, he couldn't.'

'Yes, he could.'

'Couldn't.'

'Could.'

'Couldn't.'

'*Could*. Wake up, Duddles, darling. Silly old Pongwiffy's saying you're a sissy and couldn't make mincemeat out of Hugo.'

In fact, Duddles darling was really awake, but didn't want to get involved. He still had the scars from the last time he had tangled with Hugo. That Hamster was *tough*.

'I'd help ye haul that barrel, shipmate, but I got this bad back,' he muttered, pretending he was still dreaming. He didn't fool Pongwiffy.

'There, see? He's a scaredy-cat. He's afraid of my little Hugo. I told you so.'

'That does it! Out! Out of my house this minute!' ordered Sharkadder.

'I take it I don't get the whisker, then?'

'You certainly do not. The cheek of it.'

'That's the last time I bake you rock cakes.'

'Good! This is what I think of your rock cakes.'

32

Sharkadder threw one on the floor and stamped on it. The heel came off her shoe. The rock cake remained intact.

'Right!' said Pongwiffy, hurt. 'That does it! I'm breaking friends.'

And she picked up her basket and marched out, breaking into a run as rock cakes whizzed past her head.

It seemed that the direct approach had been all wrong.

As she walked up the path to her spotless, unfriendly hovel, the Broom leapt to attention and proceeded to fussily sweep the path behind her. She put her hand on the door, and a bossy squeak commanded her to wipe her feet.

She paused, sniffed, smelt the unmistakable smell of *Reeka Reeka Roses* and decided to sleep under the stars on that old mattress in the rubbish dump. Spring-cleaning indeed!

CHAPTER FIVE
Ye Quicksande

The next morning, Pongwiffy rose at daybreak. She did some deep, healthy breathing by the compost heap, then, holding a hanky over her nose, crept into her hovel where Hugo and the Broom still slept. Moments later she marched out again with a bucket and a large soup ladle. Determinedly she set off down the path, soon leaving it and plunging deep into the trees, heading towards the quicksand.

Very few people visited the quicksand. It wasn't that much of an attraction really, consisting of a still, treacherous stretch of stagnant water where only worms, snakes and oozy things lived. Even the trees seemed darker and more sinister in this neck of the Wood.

However, it took more than a vague air of brooding menace to stop Pongwiffy. Bucket in hand, she barged through brambles and clumps of stinging nettles, lips clenched in a thin, determined line. Finally, she burst from the thicket into a small clearing, noticing just in time that the ground was spongy beneath her feet.

Very, very slowly, she edged forward. Her boots sank deep into the bubbling sludge and came up again with sucking slurps. They were two sizes too big and without laces, so Pongwiffy had the greatest difficulty keeping them on.

Balancing with great care on a tiny clump of marsh grass, she stooped, wobbled a bit, readied her bucket, and dipped her ladle in the quicksand.

Now then. Here's an interesting turn-up. Pongwiffy didn't know that this quicksand was, in fact, the home of a certain Toad. A Toad who once (and not that long before either) had spent the best part of an unforgettable evening up to his neck in batter, destined to be the main ingredient of Pongwiffy's toad-in-the-hole supper.

Pongwiffy didn't remember this. But the Toad did.

There he was, enjoying a quiet snooze on a slimy rock, getting away from the wife and tadpoles for ten precious minutes, when out of the bushes burst the Raving Lunatic who had sprinkled him with chopped parsley, stuck him in a dish of grey goo and donged him with a spoon every time he popped up for air.

The Toad remembered her all right.

The Toad noted with pleasure that the Raving Lunatic had a rather nasty bramble scratch down one arm.

He observed with glee that the Raving Lunatic had recently fallen over and banged her knee and ripped some enormous holes in her cardigan.

He was also pleased to see that the Raving Lunatic was edging towards the quicksand, stooping, wobbling, very insecure, definitely a bit nervous.

He wasn't that interested in the bucket – a rusty, battered old thing – but *he was very interested in the ladle*!

Slowly she stooped, slowly – slowly – and the Toad waited, nearly dying with pent-up giggles, the sort you get when playing hide-and-seek and the seeker is crashing around right next to you.

THEN . . .

'GERONIMO!' shrieked the Toad, kicking off, leaping high in the air, hurtling down and landing perfectly, slap bang in the middle of Pongwiffy's bony shoulder blades.

'AHHHHH!' howled Pongwiffy, arms whirling like windmills as she strove to keep her balance.

The arm-whirling didn't work, of course. Neither did the frantic grabbing of the nearest thing, which happened to be a blade of marsh grass. It did its best, but Pongwiffy was just that bit too heavy and the marsh grass wasn't built for it. It bent over and snapped! Pongwiffy pitched forward, shot out of her boots, did a clumsy somersault, and entered the quicksand head first. The bucket fell out of her hand and vanished with a slurping glug.

The ladle, however, was saved from a similar fate by the Toad, who, with a triumphant cry of 'HOWZAT!' caught it deftly by the handle as it arced through the air. A spiteful grin on his face, the Toad then waited for Pongwiffy's head to surface. As soon as it did, the Toad gave a flying leap, landed on it and proceeded to batter it with the ladle.

'Dong!' croaked the Toad, bashing away with

37

malice. 'Dong, dong, dong! There. How do *you* like it?'

'Hey! What the – look, get *off*, will you? Stop *doing* that, you crazy animal. I'll sue you for assault and battery, I'll . . .'

Booble groggle burble . . . (That's supposed to be a Sinking-in-Quicksand sort of noise. Perhaps you can do better?)

'Don't give me batter,' snarled the Toad, very worked up indeed. 'I'll give *you* batter. Now, get back down there. Dong, dong, DONG!'

It could have been nasty, couldn't it? We could have lost our poor old Pong then and there. She could have sunk without trace, the victim of a blood-crazed Toad armed with a soup ladle.

We don't, though. Help is at hand, in the form of none other than Witch Macabre's Haggis Familiar, whose name was Rory.

Now, you should know that Haggis are odd-looking creatures with a great deal of shaggy fur, two sharp horns and daft-looking ginger fringes, which hang in their eyes. They are grazing animals, normally content to spend all their time chewing the cud and mooing at passers-by. Occasionally, however, they like to enjoy what they refer to as a

Wee Wallow, and are happy to have this wallow in quagmire, marsh, swamp or bog. Best of all, though, they like quicksand.

That very morning, as luck would have it, Rory felt bored. He was left very much to his own devices during the day. (Macabre was one of those sensible Witches who sleep from daybreak to sunset, unlike Pongwiffy who, day or night, can always be found rampaging about being a nuisance, which is why she gets overtired and ratty sometimes.)

After chewing the cud for an hour or two and swaggering around his field showing off to tiny birds and harmless moles, Rory decided it was a good day for a Wee Wallow. Pausing only to collect his towel, he set off, tail flicking and horns held high, skittishly trampling pretty little clumps of daisies with his thumping great hoofs and snorting at dainty butterflies.

He was aiming, of course, for the quicksand. It was his favourite Wallow Spot. It was always nice and quiet there, and he could float around for hours practising his backstroke without people saying, 'Oh, ha, ha. Look at that stupid Haggis doing backstroke. What a show-off! Who does he think he is?' and so on.

Emerging from the bushes, Rory was very put out to find what he thought of as his own private pool already occupied! Somebody was already floundering around enjoying themselves in the thick mud, and Rory didn't like it. Particularly as that somebody looked suspiciously like Pongwiffy, who isn't the sort of person you'd care to share a bath with. Her filthy old boots were sitting forlornly on a clump of marsh grass, but apart from that she appeared to be fully dressed, with the exception of her hat. She was doing a lot of arm-waving and thrashing about, obviously having a wonderful time.

'Och, ha, ha, ha, will ye look at yon Witch doing the backstroke! Wha' a show-off! Who does she think she is?' remarked Rory in a loud, sneering way, hoping that his taunt might put her off her stroke and make her go away. Nothing of the kind. In fact, she floundered around more vigorously than ever.

'Och, ha, ha, ha . . .' began Rory again, thinking she hadn't heard, 'will ye look at yon Witch doing the ba—'

Then he broke off, for Pongwiffy appeared to be howling something at him.

'What?' returned Rory. 'Ah'll no lend ye ma toowel, if that's what ye want . . .'

41

'No, you idiot! Get – me – OUT of here, quick, I'm . . . ' *Groogle bobble blurgle.*

She was what? *Groogle bobble blurgle?*

Rory shook the fringe out of his eyes and looked again. On closer inspection, it appeared that Pongwiffy wasn't enjoying herself at all. In fact, she was having a rather horrible time. Possibly something to do with the fact that there was a demented-looking Toad battering her head with a wooden ladle, saying, 'Dong! Dong! Take that! Dong, dong, DONG!'

'Help me, Rory!' bawled Pongwiffy.

'Dong! Dong, dong, dong, dong, DONG!'

Groogle bobble blurgle . . .

At long last, Rory got the message. With a heroic moo, he reared up, pawing the air with his hooves, then charged to the rescue.

The Toad gave a startled croak, dropped the ladle and leapt for the bank, just as Rory landed with a titanic squelching splosh in the quicksand. He looked for the bubbles which indicated where Pongwiffy had floundered, dipped his head under the surface, hooked his horn into the back of her cardigan and yanked her up.

She emerged with a *plop*, spluttering and gasping,

saved in the nick of time. Which just goes to show that Haggis have got what it takes in an emergency. Even if they haven't at other times.

Triumphantly, Rory waded to firmer ground with his exhausted, squelchy burden dangling from his horn. To say that Pongwiffy was relieved would be an understatement. She had swallowed so much mud that her insides were like Sludgehaven-on-Sea at low tide. Her head ached from the ladle-battering it had received, and at one point her cardigan had ridden up most uncomfortably. Nevertheless, she still had enough energy to swear vengeance on the Toad, who had returned to his slimy rock and sat watching the rescue operation with sulky, defeated eyes.

It was an embarrassing episode – but it had a happy ending. Pongwiffy did what she set out to do. She got some quicksand. In fact, later that day, she squeezed enough of the beastly stuff out of her rags to fill a bathtub. She made a nice mess of the floor in the process too – but Hugo and the Broom were very efficient and cleaned up after her in no time at all. This was a shame. For two minutes there, with all the little puddles and trails of muddy footprints, her hovel had almost looked like home again.

CHAPTER SIX
Ye Vulture's Feathere
(Barry Gets His)

Witch Scrofula lived in a dark, festering little cave on the west side of Witchway Wood. She lived with her Familiar, a Vulture called Barry. Barry suffered from an embarrassing Personal Problem. It had to do with feathers – or, rather, the lack of them.

You see, some time ago he had commenced moulting. This, as everyone knows, is the natural process whereby birds shed their old feathers in order to grow a new batch. Barry had

44

managed the first bit of the process beautifully, losing all his feathers virtually overnight apart from a few fluffy ones growing in a scruffy ruff around his scrawny neck. However, it was now a WHOLE YEAR LATER, and he was still waiting for the new ones to grow. It was most upsetting. People were calling him Baldy instead of Barry. Besides, he was permanently chilly.

Poor Barry. Far from being a sight to strike terror into every heart, he was now a figure of fun. He had tried everything – exercise, a balanced diet, vitamins, beakfuls of quill pills, wing massage, aromatherapy – but none of them worked. He tried combing the sad, wispy little neck feathers every way, growing them long and plastering them over his naked back with grease – but they just looked pathetic and fooled no one.

Just recently, however, hope had grown in the shape of a large, glorious, glossy tail feather. There was only one, but it was a start, and Barry spent long hours preening it and admiring it with the help of a complicated system of mirrors. He almost dreaded going to sleep these days in case it fell out, but – on the other hand – maybe when he woke up another one might have grown, so there were two ways of

45

looking at it.

This particular morning, Scrofula was in her cave, washing her hair. Scrofula washed her hair several times a day, being martyr to a virulent and alarmingly stubborn form of dandruff. Even at the height of August it always snowed on Scrofula's shoulders.

Barry was outside, dozing on a low branch after a heavy lunch of garlic pills washed down with hair-restorer. He was dreaming. In his dream, he was the owner of gloriously luxuriant plumage. It was the sort of plumage that had parrots nudging each other and peacocks turning green with envy. In his dream, everyone kept asking him for preening tips and telling him he ought to be in showbiz.

Little did he know, the poor bald thing, that a certain Witch was at this very moment stealthily reaching up towards his rear end, a sharp pair of shears in her hand.

The first he knew about it was being rudely woken by a piercing scream, and he opened his eyes to see Scrofula bearing down upon him with a towel round her head and a look of utter horror on her face.

I don't think we'll stay to hear any more, do you?

46

It's just too sad.

That night, Pongwiffy proudly showed the feather to Hugo.

'There,' she said. 'One Vulture's Feathere. And I've got Ye Quicksande, of course. That makes two things already. A pity about Ye Wilde Cat's Whisker. Of course, if only you'd stop being such a disgusting little house-Hamster and give me a hand, I'd get on a lot quicker. It's funny, you know, Hugo. When I took you on, I never thought you'd neglect your duties as a Familiar. Ah well, only goes to show how wrong you can be.'

Hugo was cut to the quick. Later that night, when Pongwiffy was playing a rusty old mouth organ under the moon on the mattress in the rubbish dump, he slipped out with a pair of tweezers and returned shortly afterwards with one of Dudley's whiskers draped around his neck.

''Ere,' he said. 'Zis vat you vant?'

'It certainly is!' whooped Pongwiffy. 'Oh, well done, Hugo. Does this mean you're back on the team?'

'Ya,' said Hugo. 'Today I finish ze spring-cleanink. Now I ready to make Magic!'

Pongwiffy broke into a broad grin. Hugo was back on the team, and now she had *three* of the things needed for Granny Malodour's Wishing Water. Things were looking promising. The Locke of Goldene Hayre next.

CHAPTER SEVEN
Ye Locke of Goldene Hayre

This next part of the story concerns a certain princess. Her name is Honeydimple. I don't suppose you'll like her much.

Honeydimple has big blue eyes and eyelashes which bat. She has a put-on lisp which she thinks makes her sound cute. She has a pert, turned-up nose and a rose-bud mouth. She wears spotlessly clean white dresses and socks, takes three baths a day and skips around a lot, saying, 'Hello, treeth, hello, pretty birdth, good morning, mithter thun,' and things like that. She also screams and kicks if she doesn't get her way.

I forgot to mention that she also has the traditional long, curly, golden Princess-type hair, which she orders her maid to brush one hundred times a day whilst she (Honeydimple) smiles complacently at herself in the mirror. The hair, you'll have guessed, is the reason why she appears in this story at all.

Now, on this particular day, Honeydimple, having changed into yet another clean white frock (the third that morning), decided to go for a stroll. It was boring in the palace, because everyone was spring-cleaning. Remembering that wild strawberries were sometimes to be found in the meadow beyond the wall at the bottom of the palace garden, off she tripped in her shiny white shoes.

Honeydimple opened the gate in the wall and stepped through, taking care not to dirty her white dress. She then skipped off down the meadow, pointing her toes and tossing her hair and holding her dress out and dimpling prettily in case someone was watching her. At the same time, she carefully avoided the cowpats. It would never do to slip and spoil her lovely white frock. Seeing a

couple of open-mouthed cows staring at her, Honeydimple outdid herself. She laughed with delight at the butterflies, stooped to pick a bunch of wild flowers, threw them away because they made her white gloves dirty, and sang a little song about happiness. At this point, the cows rolled their eyes to heaven and returned to cropping the grass.

Deprived of her audience, Honeydimple gave a cross pout and flounced off to the wild strawberry patch.

And what should be sitting in the middle of the strawberry patch but the *cutest little Hamster imaginable*, with darling ears and pink paws and an adorable, twitchy little nose!

'A Hamthter! Oh, how thweet! Hello, cute little Hamthter. Are you lotht?'

She stretched out her hand. Quick as a flash, the cute Hamster scuttled out of reach and hid coyly beneath a dandelion leaf, peeking out shyly and blinking its beady little eyes.

'Coochy, coochy, come on, little Hamthter, don't be thy,' trilled Honeydimple, relentlessly advancing.

Hugo (for, of course, it was he) ran a short way further, almost to where the Wood bordered the meadow, then stopped, looked back and simpered.

Honeydimple hesitated.

'You want me to follow you? Oh, but I muthn't. Daddy thayth I muthn't go into the Wood or I'll be thure of a big thurprithe. There are *Witcheth*, you know. And a dirty old rubbith dump in the middle.'

Swallowing his pride, Hugo sat on his back legs and washed his face with his paws, doing his best to look appealing.

'Oh, how thweet, how perfectly thweet! Oh, pleathe, little Hamthter, let me pick you up. Come on, darling little Hamthter, come back to the palathe with me . . .'

Honeydimple had nearly reached the edge of the Wood now. So intent was she on capturing Hugo that she was totally unprepared for what happened next. What happened next was, a large, smelly sack came down over her and All – to cut a long story short – Went Black.

'Where am I? What happened? Have I been kidnapped?' said Honeydimple, coming round some time later. The smelly sack was no longer over her head. This was a disadvantage in one way, for it meant that she could see things. And she wasn't at all keen on what she saw.

She was bound hand and foot, tied to a table leg in some sort of scruffy old hovel. A ragged curtain hung across the one window, and it was hard to make out much detail in the dim light. But there were some strange, clashing smells in the air – disinfectant, something like mouldering roses, and something else much more horrible.

After a few exploratory sniffs, Honeydimple tracked down the source of the particularly horrible smell. It wafted from the bundle of rags dumped in the rocking chair opposite. Or was it a bundle of rags? No, perhaps it was a scarecrow. Hard to tell. As Honeydimple's nose wrinkled in distaste, the bundle of rags/scarecrow spoke.

'You're in my hovel,' it said. 'And what happened was, I put a sack over your head.'

Honeydimple opened her mouth and let out a shrill scream.

'Do you mind?' said the scarecrow. 'I've got a terrible headache, had it since this morning. I think it's the air-freshener. By the way, the answer to your third question is yes, you've been kidnapped.'

Honeydimple thought about this for a moment, wept a bit, then asked the obvious question. 'Why?'

'Because I happen to urgently need a lock of golden hair from a Princess's head, that's why. For a spell I'm working on.'

As evidence, the scarecrow produced a large pair of scissors and opened and closed them a couple of times with a sinister chuckle.

'Cut off a lock of my pretty hair? Thertainly not! Daddy would go mad!' said Honeydimple.

'Can't be helped. I need it,' said the scarecrow, who in fact wasn't a scarecrow at all but a squalid-looking old woman wearing a filthy cardigan beneath an even filthier cloak. Through her tears, Honeydimple made out a tall pointed hat hanging from elastic on the back of the door.

It seemed that she had fallen into the clutches of a Witch!

'What's more,' continued the Witch, 'I can't cut it until tonight, when the moon comes up. The recipe particularly calls for fresh hair, see. So you'll just have to be my guest for a while.'

'Out of the quethtion,' snapped Honeydimple. 'I'm not thtaying another minute in thith dirty old dump, tho there.'

If she hadn't been lying down and tied up, she would have stamped her foot. As it was, she

55

had to make do with scowling and sticking out her bottom lip.

'You think *this* is dirty? You should have seen it before they cleaned it,' said Pongwiffy with a nostalgic sigh. 'Now, that was what you *could* call dirt. What you're seeing is just a light coating of dust.'

'Well, it'th not what I'm uthed to at all. Untie me immediately. When Daddy getth to hear about thith he'll . . . oh, look! Thereth that little Hamthter! The one in the meadow! Tho you captured him too, you horrible old woman!'

Hugo came through the doorway, stopped, bristled and gave her a dirty look which Honeydimple completely misinterpreted.

'Oh, poor little thing! Look, he'th thivering with fear! Never mind, poor little Hamthter, we'll get away from thith nathty old Witch, don't you worry.'

'No, you won't,' said Pongwiffy. 'Not until full moon.'

'I thuppothe you're keeping him ath your thlave! Fanthy forthing a poor little creature like that to do all your dirty work. Never mind, little Hamthter, when Daddy rethcueth me, thith old Witch will be thrown into the dungeon, and I'll buy you a nithe

56

little cage all of your own. I shall call you Tiddleth and you shall be my pe—'

'Don't say it!' warned Pongwiffy. 'Don't use the "P" word. He doesn't like it. Gets right up his nose.'

Unlike Honeydimple, she recognised the warning signs. Tiddles was visibly swelling, and his eyes had gone red. His cheek pouches pulsed, his whiskers lashed and his fur stood on end. It was quite terrifying.

'Come on, Tiddleth, don't be afraid. Come over here and I'll tell you all about life in the palathe,' went on Honeydimple blithely. 'You'll love it, really you will. I thall buy you a little wheel and teach you trickth and – jutht a minute – what are you doing?'

Hugo had suddenly snatched the scissors from Pongwiffy's lap and was advancing on her with a face like thunder. Before she knew what was happening, Honeydimple was short of a lock of golden hair.

Honeydimple gave a sharp shriek, clutched her head and burst into loud sobs.

'Oh, bother you, Hugo!' scolded Pongwiffy, leaping from her rocking chair. 'It wasn't supposed to be cut until tonight, you idiot!'

'I not care! Zese insults I not take! She go now,

57

or I bite 'er on ze ankle!'

'Boo hoo hoo! What did he do that for, the horrible little beatht!' bawled Honeydimple.

'Well, it's your own fault,' scolded Pongwiffy. 'He's sensitive. I warned you not to make him mad. All that talk of wheels and stuff. Like a red rag to a bull.'

'Boo hoo hoo! But I only thaid he could be my pet . . .'

That did it.

'I NOT PET! I VITCH FAMILIAR!' screeched Hugo, beside himself with rage. And, as promised, he went for the ankle.

'EEEEEEEAAAAAOOOOERRGR!'

Later that day, the palace servants were surprised to hear a loud knocking at the front door, accompanied by a lot of distraught sobbing. Apparently, the noise had been going on for some time, but everyone was busy spring-cleaning and no one had heard it above the whirring of the vacuum cleaner.

When the door was finally opened, it revealed a wild-eyed, weeping, dishevelled Honeydimple with a long, unlikely story about being lured into the Wood by a mad Hamster, where she was captured by a Witch and tied up in a hovel before being set upon by the crazed Hamster again, who cut her hair and bit her on the ankle and chased her through the Wood and tripped her up into cowpats and pushed her into a pig trough, all the while calling her dreadful names in some frightful foreign language.

Honeydimple's parents, King Futtout II and Queen Beryl, were sent for and gravely listened while Honeydimple told her story again. And guess what? Instead of being soundly smacked and sent to bed, she was given a bowl of strawberries and promised a pair of ice skates and given her mother's solemn promise that Daddy would look into the matter.

Doesn't it make you sick?

CHAPTER EIGHT
Rumblings

Of course, all this activity wasn't going unnoticed. You can't go around snatching whiskers and falling into quicksand and getting attacked by toads and stealing feathers and kidnapping princesses without attracting a *bit* of attention.

There were thirteen Witches in Pongwiffy's Coven, and they all lived in Witchway Wood (which might look small on the map, but in some mysterious way seems to stretch to fit everyone in).

As well as the official monthly Coven Meeting, traditionally held on the last Friday of the month, the Witches saw quite a bit of each other on a daily basis (or nightly basis, depending on their habits). So it wasn't surprising that Pongwiffy's curious behaviour very quickly supplanted spring-cleaning as the current hot topic of conversation. As topics of conversation go, talking about Pongwiffy behind her back beat spring-cleaning hands down. The gossip spread like wildfire.

Witches Ratsnappy and Sludgegooey were sitting in Sludgegooey's kitchen having an animated discussion about a particular brand of air-freshener, when Witch Bendyshanks came rushing in.

'I say!' gasped Bendyshanks. 'Guess what? I just met Gaga and she's just seen the twins and they've just been talking to Greymatter who met Bonidle who saw Macabre who heard that Scrofula's looking for Pongwiffy *because-she-thinks-Pongwiffy-knows-something-about-Barry's-stolen-feather*!'

'*No!* Really?'

'Surely *not*!'

Ratsnappy and Sludgegooey looked suitably shocked.

'Mind you, I wouldn't put it past her,' added Ratsnappy.

'True,' nodded Sludgegooey sagely. 'She's been

acting very strangely since that quicksand business. Very strangely indeed.'

'I wonder what she was doing at the quicksand in the first place?' mused Ratsnappy. 'Macabre said she was very secretive about it all when Rory brought her home. She's up to something. I'm sure of it.'

'You're right,' agreed Sludgegooey. 'Come to think of it, I passed Sharkadder early this morning, running back from Malpractiss Magic with a load of bandages and a packet of plasters. I asked her if she'd cut herself and she said something about Dudley's cheek and how she was going to pulverise Pongwiffy when she saw her.'

'And that's not all!' burst out Bendyshanks, shrill with excitement. Ratsnappy and Sludgegooey shushed her and looked over their shoulders. Bendyshanks lowered her voice to a conspiratorial whisper. 'That's not all. My sister's boy Gary, over at the palace, said that stuck-up Princess Honeydimple came back from the Wood yesterday with a *very strange story indeed*!'

'Tell us, tell us!' urged Sludgegooey, flying to put the kettle on.

'Well, apparently, Her Royal Hoity-toityness went out into the meadow, and who should be

62

sitting in a strawberry patch wearing his best I'm So Cute face, but . . .'

And so on.

It wasn't long before the gossip reached the ears of Grandwitch Sourmuddle, Mistress of the Coven. Or rather, it reached the small, pointy red ones of Snoop, Sourmuddle's Demon Familiar, who relayed it into his mistress's ear trumpet with relish.

'What?' said Sourmuddle irritably. Like all the Witches (apart from Pongwiffy), she had been spring-cleaning. Her back was killing her, egged on by her knees. Right now, she was taking a well-deserved breather in her favourite chair. Her shoes were off and she was halfway through a large bowl of nourishing, energy-giving lice bites.

'Speak up, Snoop, I can't hear you over my own slurping. Pongwiffy's been what? Baking gruel?'

'Breaking rules, Sourmuddle! Stealing whiskers. Fooling around in quicksand. Helping herself to Barry's new tail feather without even a by-your-leave or may-I. Kidnapping princesses without filling in the proper chit. Rumour has it she's working on a secret spell, Sourmuddle. Without asking your permission. An old-fashioned one, with funny ingredients.'

63

'Is she, by thunder? Well, we'll soon see about that!'

Sourmuddle slammed down the bowl, spilling milk over her clean floor. She was a stickler for The Rules. Old-fashioned secret spells with funny ingredients were supposed to get special clearance from the Coven Mistress. You had to go to her with the recipe and be prepared to answer some very searching questions. After all, in the wrong hands, some of these old spells could be quite dangerous.

'I thought you'd want to know,' said Snoop smugly.

'I certainly do, Snoop. Er – know what?'

Sourmuddle's ancient memory let her down at times.

'About the secret spell,' Snoop reminded her.

'Yes, exactly, that's what I said,' nodded Sourmuddle, picking up the bowl and beginning to eat noisily again. 'I mean, if everyone went running around doing secret spells, badness knows what might happen. There might be all kinds of clashes. You can't be too careful where Magic's concerned. You were quite right to tell me. What else are they saying?'

'That it's high time you gave her an official

warning, Sourmuddle. And I think they're right. I think you should call a Meeting at once.'

'Excellent idea! I'll leave it up to you, then, Snoop. Get a poster organised. Tonight, Emergency Meeting, Crag Hill, Midnight, Everyone Must Attend, Bring Your Own Sandwiches . . . you know the sort of thing. On second thoughts, it looks like rain. Best be on the safe side and book Witchway Hall. Apart from anything else, I'm not sure my bum could take an hour's Broomstick ride tonight. Not after all that spring-cleaning.'

Just at that moment there was a knock at the door.

'Oh, goody, the postman!' exclaimed Sourmuddle, who was expecting a Bat on Elastic. For the past six weeks she had eaten lice bites until they came out of her ears in order to get enough tokens. She pushed the bowl aside and scuttled to open the door. Sadly, it wasn't the postman. Instead, it was Sharkadder and Scrofula with Dudley and Barry in tow. Both Familiars sported a great deal of sticking plaster and looked extremely sorry for themselves. Sharkadder and Scrofula were falling over themselves in their eagerness to complain about Pongwiffy.

'Sourmuddle, guess what Pongwiffy did! She

stole Dudley's whisker!'

'. . . after all Barry's gone through, I think it's the absolute limit . . .'

'. . . and I'd already said she couldn't have a whisker, so what does she do, she sends that sneaky little Hamster . . .'

'. . . I mean, look at the state of him . . .'

'. . . my Dudley's terribly upset . . .'

'. . . Barry's getting legal advice, and I don't blame him . . .'

'. . . Pongwiffy's really gone over the top this time . . .'

'. . . and, what's more, Sourmuddle, there's a rumour that the palace are thinking of sending a formal letter of complaint,' finished Scrofula triumphantly, 'because of the Princess Business. Did you know about the Princess Business, Sourmuddle?'

'Certainly I know about the Princess Business,' snapped Sourmuddle. 'I'm Grandwitch, remember? It's my business to know these things. In fact, I decided ages ago to hold an Emergency Meeting and thrash things out. Snoop is even now drafting a poster. By the way, Snoop, I think we should send Pongwiffy an official summons and get it delivered by hand. I don't want her pretending she doesn't know about it. Now, who shall I get to take it?'

'Us!' shouted Sharkadder and Scrofula, jumping up and down and gnashing their teeth. 'Us! Send us, Sourmuddle, we'll go!'

'Certainly not,' said Sourmuddle. 'Simmer down, the pair of you. You'll go through the proper channels. You can have your say tonight at the Emergency Meeting. Send Macabre, Snoop. No, on second thoughts, perhaps not. I don't want Pongwiffy frightened off. Tell you what – send the twins.'

Snoop sent the twins.

CHAPTER NINE
The Twins Come Calling

Up to the moment the twins came calling, things had been going surprisingly well. Not only was Pongwiffy well on her way to collecting all the important main ingredients for Granny Malodour's Wishing Water, but that very morning, a large box of basic items had arrived from Sharkadder's catalogue.

It contained everything Pongwiffy wanted – Skunk Stock Cubes, Beetle Doos, Fly Droppings, and so on. The Frogspawn was on special offer, so it worked out cheaper than Malpractiss Magic Ltd, where the prices were so high they made your nose bleed.

Her Magic cupboard was now looking much healthier. Much to Hugo's despair, Pongwiffy had rescued the old Wands and cracked crystal balls and crumbly spell books from The Dump and tenderly placed them back on the shelves, next to the rows of new, neat, winking little jars that he had carefully polished and labelled.

'Zey look out of place,' Hugo complained.

'They do,' Pongwiffy agreed. 'But don't worry, they'll soon dirty up nicely.'

'I not mean ze jars! I mean ze old rubbish you put back in.'

'Just stop complaining. I'm trying to think. I've got to come up with a way to get hold of a bobble from a Goblin's hat. It's not going to be easy. Goblins never take their hats off because they're scared their brains'll freeze up. I know all about Goblin habits because I lived next door to them once.'

'I know,' sighed Hugo. 'You tell me, many times.'

It was at this point that there was a rapping on the door. Agglebag and Bagaggle, come to deliver the summons and completely ruin Pongwiffy's day. They stood beaming on the doorstep, violins tucked

69

beneath their chins and bows at the ready.

'Hello, Pongwiffy,' said Bagaggle. 'Can we come in?' She peered hopefully into the dark recesses of the hovel. 'I think I can hear a kettle boiling, don't you, Ag?'

'I do, Bag,' agreed Agglebag. 'I expect Pongwiffy will offer us a nice cup of hot bogwater.'

'No, I won't,' said Pongwiffy.

'In that case, we'll just stand out here and play our violins. Ready, Ag? One, two, thr—'

'Come in,' said Pongwiffy hastily. She knew when she was beaten.

Happily, the twins trooped in. They gave two identical looks at the clean, tidy hovel and their mouths fell open in shock. Bagaggle clutched at her twin's arm.

'Do my eyes deceive me, Ag, or has she been spring-cleaning?' she breathed.

'I do believe you're right, Bag. It looks lovely, Pongwiffy. What's that delightful smell?'

'*Reeka Reeka Roses*,' said Pongwiffy bitterly. 'And, just for the record, I haven't lifted a finger.'

'Zat's right,' called Hugo from inside the cupboard, where he was arranging the last of the little jars. 'Me and ze Broom do it all.'

'Well, we think it's wonderful,' chorused the twins. The Broom shuffled coyly around in the corner, flushed with pride.

'I especially like the floor, don't you, Ag?' said Bagaggle. 'I've never seen it so beautifully swept.'

The Broom ventured a little way out of the corner and attempted a bow. Pongwiffy grabbed it and threw it outside, where it began to sweep the path. The twins continued to stare around. Their beady eyes didn't miss a thing. Agglebag nudged Bagaggle and pointed.

'By the way, over there on the table, isn't that a . . . ?'

'Pigeon feather,' said Pongwiffy firmly, picking it up and throwing it hastily into a drawer. Instantly, she came out in green spots, which always happens when she tells lies.

'Looked more like a Vulture feather to me,' said Agglebag.

'No, definitely pigeon. I collect them.'

'Why have you come out in green spots?' enquired Bagaggle.

'Slight allergic reaction, nothing to worry about.'

'You're allergic to Vulture feathers?'

'*Pigeon*,' insisted Pongwiffy. 'I'm allergic to

71

pigeon feathers.'

'But why collect them if you're aller—'

'*Because I do!* I'm a pigeon feather fancier and I collect pigeon feathers. All right? Satisfied? Now, how do you like your bogwater?'

'With biscuits,' said Agglebag.

'Or cake,' said Bagaggle.

'Hugo!' called Pongwiffy. 'Three cups of bogwater. And offer the twins some of those nice, fresh, home-made rock cakes. So. What brings you here? Just a social call, is it?'

'Not exactly,' said Agglebag. She reached into her pocket and withdrew an official-looking brown envelope. 'Actually, we've brought you this. It's a summons.'

'Summons? Who from? What for?'

'It's from Grandwitch Sourmuddle,' explained Bagaggle helpfully. 'She wants to make sure you come to tonight's Emergency Meeting.'

'What d'you mean, Emergency Meeting?'

'It's a Meeting you hold when there's an Emergency,' Agglebag told her. 'Right, Bag?'

'That's exactly right, Ag. You explained that beautifully,' nodded Bagaggle, and they exchanged happy smiles.

'But I'm busy!' wailed Pongwiffy. 'I've got something planned for tonight. I haven't got time to go to some old meeting. What's it about, anyway?'

'Who knows?' chorused the twins innocently, rolling their eyes.

'Well, I bet it's not important. Tell Sourmuddle I'm poorly. Better still, tell her I wasn't in and you couldn't deliver the summons.'

'Oh, we can't do that, can we, Ag?' said Bagaggle, terribly shocked.

'Certainly not, Bag,' tutted Agglebag. 'That'd be telling fibs. Besides, she's very keen that you should be there.'

'Well, I don't know why,' said Pongwiffy uneasily.

'Something to do with Sharkadder and Scrofula, I think,' said Bagaggle. 'They've been complaining about you. Something about missing whiskers and feathers.'

'I can't think what they mean,' said Pongwiffy. 'Whiskers? Feathers? What's that got to do with me?'

'Well, you can ask them yourself,' said Agglebag, who was staring out of the window. 'They're coming up the path. They're nearly at the door. Badness me, they do look cross. Come and see how cross they

73

look, Pongwiffy. Pongwiffy? Where is she, Bag?'

'Vanished in a smelly puff of smoke, Ag,' explained Bagaggle. 'Hugo's gone as well, look.'

Sure enough, there was a small, green, evil-smelling cloud hovering in the place where Pongwiffy had been standing. The door to the Magic cupboard swung open and there was no sign of Hugo.

'Say what you like, Bag, she's fast,' said Agglebag admiringly.

'She needs to be if Sharkadder and Scrofula are on the warpath, Ag.'

'Oh, but they're not. Well, not at this very minute. I said that for a joke, to see what she'd do.'

'Good. That means we can eat all the rock cakes.'

Chuckling, the twins eagerly helped themselves to a cake each and attempted a bite. There came the sound of teeth grinding on granite. Hastily, they lowered their arms, looked at each other and pulled a face.

'Perhaps not,' they chorused.

CHAPTER TEN
The Demon Barber

'Phew! That was a close one!' gasped Pongwiffy, staggering forward a few paces before buckling at the knees and slithering gratefully down the nearest tree.

'Ssh. Don't speak,' begged Hugo, who was lying down in a clump of grass, very pale round the pouches. 'I still vaitink for tummy to catch up.'

'The trees are whizzing round! I can't stop them! Remind me not to use that spell again,' groaned Pongwiffy, crawling off on all fours and collapsing into a nearby bush.

She had transported them into a large glade on the other side of Witchway Wood, using the first transportation spell that had come into her mind. Unfortunately, like most of Pongwiffy's spells, it was one of those old-fashioned, wonky ones which did the trick but came with nasty side effects. It got you out of there fast, but you certainly paid for it.

They both lay quietly moaning for a while, wishing they hadn't had so much breakfast. At one point, Pongwiffy remarked that there was something familiar about that tall tree over there, the one with the rope ladder and the red and white stripy pole, and that if only it would stay still for a moment she'd know what it was. A bit later, Hugo remarked that he would sooner have taken his chances with Sharkadder and Scrofula. On the whole, Pongwiffy was inclined to agree with him.

It was fate, of course. One chance in a million. But things like fate and coincidence and one-in-a-million chances are always cropping up in Witchway Wood. There they were, Pongwiffy and Hugo, lying down quietly, conveniently hidden by grass and bushes, when who should come along the path but . . .

THE GOBLINS! Yes, here they come, all seven

of them, stomping along in single file. Plugugly, Stinkwart, Eyesore, Slopbucket, Sproggit, Hog and Lardo. Those are their names. They live in a damp cave on a particularly horrible mountain which borders Witchway Wood. Right now, they are off on one of their doomed-to-failure hunting trips. You can tell this because their faces are smeared with soot, they are carrying the Traditional Goblin hunting bags (the ones with the Traditional holes cut in the bottom) and they are singing a loud hunting song.

'*Oh, a-hunting we will go,*' sang the Goblins, horribly out of tune.

> '*A-hunting we will go,*
> *We'll bump the trees*
> *And hurt our knees*
> *And then we'll stub our toe.*'

'Well, well, well,' hissed Pongwiffy, suddenly alert and cured of all queasiness. 'What have we here?'

'Goblins!' gloated Hugo, also perking up considerably. 'Ve in luck, Mistress. Vat ve do? Jump out at zem and grab ze bobbles off zeir 'ats?'

'No. I don't want to draw any more attention to

77

myself. We've got to be subtle. Stay hidden. I want to watch. I wonder why they're out hunting today? It's not Tuesday, is it?'

(Tuesday is the Goblins' traditional hunting night. They rarely come down into Witchway Wood at any other time, because Witches and Goblins don't like each other. The Witches think the Goblins are stupid and the Goblins think the Witches are spiteful. They both have a point.)

The Goblins rounded the corner, and further conversation was impossible. Apart from anything else, you couldn't hear yourself speak above the dreadful singing.

'*A-hunting we will go,*' warbled the Goblins.

> '*A-hunting we will go,*
> *We'll trip on logs*
> *And drown in bogs*
> *And then . . .*'

'Halt!' shouted the Goblin at the front, stopping suddenly. There was a squeezed concertina effect as the Goblins piled up on each other, shouting alarmed cries of 'What happenin' up front there, Plugugly?' and 'Is we attacked?'

'I is gettin' tired o' dis song,' explained Plugugly, who was the Goblin at the front. He usually got stuck at the front, not because of his powers of leadership but because he was the biggest and therefore best equipped to carve a path when the going got rough. Like a snowplough, but more stupid.

'What you mean, tired of it?' objected Eyesore. ''Ow can you be tired of it?'

'Well, I am,' insisted Plugugly stubbornly. 'It depressin' me. All dis talk o' hurtin' knees and fallin' in bogs an' dat. I fink we should sing anudder one. Fer a change.'

'We don't know anuvver huntin' song,' pointed out Hog.

'Ah, but we ain't *really* goin' huntin', so it don't 'ave ter be a huntin' song, do it?' remarked Slopbucket, who was immediately rounded on and soundly criticised.

'Ssh! Idiot!'

'We said we wasn't goin' ter say nuffin, remember?'

''E's blown the gaff!'

'Talk about mouf, you could lose a battleship in 'is mouf!'

79

'Sorry,' said Slopbucket, going red, aware of his indiscretion the minute he had said it. 'Slipped out. Sorry.'

'We could sing "'Ere We Go",' suggested young Sproggit, hopping from boot to boot in his eagerness. 'One o' my favourites, that.'

''Ow's it go again?' asked Hog. 'I've forgotten the words.'

''Ere we go, 'ere we go, 'ere we go,' supplied Sproggit. ''Ere we go, 'ere we go, 'ere we go-oh, 'ere we go, 'ere we go, 'ere we go, 'ere we go-oh, 'ere we go . . .'

'Oh yeah,' said Hog. 'I remember now.'

'Acherly, there ain't no point in singin' anyfin',' remarked Stinkwart. ''Cos we've arrived. We're 'ere. 'Oo's gonna ring the bell?'

This was the cue for all the Goblins to huddle together in terror and try to push each other to the front. Apparently, no one wanted to ring the bell.

'Vat zey do?' whispered Hugo from behind his grass. 'Vy zey frightened?'

'I don't know,' muttered Pongwiffy. 'But I'll tell you one thing. I've suddenly recognised that tree over there! The tall one with the rope ladder and the stripy pole sticking out, see? Come to think of it, that pole never used to be there. But it's definitely the same tree. There's a tree house right up the top of that tree, and I happen to know who lives there.'

'Oh. Who?'

'A nasty little Tree Demon, that's who. Did I ever tell you about the awful experience I had when I was house-hunting? It was all Sharkadder's fault. This is before your time, of course . . .'

'Ssh!' said Hugo. 'Look.'

By some mysterious process known as Pushing, the Goblins had unanimously elected Plugugly as official bell-ringer. Unwillingly, with much hesitation and backward glancing, he approached the tall tree with the rope ladder, the one that Pongwiffy recognised despite the addition of the mysterious striped pole, and gave the bell-rope that hung there a reluctant little tug. At once, an almighty clanging sounded high up in the branches. Plugugly staggered back a step, dropped the bell-rope as if scalded and ran back to the doubtful safety of the group.

'Coming, sir, coming, sir, just one minute if you *please*!' came the bad-tempered screech from on high.

The foot of the rope ladder shook, there was a

81

flash of green, and suddenly a small Tree Demon was standing at the foot of the tree. He wore a white coat with a large breast pocket which contained an assortment of vicious-looking razors, scissors and combs. His pinched green face wore an expression of extreme irritation.

'Yes?' he shrieked. 'What can I do for you, gentlemen?'

'I don't believe it!' gasped Pongwiffy. 'Now I've seen everything! The little stinker's gone and set himself up as a Demon Barber!'

CHAPTER ELEVEN
Ye Bobble off ye Hat of a Gobline

'And how would sir like it?' asked the Tree Demon, tapping his foot, rolling his eyes and whetting his razor impatiently.

Plugugly cleared his throat unhappily and didn't say a thing. He had been forced at comb-point to sit on a stump in the middle of the glade. He had been draped in a towel. The traditional saucepan he always wore on his head had been forcibly removed and placed out of reach on a nearby branch. He felt terribly insecure without it.

'Well?' prompted the Tree Demon, who didn't suffer fools gladly.

Plugugly licked his lips and tried to think whilst the Tree Demon climbed up behind him on a handy log and clashed a huge pair of scissors experimentally in the air. The rest of the Goblins stood around and stared in open-mouthed horror.

(Goblins have a terrible fear of having their hair cut. For them, having their hair cut is sissy stuff which falls into the same category as washing. They hate it so much, they only do it once a year. When the time of the Haircut rolls round again, they get into a terrible state. They are so convinced that everyone will laugh at them that they try to keep the whole venture undercover. That's why they were pretending to be going hunting, so no one would know what they were up to.)

'Come along, come along, come along, come along, sir, *if you please*!' spat the Tree Demon. As a hairdresser, his sinkside manner left a lot to be desired. 'There are other gentlemen waiting, you know.'

'I want it long,' Plugugly suddenly burst out. 'Long an' greasy!'

'I see,' nodded the Tree Demon, stroking his chin

professionally. 'Long and greasy. Anything else, sir?'

'Sideburns,' instructed Plugugly, suddenly hopeful, adding, 'an' one o' dem wotsits – quiffs.'

'Right away, sir,' said the Tree Demon.

The scissors flashed, and in seconds Plugugly was the horrified owner of the shortest back and sides it is possible to have without being pronounced clinically bald. The general effect was of huge jug-handles stuck on either side of a crimson pimple. The watching Goblins all gasped, pointed, then disloyally fell about laughing.

Behind their bush, Pongwiffy and Hugo did the same.

'There we are, sir,' said the Tree Demon, simultaneously flashing a mirror around, snatching the towel away and picking Plugugly's pocket. 'Very nice, very smart, that. Don't forget your saucepan, sir. Pay on your way out. Next!'

The Goblins immediately sobered up. Nobody wanted to be next.

'You,' hissed the Tree Demon, pointing at Lardo, who had been laughing louder than anyone.

'Me?' gulped Lardo, quaking. (He probably had an even bigger fear of being parted from his hat than the rest of the Goblins. It was his comforter.

He needed it. He sucked the bobble when he went to sleep. He had lost it once, and all sorts of bad things had happened.)

'Yes, you! The short, fat, stupid one. Take your hat off, hang it on the branch and get over here. I haven't got all day.'

'This is it,' mouthed Pongwiffy to Hugo. 'Now's our chance!'

Poor Lardo. Slowly he shuffled forward, removed his hat with trembling hands and hung it carefully on the branch next to Plugugly's saucepan, as instructed. He then reluctantly approached the dreaded stump where the scissor-happy Tree Demon was holding out the towel and flapping it like a matador.

'What's it to be, sir?' asked the Tree Demon, tucking Lardo up firmly and menacing him with a large pot of shaving cream. 'The Usual?'

Lardo whispered something.

'Speak up, sir, speak up if you *please*!' said the Tree Demon.

'Curls,' said Lardo, and blushed.

'Certainly, certainly. Would that be *golden* curls?'

Lardo confirmed that, yes, golden curls would be most acceptable.

87

'Golden curls coming right up, sir. Shocking weather we been having,' observed the Tree Demon, and went to work. In no time at all, Lardo emerged with the second short back and sides of the day. This time, it was Plugugly's turn to laugh until he was sick.

'There we are, sir, lovely cut, that!' insisted the Tree Demon, trying to force Lardo to look at himself in the mirror.

Lardo gave a little sob, threw off the towel and ran the gauntlet past the hysterical Goblins to where his beloved hat hung on the tree. He snatched it up and was about to ram it on, when he suddenly noticed something.

'All right, who's got it?' he asked plaintively. 'Enough's enough. You've gone too far this time. Who's the joker what's taken me bobble? Eh? Eh?'

Needless to say, nobody owned up.

Back at Number One, Dump Edge, Pongwiffy and Hugo were celebrating. Pongwiffy was dancing on the table doing a wild Spanish dance, Lardo's bobble clutched between her teeth like a wilting rose.

'We got it! We got the bobble!' she crowed. 'I just can't believe our luck, Hugo. It's almost as though it's meant to be. Put the kettle on. I fancy a huge mug of bogwater with three sugars to celebrate. No sign of Ag and Bag. Or Sharky and Scrofula, for that matter. I wonder where they've all got to?'

'Who knows?' said Hugo. 'It look like ze twins leave in hurry. Zey not drink ze bogwater. Only two bites out of rock cakes.'

(In fact, the twins were currently sitting in a dentist's waiting room. Bagaggle was waiting to have a piece of Pongwiffy's rock cake chiselled from between her teeth, and Agglebag was holding her hand and reading out soothing horoscopes from old back issues of *Witches' Realm*.)

'They've left the summons, though,' said Pongwiffy, pointing at the ominous brown envelope with a little sigh. There was always something that had to spoil things.

'Aren't you going to open it?' asked Hugo curiously.

Pongwiffy carefully placed the precious bobble in her Magic cupboard, alongside Dudley's whisker, the quicksand, Barry's feather and Honeydimple's hair. She then picked up the brown envelope and

89

opened it. Inside was a piece of paper. It said: I SUMMON YOU TO APPEAR AT TONIGHT'S MEETING. THAT'S AN **ORDER**!

'Huh,' said Pongwiffy. 'What a cheek. Sourmuddle's really throwing her weight around these days. You know what I'm going to do about *that*, don't you?'

'Vat?' asked Hugo, eyes round.

'Go to the Meeting,' said Pongwiffy lamely.

CHAPTER TWELVE
Banned

Witchway Hall is the focal point of community life in Witchway Wood. It is used for parties, ping-pong and protest meetings. It is also used for fund-raising events and theatrical performances. In a typical week, there might be a rabble-rousing meeting of the Hamsters Are Angry Movement (HAM) chaired by Hugo, the finals of the Lady Ghouls' Darts Championships, a Witchway Rhythm Boys' practice session, Troll country dancing (interesting), a Zombie jumble sale, a Banshee concert, a rehearsal of the Skeleton Amateur

Dramatics Society (SAD), a Friends Of the Goblins Reunion Dinner (always poorly attended) and the ever-popular Beginners' Class in Demon Basket Weaving run by Snoop on wet Sunday afternoons.

In view of its popularity, the Witches were lucky to get Witchway Hall at such short notice. Normally, at midnight on a Tuesday, the Gnome Debating Society would have been in full swing. Well, actually, it wasn't so much *luck*. It was more that Snoop had a few words in the chief Gnome Debater's ear. Nothing unpleasant, you understand, just a few quiet words about Witches and Tuesday Nights and the Importance Of Emergency Meetings and the Inconvenience Of Being Turned Into A Frog, and so on.

For once, the chief Gnome Debater didn't argue.

So. There they were in Witchway Hall. It was midnight, it looked like rain, just as Sourmuddle had predicted, and the Emergency Meeting was due to start.

Thirteen chairs had been set around the long trestle table. Eleven were already occupied by Witches' bums. Well, to be strictly correct, only nine had actual bums on. Witch Gaga was standing on her head on the tenth, and Witch Macabre wasn't sitting down yet. But her bagpipes were, which was almost as bad. Various Witch Familiars were skulking, slithering and generally milling around, according to their disposition.

Sourmuddle hadn't yet arrived.

There was also no sign of Pongwiffy.

Sharkadder and Scrofula had come early and grabbed the seats on either side of Sourmuddle's chair. It was plain that they were terribly put out. They both sat in stony silence with their arms folded and their noses in the air, refusing to join in the general chit-chat, and Barry and Dudley did likewise. All about them buzzed tantalising talk of spells and spring-cleaning and recipes and who was hot favourite to win the Spell of the Year Competition and the trouble with Brooms today, and so on, but nothing could tempt them to relax. As the injured parties, they were determined to milk the Emergency Meeting for all it was worth.

To be sure, Scrofula and Barry didn't look well at all. Scrofula's hair was greasier than ever, and her shoulders looked like the wastes of Greenland. Barry hunched mournfully on the back of her chair and tried to ignore the draught around his rear end. Every so often he shook his head slowly, sighed,

93

said, 'Why me?' in a small, dry voice, then gave a pathetic little cough. On top of everything, he had another cold coming on.

In contrast, Sharkadder was rather enjoying all the drama. She had gone to a great deal of trouble to make herself up as a tragic victim. She was all in black, and had painted dark panda shadows beneath her eyes. Every so often she dabbed at them dramatically with a black lace hanky. Dead Eye Dudley crouched vengefully at her feet, muttering dark curses and glaring balefully around, daring anyone to say one word, just one word, that's all, about his swollen cheek.

Agglebag and Bagaggle were there, telling a dental horror story to anyone who cared to listen. That didn't include Greymatter, who was sitting next to them, busily writing a poem in an old exercise book. Speks, her Owl Familiar, peered thoughtfully over her shoulder and made creative suggestions every so often.

'. . . and we think Pongwiffy left the rock cakes to tempt us on purpose, so that Bag would break her tooth!' finished up Agglebag. 'What do you think, Greymatter?'

'I beg your pardon?' said Greymatter. 'What did

94

you say, Agglebag? I'm trying to write a poem here, if you don't mind.'

Further down the table, Sludgegooey, Ratsnappy and Bendyshanks were playing cards. Bonidle, as always, was collapsed face down on the table, fast asleep. Over by the door, Witch Macabre was having a loud argument with the caretaker, a sullen Troll by the name of Clifford. The row appeared to be about the state of the tea urn, although they were both bellowing so loudly no one could be sure.

Several curious onlookers skulked in the shadowy background. A couple of Skeletons lurked in the darkness of the back stalls. A few Ghouls and the odd Gnome were attempting to mingle with the Familiars and make themselves inconspicuous. There was nothing like a good Emergency Meeting to bring them all out of the woodwork.

'All right, settle down, settle down!' Sourmuddle came bustling in with a flask, a bag of boiled sweets, her reading glasses and the Rule Book. Snoop walked behind carrying a bin liner full of essentials.

'No, no, don't bother to stand,' ordered Sourmuddle, as a few Witches made a half-hearted attempt to rise. 'This isn't a proper Coven Meeting, so we can dispense with the formalities. It says so in the Rule Book. Just sit up straight and shut up. All non-Witches out!'

Immediate consternation in the shadows. Sourmuddle held firm.

'Yes, I'm talking to you Ghouls over there. And you lot hiding in the back stalls – don't think I can't see you. This is a private meeting. Witches and Witch Familiars only.'

'It doesn't say so on the poster,' protested a Gnome.

'I don't care about the poster,' said Sourmuddle firmly. 'I make the rules around here. Out. Make sure they go, Macabre. That includes you, Clifford. By the way, I hope you've cleaned out that tea urn?'

Grumbling, the banished ones were chased from the hall by Witch Macabre, to a chorus of catcalls, raspberries and mocking laughter.

'Right,' said Sourmuddle as soon as the door had closed behind them. 'Are we all here? Then sit down, Macabre, and let's get cracking.'

'I don't believe we *are* all here actually, Sourmuddle,' remarked Sharkadder, pointing to the one remaining empty chair. 'Correct me if I'm wrong, but I believe I'm right in saying that Pongwiffy's not here. Which is exactly what Scrofula and I expected, of course, and why we're disappointed you didn't give us permission to go round and pulverise her this afternoon, like we wanted to. Right, Scrofula?'

'Right, Sharkadder.'

'Sit down, Sharkadder. We'll conduct this Meeting in a proper manner,' ordered Sourmuddle sharply. 'Pongwiffy's got a right to tell us her side of the story. We've only got your word for it that she stole Dudley's whisker to put in some secret spell or other.'

'But she's not coming, Sourmuddle! Don't you see?' shrieked Sharkadder. 'Even though you made a special point of telling her, she's *not coming*! She's afraid to face the music.'

'What music?' said a voice from the wings. 'Sorry I'm late, Sourmuddle. Couldn't get my Broomstick started. It's the damp. Poor thing's got a terrible cough. Keep meaning to get it seen to, but you know how it is. Evening, girls. Have I missed much?'

Cheerfully, Pongwiffy approached the table and plonked herself down in the one empty chair. Hugo rode on the brim of her hat. He winked cheekily down at Dudley, who flicked his tail and looked the other way. Barry gave him a long, hurt, sorrowful look, then pointedly turned his back.

'So,' said Pongwiffy. 'What's all this about facing

music? I'll face anything but Ag and Bag playing violins. I had enough of that earlier. Did you enjoy the rock cakes, you two? Sorry I had to leave a bit smartish. I just remembered something I had to do.'

'That's enough of the chit-chat, Pongwiffy,' said Sourmuddle severely. 'I'm just about to start this Meeting, if you don't mind.'

'Certainly, Sourmuddle, certainly. I'm sure I don't want to hold things up longer than necessary. I'm as keen to get away early as the next Witch. By the way, what's it all about? What's so important that it can't wait? Some of us have got things to do.'

'So I've heard,' said Sourmuddle tartly. 'In fact, Pongwiffy, rumour has it that you've been doing rather too much lately. That's why we're holding this Emergency Meeting. I've been getting complaints. About you. In fact, I've got a whole list of charges against you.'

'No!' cried Pongwiffy. 'Me? Surely not!'

'Don't put on an act, Pong. You know you're collecting the ingredients for a secret spell!' shrieked Sharkadder, pointing an accusatory talon. 'We're not that stupid, are we, Scrofula?'

'We certainly are not,' agreed Scrofula, shaking her head vigorously and causing another avalanche to cascade on to her shoulders.

'You stole my Dudley's whisker, you did, Pongwiffy, and I'm going to get you for it!' screeched Sharkadder. Pongwiffy tried her best to look innocent. No one was taken in.

'Sit down, Sharkadder, before Macabre throws you out!' commanded Sourmuddle, putting on her reading glasses and holding at arm's length an old envelope covered in scribbled notes. 'Do you deny, Pongwiffy, that in the past few days you've stolen or arranged to have stolen a whisker belonging to one Dead Eye Dudley, misappropriated a feather belonging to one Barry Vulture, and kidnapped that awful Princess Honeydimple against her will and hacked her hair off?'

'I categorically deny everything,' said Pongwiffy, and immediately came out in those pesky green spots. It really was most inconvenient.

'You see? You see? Look at her fib rash!' squawked Sharkadder. 'She *is* working on a secret spell, Sourmuddle, I know it! She's taking advantage of everyone being so busy doing spring-cleaning that we won't notice!'

'Aye!' chipped in Macabre. 'Why else would she want quicksand? I mean, nobody uses quicksand any more, do they? Quicksand's old-fashioned. Only very old spells call for quicksand.'

That was the signal for everyone else to join in.

'All those peculiar things she wanted in Malpractiss Magic, I mean it stands to reason . . .'

'Skulking around all hours of the day and night, avoiding everybody . . .'

'And what about my Barry's feather? Don't forget that . . .'

'Yes, and do you know, I've seen her . . .'

'Obviously hiding something . . .'

'Attacking us with rock cakes and vanishing in a puff of smoke . . .'

Pongwiffy listened to it all with growing alarm. It seemed that everyone had a complaint against her. Nobody was on her side. Even Greymatter's poem was about her and was distinctly unflattering. It went like this:

> *Uplift thee, muse! And tell how old Pongwiffy*
> *(A Witch who has a smell distinctly iffy)*
> *Has taken things that were not hers to take:*
> *A feather, hair, a whisker and some cake.*

'I didn't take any cake!' protested Pongwiffy,

but nobody heard her except Greymatter, who mumbled something about poetic licence. It seemed that everybody was trying to outdo everyone else in telling stories about her which would get her into trouble. The general feeling was definitely anti-Pong.

'Order! Order! That's enough,' commanded Sourmuddle. 'Deny it all you like, Pongwiffy, but in my opinion there's an airtight case against you. It's clear as crystal balls that you're working on a secret spell.'

'All right,' cried Pongwiffy. 'All right, so I am! I admit it! But so what? We're Witches, aren't we? We're supposed to be working on spells, remember? Not polishing the silver and washing-up! Spring-cleaning's for sissies!'

There was a lot of angry muttering. Some of the loudest came from the brim of her hat. Even Hugo wasn't with her on this one.

'Ah,' said Sourmuddle. '*Spells*, yes. But *secret* spells? Not without clearing it with me first.'

'But . . .'

'It's in the Rule Book. Paragraph nine, item fourteen: No Pinching Items From Fellow Witches Or Their Familiars To Use In Spells Unless

101

Given Express Permission By Grandwitch. And I certainly don't recall giving you permission. What is it, anyway? What does it do, this spell of yours? Where did you get it from?'

'I'm sorry, I'm afraid I'm not at liberty to tell you that,' said Pongwiffy.

'Oh really? Well, in that case, I'm going to ban you. Hand over your Magic Licence, Pongwiffy.'

'But . . .'

'No more buts. Hand it over. That's an order.'

There was quite a bit of unsympathetic tittering as Pongwiffy reached into her rags and drew out an old, crumpled, yellowing piece of paper. With a sulky sniff she handed it to Sourmuddle, who examined it through her reading glasses.

'Hmm. As I thought. Two endorsements already. Right, I'm adding a third. That means you're banned from making magic of any kind, secret or otherwise, for *one whole week*!'

'But, Sourmuddle . . .' protested Pongwiffy.

'Not only that,' continued Sourmuddle sternly, 'you will also go and say you are humbly sorry to everyone you've offended. You will write a grovelling note to King Futtout apologising for kidnapping that ghastly daughter of his. Plus you

102

will come and clean my boots every morning for the next six weeks. That'll teach you to not clear things with me first. Right, that's settled. Meeting over. Whoopee! Sandwich time! Who wants to see my Bat on Elastic?'

Everyone did except Pongwiffy.

CHAPTER THIRTEEN
Ronald

Sharkadder's nephew Ronald was feeling delighted with himself. Feeling delighted with himself was not a new sensation. Ronald was the sort of person who usually felt delighted with himself. However, right now he felt *particularly* delighted, and the reason for this was that he had just been hired by the palace! His first proper job.

Imagine! A Royal Wizard already, and he'd only just qualified. Ten bags of gold a year, two weeks paid holiday, expense account, turret of his own, as much as he could eat and drink and the possibility of the Princess's hand in marriage! And all he had to do in return was to do something about the Witches in Witchway Wood. Apparently, they had been getting above themselves recently, and the King (Futtout II) was anxious that they should be made to toe the line.

Do something about the Witches? Nothing to it! Why, his own aunt was one! He'd simply have a word with Aunt Sharky, get her to speak severely to some of her more boisterous cronies and Bob's your uncle – or, rather, Sharky's your aunt, ha ha – he'd got it made! What could be easier?

The interview with King Futtout had gone without a hitch. It had been more a case of Ronald interviewing the King than the King interviewing Ronald.

'Are you . . . erm . . . sure you've got enough experience, Mister . . . erm . . . ?' King Futtout had quavered, fixing him with anxious, wet spaniel eyes. Futtout was small and thin and droopy and ineffectual. He didn't really speak, he just apologised. He was the sort of person who says, 'Awfully sorry' to you when you stand on his foot.

'Absolutely!' Ronald had replied grandly. He had just caught sight of his reflection in the throne room mirror. He knew he looked good. He was wearing the eye-catching, traditional red and purple tall pointy Hat of Knowledge and the matching ceremonial Robe of Mystery. His Mystic Staff was in his hand, and thrown casually over his shoulders was his Cloak of Darkness, the one with the star-spangled dark blue lining which he'd paid an arm and a leg for.

His face had recently been trying very hard to grow a beard, and he was almost sure he could see the beginnings of a wisp on his chin. Best of all, much to his relief, his spots had responded well to the evil-smelling spot cream Aunt Sharkadder had sent him in the post.

Yes. He looked good all right.

Looking so good made him even more confident than usual (which was very confident indeed).

'No probs, honestly. Do something about the Witches, you say? Nothing to it. I'm an expert with Witches. Hey, listen, when we Wizards snap our fingers, those Witches jump, right? I'm your man. Bank on it. Absolutely.'

'It's just . . . erm . . . experience . . . bit young, perhaps . . . you know . . . ? Confess I haven't actually heard of Mighty Ronald the Magnificent . . . erm?'

worried King Futtout.

'I've just qualified,' explained Ronald. 'I got honours. Don't worry, I'm up to the job. I'm a member of the Wizards' Club, they all know me up there. You want to see my certificate?'

'Oh no, no, that won't be necessary . . . erm . . . I'll just have to clear things with Beryl, my . . . erm . . . wife,' King Futtout apologised. 'The Queen, that is. You know how it is? I've never appointed a Wizard before . . . not sure what to look for . . . erm . . . ha ha . . . erm . . . ?'

'Sure, sure. Absolutely. Fine by me. Go right ahead. Wheel her in.'

'And my daughter?' begged King Futtout, wringing his hands. 'You don't mind if I just . . . erm . . . have a quick word . . . erm . . . with Honeydimple? She expects to be . . . erm. Consulted. Erm . . . mind of her own, you know how it is with these girls nowadays, ha ha . . . erm . . . ?'

'Be my guest,' said Ronald graciously. 'I wouldn't mind a quick look at her anyway. If I'm having her hand in marriage.'

King Futtout looked unhappy, opened his mouth to speak, then closed it again and gently rang a little bell which sat on his desk. After a painfully long pause, a footman sauntered in with his hands in his pockets. The King apologised for bothering him and asked if he could possibly beg the Queen and Princess Honeydimple to spare a moment if it wasn't too much trouble.

The footman wandered away, and Ronald and the King stared at each other and tried to think of something to break the embarrassing silence.

'So. These witches,' Ronald said. 'Been giving you a spot of trouble, have they?'

'They most certainly have,' confessed King Futtout with a little shiver. 'Just my luck the palace backs on to Witchway Wood. That's where they all live, you know. I wish they didn't. I'm terrified of them. As a matter of fact, I'm getting quite desperate. Hiring a Wizard was all I could think of. This latest nasty business with Honeydimple . . . most upsetting . . .'

'Quite, quite, absolutely, tut tut,' sympathised Ronald. He refrained from mentioning that his aunt was a Witch. Having a Witch in the family wasn't something you boasted about. Especially if you were a Wizard. Wizards always looked down on Witches. It was traditional.

'You see, stealing from the herb garden I can take,'

108

King Futtout was saying. 'I don't even make a fuss when they buzz the turrets with their Broomsticks at night. I put up with the sound of their cackling and the awful smells drifting over from their brews – and you should try being here when the wind's in the east! And as for that rubbish dump . . .'

Ronald gave a solemn nod. He too had smelt Pongwiffy's tip.

'I've said nothing about what their Bats have done to the coach paintwork and what their Cats have done to the lawn,' continued King Futtout, on the verge of tears. 'I even turn a blind eye when that Haggis creature with the orange fringe comes and practises backstroke in the royal swimming pool. But kidnapping the Princess and setting a Hamster on her is quite another matter, don't you think?'

'Oh, yes,' agreed Ronald. 'Absolutely. Definitely out of order. Er – did you say Hamster?'

'Yes. Small, golden Hamster with a stupid accent. Cut her hair off and bit her ankles. A shocking bully she said it was.'

There was a long pause.

'Oh, all right, I know it sounds unlikely,' said King Futtout. 'Honeydimple exaggerating again, I suppose. I wouldn't make a fuss myself, of

109

course, but the wife . . . Queen Beryl, that is . . . Look, I'd be grateful if you didn't mention the . . . erm . . . the, you know, hand in marriage business? To Honeydimple? Not at this stage, you . . . erm . . . you understand?'

'Oh, quite,' said Ronald. 'Right. Absolutely.'

'They're making me write an official letter of complaint,' confessed King Futtout worriedly. 'Beryl and Honeydimple, that is. They want me to send it to the erm . . . Coven leader.'

'Grandwitch,' Ronald told him. 'She's called the Grandwitch.'

'Oh . . . erm? Frankly . . . erm . . . I'm a bit nervous.'

'May I see?' asked Ronald. 'Glance over it? Professional eye, so to speak?'

'Oh, erm, erm, of course!' cried King Futtout, scrabbling in his desk and coming up with an old envelope which he thrust gratefully into Ronald's hand.

'Is it too . . . erm . . . strong, do you think?' he asked, anxiously searching Ronald's face as he read it. 'I mean, they are Witches. I don't want to, you know. Erm. Upset them.'

'Not strong enough,' said Ronald, shaking his

head. 'Not strong enough by half. You need to be firm with Witches. Where you say you're "a bit annoyed", I mean, it hardly sounds as though you're putting your foot down, does it?'

'Erm,' said King Futtout woefully. 'Erm . . . no, I suppose it doesn't.'

'Don't you worry,' Ronald reassured him. 'Leave it all to me. I can deal with Witches all right.'

'Nothing would make me happier than leaving it all to you,' admitted King Futtout longingly. 'I just hope Beryl and Honeydimple agree. I wonder where they can be?'

It transpired that Queen Beryl was visiting her mother, and had been there for the past week. Nobody had bothered to inform the King. So Ronald was spared the experience of being interviewed by her. (Just as well. Queen Beryl was a very different kettle of fish.)

Honeydimple turned up an embarrassing two hours later.

'Hello . . . erm . . . darling, sorry to bother you,' said King Futtout when she flounced into the room. 'Come and give Daddy a kiss. This is the Mighty Ronald the Erm.'

'Who?' snarled Honeydimple. She was wearing a

grubby dressing gown, a large straw hat (to disguise the fact that she had a huge hank of hair missing) and a petulant expression. She didn't even bother to bat her eyelashes. It was clear that she was far from over her distressing experience.

'Magnificent,' Ronald told her firmly. 'Ronald the Magnificent.'

She wasn't what he expected at all. For a start, she was years too young for him. Just a kid. And even when she grew up, he didn't think he could take that hat. Or that pout.

'Ronald's going to be our new Wizard,' explained King Futtout anxiously. 'Daddy's thinking of hiring him. I've told him all about your . . . erm . . . you know . . . Dreadful Experience. He says he can handle Witches. With him at the . . . erm . . . helm, we should have no more trouble. Right, Ronald?'

'Absolutely no probs,' agreed Ronald airily.

'There you are, you see, sweetheart. So. What d'you . . . erm . . . think of him?'

'Yeuk,' said Honeydimple, wrinkling her nose. 'He'th got thpotth. Yeuk.' It was at that point that Ronald decided he wasn't the marrying kind.

CHAPTER FOURTEEN
Tea at Sharky's

'It's awfully nice of you to invite me and Hugo to tea, Sharky,' said Pongwiffy, surreptitiously poking her finger into the trifle. Sharkadder was too busy running to and fro between the larder, the mirror and the overflowing table to notice. 'After everything we've done. The whisker and that. We're most grateful. Aren't we, Hugo?'

'Hmm? Oh, ya,' agreed Hugo vaguely, his eyes on a bowl of bright green frog jelly sprinkled with ants' eggs in the form of an artistic R (for Ronald).

'Oh, that's all right, Pong,' said Sharkadder, trying

to find room for a fungus sponge. 'You've suffered enough. I forgive you. Dudley hasn't, but I'm sure he'll come round.'

They all glanced at Dudley's basket. Right now, it was empty of Dudley, who had stormed out in disgust the minute he had heard that Pongwiffy and Hugo had been invited to Sunday tea after all. In fact, there had been quite a row about it. It had gone something like this:

DUDLEY: (*shocked disbelief*) Tea? After pinchin' my whisker, you've gone and invited 'em ter tea?

SHARKADDER: (*uncomfortably*) Yes, yes, don't go on about it.

DUDLEY: (*still incredulous*) Today? Tea today? With Ronald coming?

SHARKADDER: (*irritably*) Well, what was I supposed to do? I mean, she said she was sorry, you saw her, and she got down on all fours and blubbed on my knees! I had to think of my stockings. Besides, she is my best friend. I think we should show a little forgiveness to our best friends. After making them suffer terribly first, of course. That goes without saying.

114

DUDLEY: Forgiveness? But us be in the Witch business! Whatever 'appened to Vengeance?

SHARKADDER: We've had quite enough Vengeance, Dudley. Actually, I don't mind admitting it, I feel quite sorry for her. Just think. Banned, Dudley. Another endorsement on her licence and banned from making Magic for a *whole week*! I've invited her to tea to cheer her up and, quite frankly, I don't know what you're making such a fuss about. It's not as if it was your only whisker. I mean, you've got plenty more.

DUDLEY: (*leaving in outrage*) That does it. I'm off.

The row had happened hours ago, and Sharkadder hadn't seen him since. It was now nearly tea time. Pongwiffy had arrived early as usual (in the middle of lunch, actually) and was sitting at the table snaffling food as Sharkadder bustled to and fro with trifles and tarts and dainty little sandwiches with the crusts cut off and jugs of yellow custard and a big cake with WELCOME RONALD picked out in green icing.

'What time is Ronald coming?' Pongwiffy asked innocently, scooping a jam tart into her mouth.

'Any time now.'

'Oh good,' said Pongwiffy. 'And how are his spots these days?'

Sharkadder stopped with a plateful of bat biscuits and gave her a warning look.

'That's quite enough of that,' she scolded. 'You be polite to Ronald, do you hear? He's a real Wizard now; he's passed his exams. He's going places, and I won't have him mocked.'

Just at that moment, there came three loud, important-sounding knocks at the door. They weren't the sort of knocks to ignore. They were knocks of substance. Stern, Open-Up-I-Haven't-Got-All-Day sort of knocks. The knocks of a Wizard who had passed his exams and expected to go places.

'That'll be him now!' cried Sharkadder, spinning round in a tizzy. 'Oh dear! He's early! Is my hair all right? Is my nose shiny? Go and answer the door, Pong, while I put on more lipstick. Don't you dare let him in until I say so.'

She snatched off her apron, raced to her dressing table, and disappeared in a cloud of powder while Pongwiffy went to answer the door.

Outside stood Ronald in all his glory. Hat of

Knowledge, Robe of Mystery, Mystic Staff, Cloak of Darkness, the lot. In fact, he looked exactly the same as he did when we last saw him, except that his spots were worse. (This usually happened with Sharkadder's beauty preparations, which were very hit and miss.)

'Oh,' said Ronald heavily. 'It's you, Pongwiffy. I didn't know you were invited.'

'Well, I am, so there,' said Pongwiffy with satisfaction. 'Spotty,' she added in an undertone. She and Ronald had never liked each other.

'Come in, Ronald, come in!' trilled Sharkadder from inside. 'Whatever are you thinking of, Pong, keeping Ronald waiting on the doorstep!'

'You might as well give me your cloak, then,' said Pongwiffy, deceptively casual. 'I'll hang it up for you.'

'No, thank you,' said Ronald, pushing past. 'It's new. I don't want you touching it.'

'You'll be hot,' Pongwiffy warned him. 'It's really boiling in there. She's been cooking all afternoon – it's like an oven. You'll be much more comfortable with your cloak off.'

'Since when did you care for my comfort?' asked Ronald suspiciously. 'Anyway, a Wizard and his

117

Cloak of Darkness are Never Parted. Except behind the secret portals of the Wizards' Clubhouse. And when we're in bed. I thought you would have known that, Pongwiffy. By the way, is that a Hamster on your hat? And has it got a stupid accent, by any chance?'

'It is,' said Hugo, bristling. 'It has. Vat of it?'

'Aha! I knew it! I've been hearing all about you! King Futtout's been complaining about you, if you must know. I might have known it'd be something to do with you, Pongwiffy . . .'

At this point, Ronald was interrupted, as Sharkadder swooped down upon him with glad cries and attempted to smother him in lipsticky kisses.

'Please, Aunt Sharkadder,' protested Ronald, wriggling out of her embrace, smoothing down his robe and straightening his hat, which had been knocked crooked. 'Please. Do you mind . . . the robes . . .'

'Oh, but look at you!' cried Sharkadder fondly, fussing around and picking imaginary bits of cotton from his shoulder. 'Look at you in all your fancy finery! When I think I used to dandle you on my lap and conjure up little green explosions to make you cry. Little did I know you'd grow into such a tall, handsome young man. Of course, good looks run in the family. Pity about the spots, though. Didn't you use that new cream I sent you?'

'Can we have tea now?' asked Pongwiffy from the tea table, through a mouthful of custard. 'I don't know about anyone else, but I'm starving.'

'Me too,' announced Hugo, from somewhere inside the dish of green jelly.

'Badness me, whatever am I thinking of? Where are my manners?' cried Sharkadder. 'Sit down, Ronald, do. Pongwiffy, get your fist out of that trifle and pull Ronald up a chair. Then we can sit down and have tea and Ronald can tell us all about his interview at the palace.'

And she ran to turn the kettle off.

'Nice cloak,' remarked Pongwiffy. 'I like the stars on the lining. Very smart. What, glued on, are they? Or sewn?'

'I really have no idea,' said Ronald.

'You'd better take it off if you're having tea. It being so new and all,' remarked Pongwiffy helpfully.

'No, thank you,' said Ronald. 'I told you before. I don't want to take it off.'

'You might spill something down your front,' said Pongwiffy.

'No, I won't,' said Ronald, staring at her.

'*I* might spill something down your front,' threatened Pongwiffy.

At that point, Sharkadder came hastening back with the teapot.

'Right, shall I be mother? Now, do help yourself to a sandwich, Ronald. There's spiderspread, grasshopper in mayonnaise or slug and lettuce. I've cut the crusts off. Here's your tea. Strong with three sugars in a proper cup and saucer, just how you like it.'

'Where's *my* tea?' complained Pongwiffy.

'It's coming, it's coming, just wait. I do hope everything's to your liking, Ronald. I'm afraid it won't be up to the standard of the meals you get at the Wizards' Clubhouse.'

'Oh absolutely,' agreed Ronald. 'Some pretty amazing spreads we get there, I can tell you. Three courses at least. And paper serviettes.'

'You hear that, Pong?' breathed Sharkadder, terribly impressed. 'Three courses! And paper serviettes. Well I never.'

'Oh yes,' said Ronald, warming to his theme. 'Three courses and a clean tablecloth every day. And our own goblets with our names on.'

120

'Clean tablecloths!' breathed Sharkadder, enthralled. 'Own goblets! So sophisticated! Imagine, Pongwiffy.'

'So what?' growled Pongwiffy. 'So what if there are clean tablecloths? Who cares? I hate clean tablecloths. Don't encourage him, Sharkadder.'

Sharkadder ignored her.

'You know what I'm dying to hear about, Ronald?' she trilled, and gave a girlish little skip. 'The password! Tell us about the password, do! It's too, too thrilling!'

Ronald shook his head.

'Sorry,' he said importantly. 'No can do, Aunt. All very hush-hush. Only We Wizards know it.'

'It's probably something really stupid and obvious, like Open Sesame,' said Pongwiffy.

Ronald gasped.

'How do you know?' he cried, then went bright red and clapped his hand to his mouth.

'Because you Wizards have no imagination,' explained Pongwiffy.

'Well, I'd sooner you didn't mention it,' Ronald muttered. 'As I said, only We Wizards are supposed to know it. And the servants, of course.'

'Servants? You have servants up at the Wizards'

121

Clubhouse?' said Pongwiffy, suddenly perking up.

'Certainly. Cooks. Butlers. Waiters,' Ronald told her loftily.

'You mean someone else washes your dirty socks?' Pongwiffy wanted to know.

'Of course,' said Ronald. 'We Wizards don't have time to do all the menial tasks. Especially Those Of Us With Proper Jobs,' he added proudly.

'Oh, Ronald!' cried Sharkadder, thrilled to pieces. 'You did it! You got the job up at the palace! Oh, you clever, clever boy! Tell us all about it, then. How much does it pay? How many weeks holiday? Are there banquet vouchers? What are your duties?'

'Well – actually, I was about to come to that,' said Ronald. 'There's something I wanted to discuss with you, Aunt. A small favour.'

'Oh yes?' said Sharkadder. She was still smiling a wide, toothy smile, but her voice bore a hint of frost. She was suspicious of people who asked favours, as anyone who knows Pongwiffy has a right to be. 'And what might that be, Ronald?'

'Well, King Futtout tells me there have been . . . well, a few problems with you Witches lately. I'm afraid he's rather upset. And quite frankly, Aunt, it's got to stop.'

There was a long pause, during which Sharkadder and Pongwiffy looked at Ronald. Even Hugo stuck his head up over the jelly dish and treated him to a long, hard stare.

'Problems, Ronald?' said Sharkadder in a silky voice. 'What sort of problems?'

'Oh, you know. Bat droppings on the lawn. Unlawful use of the swimming pool. Er – some unfortunate business with the Princess – er . . .'

Ronald tailed off. Suddenly he began to feel a little uncertain.

'So?' asked Sharkadder. 'That's Witch Business. I wouldn't like to think that you were interfering in Witch Business, Ronald.'

'Quite right, Sharky,' chipped in Pongwiffy. 'You tell him. It's bad luck to stick your nose in Witch Business. I'd have thought you'd have known that, Ronald. All those exams.'

'I just thought, you know . . . maybe a few words in the right ear . . .'

At this point, Ronald's confidence deserted him completely. His throat went dry and he badly wanted a drink. He lifted the brimming cup to his lips and attempted to take a sip.

It was then that Pongwiffy leaned across the table

and violently joggled his elbow, crying, 'Ronald! You've just spilt some tea on your lovely new cloak! Take it off immediately. I'll get a cloth!'

'Oh, Pongwiffy, how could you be so clumsy!' wailed Sharkadder, rushing forward and dabbing violently at Ronald with the first thing that came to hand, which happened to be the blanket from Dudley's basket. So enthusiastic was she that Ronald toppled backwards out of his chair and landed on the floor with a little scream.

Just to complicate things still further, Dudley chose that very moment to stage his return. He came leaping in through the window and came face-to-face with his old enemy Hugo, who, by way of greeting, stuck his tongue out and flicked a spoonful of frog jelly in Dudley's one remaining eye. An interesting chase followed, resulting in a lot of food ending up on Sharkadder's newly spring-cleaned floor.

Meanwhile, under the table, Ronald fended off Pongwiffy as she attempted to forcibly divest him of his cloak. She would have succeeded too, if Sharkadder hadn't come to the rescue.

It is best to draw a veil over the rest of the proceedings and skip straight to the outcome.

The outcome was that Pongwiffy and Hugo were thrown out of the tea party in disgrace. Once again, Pongwiffy was minus a best friend. She didn't even get one star from the Cloak of Darkness, let alone seven.

But she did get a good tea.

And an idea.

CHAPTER FIFTEEN
Seven Stolen Stars

The Wizards' Clubhouse perched high in the Misty Mountains, some distance from Witchway Wood. (Wizards don't tend to go in for woods much. They don't enjoy roughing it. They prefer proper amenities, such as street lighting. Wizards like to stroll around in expensive robes, talking wisely in loud voices, and while they are doing this, they prefer not to step into a bog.) Even better than strolling around talking loudly and wisely was sitting down being waited on. That's why most Wizards tended to live at the Clubhouse.

The Clubhouse was, as you might expect, very posh indeed. It sat glittering proudly at the top of a steep, imposing driveway consisting of yellow and pink crazy paving with silver grouting. There were curly bits and twiddly bits and bits which squirted coloured water. There were spirals and murals and gargoyles and symbols. Someone had gone mad with a lot of gold paint. The Wizards' flag (a sort of messy mishmash of crossed staves and lightning bolts and stars and moons and stuff) flew from the topmost turret.

'So *that's* the famous Wizards' Clubhouse,' said Pongwiffy, peering round an ornamental fountain. 'Don't think much of it, do you? Give me a nice filthy hovel any time. All those fancy spires and portals and stars and carved knockers and stuff. Bad taste, I call it.'

'Ssh,' hissed Hugo. 'Keep voice down.'

'And the colours! Yuck. Makes my eyes water. All that pink and gold. What's wrong with nice plain serviceable black, I want to know?'

'Mistress! Please!' begged Hugo. 'Ve don't vant to be catched.'

'Oh, stop being such an old worry-pouches. If I'd known you were going to be like this I wouldn't

127

have brought you with me. Where's all that famous Hamster swashbuckle you're always talking about? Where's your sense of adventure? All that spring-cleaning's turned you soft. Now, where's my disguise?'

Obediently the Broom came scuttling forward with a badly wrapped newspaper parcel.

'I still say you crazy,' said Hugo in a sulky voice. He didn't like being called soft. 'If Sourmuddle find out about zis, she throw you out of Coven. Zen I out of job.'

'Serve you right,' said Pongwiffy. 'In fact, just recently, I've been wondering if you're up to the job. It seems that if I want anything done I have to do it myself. Anyway, it's taken me ages to get all the ingredients together and I'm not stopping now. I've only got the seven stars to go. If all goes well, we can make the potion tonight. Now, how do I look?'

Hugo looked at her. Slowly, he shook his head. 'It von't vork,' he said.

'Yes, it will. I am the very image of a rosy-cheeked washerwoman.'

'No, you not,' argued Hugo. 'Vashervimmin alvays clean. You filthy.'

'But I've got the frilly apron and the cap and everything!' Pongwiffy was hurt. She had indeed gone to a lot of trouble to look the part, even making sure that a handful of clothes pegs and an old bar of soap (stolen, naturally) protruded from her apron pocket.

'Zey filthy too. I tell you it von't vork.'

'Well, whose fault is all this anyway!' cried Pongwiffy crossly, stamping her foot. 'If you hadn't thrown out my Cardigan of Invisibility, we wouldn't have to bother with all this disguise nonsense!'

'I not throw it out!' denied Hugo.

'Oh ha! Next thing you'll be saying you didn't even see it!'

'Of course I not see it! How I see it? It invisible!'

'Oh, pass the laundry basket. I'm not standing around here arguing with you a minute longer! I'll show you how it's done. Stay here and keep watch with the Broom. And be prepared for a quick getaway.'

Bad-temperedly, Pongwiffy snatched up her most important prop – the battered red plastic basket she had found on the rubbish dump – and marched up the crazy-paving path which led to the star-studded front doors of the Wizards' Clubhouse.

'Not zat one! Not ze front door! Go to ze tradesman's entrance at ze side!' called Hugo. But he was too late. Pongwiffy had already knocked, using the heavy carved knocker.

Not content with that, she gave the bell-rope a determined yank and at the same time kicked the door sharply with the toe of her boot.

'Open up,' bawled Pongwiffy over the clanging. 'Hurry up in there, get a move on!'

'She blow it!' moaned Hugo to the Broom. 'I know it! She blow it! She overconfident. I not look.'

Pongwiffy tapped her foot impatiently. She was just about to kick the door again, when there came an unpleasant crackling noise from one of the decorative stars. Pongwiffy gave a little jump.

'This is a recorded message,' shrieked a harsh voice in Pongwiffy's ear. 'Oozat? Wachoo want? Please speak clearly after the tone or belt up and go away.'

There was a terrible burst of static, then silence.

'Washerwoman,' bellowed Pongwiffy into the star. 'Harmless old washerwoman, come to collect the dirty clothes.'

Immediately, she came up in green spots.

'Password?' grated the voice.

'Open Sesame, of course,' squawked Pongwiffy. 'Hurry up, I haven't got all day. I've got to get back to my – er – mangle. Oh yes, there's a mountain of ironing I've got to do. That's because I'm a washer-woman.'

There was a pause, followed by a great deal of interference from the primitive intercom. (Wizards are creative types. When it comes to anything the slightest bit technical, they're all thumbs.) Then, slowly and dramatically, with a good deal of theatrical squeaking, the doors swung open and Pongwiffy strode into the vestibule.

Inside, it had been done out in red flock wallpaper. Dreary organ music issued forth tinnily from a couple of cheap wall speakers. Dull portraits of miserable-looking bearded ancients in pointy hats stared down from the walls. There was a headache-inducing, swirling, multicoloured carpet. There was a polished desk marked RECEPTION behind which a bored-looking female Zombie with large brass earrings and a tangled mass of green hair chewed gum and read a magazine.

Pongwiffy marched over to the reception desk and briskly rang the bell.

'Yeah?' said the Zombie, not even looking up.

She was reading an article entitled 'Scott Sinister – Man or Myth?'

'Where's the cloakroom?' said Pongwiffy. 'Dearie.'

Slowly, the Zombie looked up and stared rudely. Pongwiffy gave her what she imagined to be a broad Honest Washerwoman smile.

'Oooja saya wuzagin?' said the Zombie. She wore a badge proclaiming that she was Brenda and that she was At Your Service.

'Harmless old washerwoman. Mrs Flushing's my name. From the new laundry down the road,' said Pongwiffy.

'Nobody's said nuffink to me,' said Brenda, pulling her gum out to arm's length in a long grey string then letting it coil back down into her mouth.

'You mean they haven't told you?' cried Pongwiffy. 'About the new arrangement? How I'm to come and collect the dirty cloaks every Wednesday? Well, if that doesn't beat all. You'd think they'd have told you. You're not expecting me, then?'

'No,' said Brenda, blowing a bubble. ''Ere. You're covered in green spots, you are.'

'Oh, am I? Really? Probably my allergy. I'm allergic to multicoloured carpets. Frightened by

132

one as a child. Terrible thing. Oh well, can't stand chatting here all day. This way, is it? To the little boys' room? Down this passage?'

''Ere, jussa minute, you can't . . .'

'Don't worry, dear, I'll find it.'

And Pongwiffy marched purposefully off down a long passageway, leaving Brenda with an uncertain expression on her face.

The lounge was packed with Wizards. For the most part, they sat silently in overstuffed armchairs, glancing impatiently at their watches, snoozing, doing the crossword, leafing through back copies of *Wizards' World* or merely dribbling into their beards whilst waiting for the dinner gong.

It was hard to know they were Wizards when they were without their Hats of Knowledge and Cloaks of Darkness. Bald heads and very old woolly jumpers predominated. An ancient retainer creaked around amongst them, handing out small glasses of smoking green stuff.

Ronald was standing casually at the window, pretending not to mind that all the chairs had been taken so there was nowhere for him to sit. Neither

133

had there been a peg available in the cloakroom. He was the new boy, so everyone tended to ignore him. He was, he noticed, the only one who hadn't been offered a glass of the smoking green stuff.

'Hasn't our Brenda got round to ordering a chair for you yet, young Ronald?' jeered a rat-faced Wizard, from the depths of the comfiest sofa. His name was Frank the Foreteller and he specialised in Foreknowledge.

'Actually, I rather like standing,' said Ronald.

'I knew you were going to say that,' cried Frank the Foreteller triumphantly, slapping his knee. 'I knew he was going to say that,' he repeated to the room at large. Several Wizards looked up from their newspapers and stared at Ronald as though they were seeing him for the first time.

'You're looking flushed, young Ronald. Why don't you take your cloak off?' suggested Frank the Foreteller, winking at the watching Wizards, really rubbing things in. 'We're all informal here, lad – you don't have to stand on ceremony.'

'Actually, I don't have a peg,' said Ronald stiffly.

'I know you don't,' crowed Frank the Foreteller. 'And I can foretell you won't have one for a long time to come,' he added spitefully. 'And how did the

134

interview go, young Ronald? Applied for a post at the palace, eh?'

'Well, yes, I . . .'

'Don't tell me, don't tell me, you got the job. I knew that. Saw it in the tea leaves yesterday. So old Futtout wants you to do something about the Witches, eh?'

'Well, I . . .'

'Yes, yes, I know, you don't have to tell me. Of course, you know you've bitten off more than you can chew, don't you?'

'I don't think I . . .'

'Oh yes, oh dear me yes. Tricky business, dealing with Witches. You're going to come a cropper.'

'King Futtout has every conf—'

'Yes, when it comes to handling Witches, some have got it and some haven't.'

'Look, I really . . .'

'No point in arguing, young feller. I know. I can foretell. I can foretell most things. In fact, I can foretell the dinner gong's about to go.'

There really was no point in talking to him. Ronald turned away. As he did so, he caught a glimpse of someone – a servant, no doubt – hurrying past the doorway carrying what looked like a heaped pile of clothes in a basket. For a moment, there was an unpleasant, somehow familiar smell in the air. He couldn't quite place it, but he knew he'd smelt it before. It was on the tip of his nose . . .

The gong went. There was a united sigh of relief, and a general stirring and cracking of bones as the Wizards heaved themselves out of their armchairs and made for the door, eager to be first in the queue for the dining room.

The exodus was halted by the sudden appearance of Brenda in the doorway. She was breathing heavily and was rather flushed, as though she had been lumbering a shade faster than usual.

'You can orl siddown again,' announced Brenda. 'That weren't the dinner gong. Dinner ain't ready yet. That were the emergency gong. I just come up to tell you we bin robbed, see? Loada cloaks gawn from the cloakroom. An' before you start, it weren't my fault. She said she wuz a washerwoman. 'Ow wuz I to know?'

There was instant panic amongst the Wizards. This was grave news indeed! Not only were the cloaks stolen, dinner wasn't ready!

Ronald couldn't resist it. He turned to Frank the Foreteller.

'Pity you couldn't have foretold that,' he remarked with a smirk.

He could afford to be smug. You see, *he was the only one who hadn't hung his cloak up in the cloakroom*!

CHAPTER SIXTEEN
Brewing Up

It was full moon – or, as Granny Malodour would have put it, Fulle Moone. In the hovel, preparations were well under way. The fire was lit and the cauldron was giving off promising gloppy noises. Rich brown muddy fumes curled into the air, mingling unpleasantly with the all-pervading smell of *Reeka Reeka Roses*. Pongwiffy peered in at the brew, sniffed, stirred, tasted and gave a nod.

'The quicksand's nearly ready. How are you getting on with the chopping?'

'I done ze visker and ze fezzer and ze golden hair.

I still got ze bobble and ze stars to do.'

'Well, get a move on,' snapped Pongwiffy. 'We've only got until the cock crows, you know.'

'Chop, chop, chop, all I do is chop. It make my paw ache. I sink it my turn to stir now.'

'Certainly not! Haven't you heard the old saying? Too Many Witches Spoil The Brew. Familiars chop, Witches stir. That's the way things are done. Keep chopping or you're fired.'

She hunched down grumpily in her chair, bit her nails and scowled. It wasn't like her to be so bad-tempered when she was brewing up. It was just that, somehow, things didn't *feel* right. There simply wasn't an atmosphere. Everywhere was too clean and tidy. There were too few shadows; there was far too much hygiene. Even the cauldron had been scraped out and there were none of those interesting little black bits to drop into whatever was cooking.

Pongwiffy sighed deeply. She missed the dirt and the cobwebs and the little black bits. In the past there had always been dirt and cobwebs and little black bits when she made a brew. There was *supposed* to be dirt and cobwebs and little black bits. It was traditional.

'If you only let me use uzzer paw . . .'

'No.'

Firmly, Pongwiffy tapped Granny Malodour's Spell Book, which lay crumbling away before her on the kitchen table.

'No. The recipe says "Using thy left hand only." We've got to do it right. The important thing about making a decent brew is to get the details right.'

'Vy ze Broom not help?' sulked Hugo.

'Because I've posted it outside on guard duty. I've told it to give three loud knocks as a warning signal if anyone comes. We don't want unexpected visitors, do we?'

'Hmm. I just hope all zis choppink vorth it,' said Hugo doubtfully. 'Suppose it not vork? Sometimes zese old recipes . . .'

'You just don't understand, do you? This is Granny's Wishing Water, Hugo. Granny's spells *always* work. And if it doesn't, I shall blame you. It'll be because the lock of hair isn't fresh . . .'

She broke off as there came three thunderous knocks on the door. Hugo jumped into the air and the knife he was holding dropped from his numb paw. Quite a bit of chopped hair spilt on the floor. Guiltily, Pongwiffy snatched up the cauldron lid and slammed it down over the illicit brew.

'It her!' gasped Hugo. 'It Sourmuddle! Now you done it! She caught us! Now vat ve gonna do?'

'Stall her,' hissed Pongwiffy, throwing Granny Malodour's Spell Book under the nearest cushion and spraying the air liberally with *Reeka Reeka Roses*.

Then a voice spoke.

'Pong?' it said. 'Is that you in there, Pong? It's all right, you can open up. It's only me, Sharky.'

Gasping with relief, Pongwiffy scuttled across and threw open the hovel door. Sure enough, outside stood Sharkadder. She had obviously come in a hurry, because her Broomstick looked all in. In one hand she held her handbag. In the other was a large, fragrant, still-warm, home-made fungus sponge. Pongwiffy's Broom stood on the doorstep, twiggy arms out-stretched, boldly blocking her way.

'Hello, Pong,' said Sharkadder, holding out the sponge. 'Tell your idiot Broomstick to get out of my way, will you? I've brought you a cake as a peace offering. Just out of the oven.'

'Sharky! What a sight for sore eyes! Come in, come in!' cried Pongwiffy, never one to turn down an offer of friendship. Or cake, for that matter. 'I just can't tell you how pleased I am to see you.

141

Broom! Get out of Witch Sharkadder's way this minute!'

Huffily, the Broom moved to one side and threw itself against the hovel wall. Sharkadder propped hers next to it, and the two of them began the low, mutinous rustling which is the Broom equivalent of discontented whispering.

'Come on in, then,' said Pongwiffy, reaching for the sponge. 'I suppose you've come to make up?'

'No, I made up before I came,' explained Sharkadder, following her in. 'Doesn't it show?'

It did. Her hair was frizzed, her face was chalky white, she was wearing her longest spiderleg eyelashes and a great deal of beetroot-coloured lipstick.

'But if you mean have I come to make friends again, yes I have,' she added. 'I've decided to forgive you again, Pong. I've been talking it over with Dudley, and I've come to the conclusion that Ronald was every bit as much to blame as you for spoiling my tea party.'

'Oh yes?' said Pongwiffy, biting into the fungus sponge. 'And Dudley? What conclusion did he come to?'

'The opposite,' confessed Sharkadder. 'He says

142

it's all your fault. I must admit I agreed with him. Until Ronald sent me a *dry-cleaning bill*!'

'Never!' cried Pongwiffy. 'And you his aunty? Surely not!'

'Yes, he did. The cheek of it. It arrived this morning. And there was me thinking it was a letter saying thank you for the lovely tea. And not a word about the spot cream I gave him either. No manners at all.'

'I told you so,' Pongwiffy reminded her. 'If that's not a typical Wizard. I always said Ronald was a snobby little swankpot, didn't I?'

'And you were right. My badness, it's clean in here, isn't it?' Sharkadder suddenly exclaimed. 'I do believe you've swept the floor! And all your cobwebs have gone. It doesn't look like your hovel at all, Pongwiffy.'

'I know,' said Pongwiffy, with a bitter little glance at Hugo, who sucked in his pouches and looked obstinate.

'Anyway, as I told Dudley, "Friendship's Thicker Than Bogwater",' continued Sharkadder. 'Besides, I know you're up to something and I want to know what it is.'

Sharkadder's long white nose sniffed the air.

'Aha! I thought so! I detect hot quicksand. You're working on your secret spell, aren't you? Is that a brew you've got going over there in the cauldron? Let's have a look.'

Sharkadder swept across, lifted the cauldron lid and examined the bubbling quicksand with a critical eye.

'Smells awful. Is Dudley's whisker in there?' she asked.

'Not yet.'

'Hmm. There's none of your usual little black bits. What is it, anyway? Come on, Pong, you might as well come clean.'

'Come clean? Me? Never!' said Pongwiffy with a shudder. 'But I suppose now you're here and we're friends again, I might as well tell you everything. Keep your eye on the cauldron while I put the kettle on. Hugo! What did I just tell you? Get on with that chopping.'

And while Hugo got on with the chopping, Sharkadder stirred the cauldron and drank bogwater and Pongwiffy ate the sponge and showed her Granny Malodour's recipe and told her all about the difficulties she'd had getting hold of the ingredients.

'Well!' said Sharkadder, when she had finished.

144

'Well, I never did. So *that's* what it's all about! You've got the recipe for Granny Malodour's famous Wishing Water! Well, well, well. Lucky old you. I've always wanted to try that stuff. You should have told me that's what you were planning, Pongwiffy. I'd have pulled out one of Dudley's whiskers myself. And if it comes out right, you mean to enter it for the Spell of the Year Competition, did you say?'

'Most definitely,' agreed Pongwiffy. 'So you see why I wanted to keep it a secret?'

'I suppose so,' said Sharkadder doubtfully. 'Although I still think you could have told *me* about it. After all, I am your best friend.'

'You didn't want me to come in,' Pongwiffy reminded her. 'You wanted to get on with the spring-cleaning, remember? You said you didn't want me smelling the place up.'

Sharkadder looked sheepish.

'You caught me at a bad moment,' she confessed.

'Not to worry. I forgive you,' said Pongwiffy graciously. 'And I tell you what!' she added, in a spirit of generosity. 'You can help me! We'll do it together, and we'll both enter it for the competition. It'll be a joint entry. Pongwiffy and Sharkadder's Wonderful Wishing Water. It's got a certain ring to it, don't you think?'

Sharkadder thought about it. She'd been far too busy spring-cleaning to give much thought to the Spell of the Year Competition. She had vaguely thought about entering her new spot cream, the one she'd tried out on Ronald, but looking at him she suspected it still needed a bit of work. That was the trouble with spring-cleaning. It left no time for Magic.

'Think of the prizes,' Pongwiffy tempted her.

Sharkadder thought of the prizes. There were some good ones. A large silver cup with your name on, for a start. Plus a year's interest-free credit at Malpractiss Magic Ltd, two carefree weeks in the drizzle at Sludgehaven-on-Sea, timeshare on a flying carpet, a year's subscription for *The Daily Miracle* and, for some strange reason, a lifetime's supply of *Reeka Reeka Roses*.

'We're sure to win,' said Pongwiffy confidently. 'Besides, I'm really looking forward to trying Granny's Wishing Water again. I tell you, Sharky, this stuff is Magic! It really works. One sip, one wish. Simple as that. Imagine, Sharky. Your heart's secret desire.'

Sharkadder had a fleeting daydream for a moment

that involved a small, exclusive dress shop in a better part of the Wood and a career in modelling.

'All right, then,' said Sharkadder. 'What can I do to help?'

'Chop,' said Pongwiffy and Hugo together.

CHAPTER SEVENTEEN
Ronald Tells

'Who did you say you were again?' said Sourmuddle snappily, fumbling for her glasses. She was standing on her doorstep in her nightie in the drizzle in the dark at a stupid hour of the night while some pushy, pimpled pest in a pointy hat shouted down her ear trumpet, and she didn't take kindly to it.

'RONALD! I'M RONALD!'

'Well, Donald, let's just get one thing clear before I catch my death. I don't want double glazing or patio doors or a cheap ironing-board cover or a selection of alpine scenes hand-painted on velvet. Neither do I want my garden weeding or my windows washing or my chimney swept. What I *do* want, Roland, is a decent night's sleep. So why don't you just run along before I lose my temper and turn you into something nasty?'

'I'M NOT SELLING ANYTHING!' bellowed Ronald. 'I'M A WIZARD.'

'A what?'

'A WIZARD!'

'Here,' said Grandwitch Sourmuddle, polishing her glasses with the end of her nightcap. 'Here, you remind me of someone, you know.'

'I'M RONALD! SHARKADDER'S MY AUNT!'

'Wait a minute, wait a minute, it's on the tip of my – ha! I know who it is! Sharkadder's awful little nephew! The stuck-up one with the pimples. The one who wants to be a Wizard when he grows up. Rudolph or something. You're the spitting image.'

'RONALD!' screamed Ronald through tortured tonsils. 'RONALD! IT'S ME! I *HAVE* GROWN UP. I *AM* A WIZARD AND I'M HERE ON OFFICIAL BUSINESS! I WISH TO MAKE A FORMAL COMPLAINT ABOUT ONE OF YOUR WITCHES!'

149

'Complaint? What have you got to complain about? You're not standing on your doorstep in your nightshirt, are you? If anyone's got a complaint, it's me. And stop shouting like that, you're giving me a headache. Think I'm deaf or something?'

'IT'S ABOUT – it's about Pongwiffy, Grandwitch Sourmuddle. She's really overstepped the mark this time.'

'Eh? Pongwiffy? What about Pongwiffy? If you're referring to that Princess Business, young Randolph, I've already dealt with that. I've told her to write to the palace and apologise.'

'No, no, it's much worse than that. Earlier today, cunningly disguised as a washerwoman, she infiltrated We Wizards' private Clubhouse and stole a number of cloaks. These were later retrieved from the bottom of an ornamental fountain. Upon examination, we found that several valuable stars had been forcibly removed. The owners will, of course, be claiming compensation.'

'Hold your horses, sonny,' snapped Sourmuddle. 'Are you quite sure about this? You're making a serious allegation, you know.'

'Absolutely,' agreed Ronald eagerly. 'I'm glad you see it our way, Sourmuddle. Stealing Wizards' cloaks is a serious business.'

'The cloaks? Who gives a bat squeak for the cloaks? No, what I'm annoyed about is that I personally banned Pongwiffy from all Magical activity for one entire week. She's not allowed to read so much as one tea leaf. Are you saying she's still running about making a nuisance of herself? In defiance of my orders?'

'Yes,' said Ronald, nodding vigorously. 'Yes, that's exactly what she is doing. Absolutely.'

'Wait there on the doorstep while I get my dressing gown,' ordered Sourmuddle. 'And don't touch anything. I don't trust you Wizards.'

'Can't I come in? It's drizzling.' Sourmuddle's answer was to shut the door firmly in his face. Ronald turned his collar up, shuffled about on the step and allowed himself a little smile. Despite the weather, for once things were going quite well.

CHAPTER EIGHTEEN
Caught in the Act

Things were also going quite well at Number One, Dump Edge. All the ingredients had been added to the brew, which was now bubbling nicely and giving off gratifyingly black, oily fumes.

'Mmm. There's something *about* the smell of Skunk Stock,' said Pongwiffy, sniffing appreciatively and throwing in a cupful of Frogspawn. 'Grab another handful of those Fly Droppings, Hugo. I like a nice bit of seasoning. Right, Sharky, what's next?'

'Sit with thy nose pointing due north and thy

boots on ye wrong feet,' read Sharkadder. 'Recite thou ye following chant . . .'

'Wait, wait, which way's north?'

'That way,' said Sharkadder and Hugo, simultaneously pointing in opposite directions. At this point, both Brooms had to be brought in and consulted. (Brooms have a kind of inbuilt compass, which is situated approximately halfway up their sticks. They might not know much, but they certainly know north.)

It was very soon established that Pongwiffy had to sit looking out of the newly glazed window overlooking her beloved rubbish dump. The Dump had swollen considerably, mainly because of all the extra junk that Hugo and the Broom had removed from the hovel. Pongwiffy sighed as she looked out over it, wiped away a nostalgic tear, then concentrated on the business in hand.

'Right, I've swapped my boots around. Where's the chant? Pass me Granny's Spell Book, Sharky. Hurry up, it's nearly dawn and my feet are killing me.'

'Why have I got to do all the menial tasks?' grumbled Sharkadder, whose arm ached from chopping. 'Why can't I do the chant?'

153

But she did as she was told.

'Right,' said Pongwiffy. 'Here goes. Leap around the cauldron, all of you. Brooms included.'

'Where does it say that?' Sharkadder wanted to know. 'Where in that spell does it say we have to leap?'

'It doesn't. I just think it adds to the atmosphere, don't you? Just stop whining and do it, all right?'

Sighing, Sharkadder gave a small leap and waved her long arms around. Hugo did a spirited tap dance and the two Brooms hopped about obligingly, in a better mood now that they had been consulted about north. Pongwiffy waited a moment or two to let them all get into the swing of the thing, then began to chant in her best professional cackling voice.

Snap and crackle, scream and cackle.
Can't catch cows with fishing tackle.
Bubble, brew, the way thou oughter.
Then turn into Wishing Water!

She signalled the dancers to halt. Puffing a bit they jogged to a stop and listened. Nothing happened.

'Where's the cock crow?' said Pongwiffy with a

154

worried frown. 'The cock's supposed to crow.'

'Keep going,' panted Hugo. 'Say it again. You supposed to continue ze chantink.'

'It'd better work this time,' said Sharkadder with a sniff. 'I'm not leaping much more, I tell you. These shoes aren't made for leaping.'

Snap and crackle, scream and cackle,
Can't catch cows with fishing tackle.
Bubble, brew, the way thou ...

That did it. The brew gave a convulsive heave and boiled over. Where the brew met the fire, the flames turned green and blazed up dramatically.

'Vow!' said Hugo. 'Zat amazink!'

There was a hissing and a fizzling and a spluttering and puffs of lime green smoke. Little crackles of shocking pink lightning arced above the cauldron. The startled cauldron-dancers drew back in alarm as pink and green sparks rained down and Pongwiffy hastily reached for a jug of flowers, just in case. There was an eye-watering, multicoloured eruption of light.

And then, far away, the cock crowed. Five times. Just like it was supposed to do. And with the first crow, the miniature firework display above the cauldron fizzled out, leaving an unappetising purplish liquid simmering sluggishly in the bottom.

Pongwiffy peered in and gave a deep sniff. 'That's it!' she said excitedly. 'Wishing Water! It's come out just the way I remember it! Colour, smell, everything! This is the moment we've been waiting for. Hugo, fetch me the ladle. I'm having first taste.'

'Oh no, you're not, Pongwiffy,' said a voice from the doorway. It was accompanied by a theatrical rumble of thunder.

Everyone turned round. There stood Sourmuddle in fluffy tartan slippers and a quilted blue dressing gown that had seen better days. Behind her stood Snoop, rubbing his eyes and looking like he'd just woken up. And behind *him* stood Ronald, wearing a malicious little smile.

'Oh, Sourmuddle, it's you,' said Pongwiffy with a gulp. 'What a lovely surprise. Just in time to sample my new brew.'

'I'll take charge of that,' said Sourmuddle sternly. 'Making Magic behind my back indeed! After I've banned you! And what are you doing here, Sharkadder?'

'Trying to stop her,' explained Sharkadder. 'I

156

wasn't dancing around the cauldron or anything. Oh, dear me, no.'

'Hello, Aunt,' said Ronald with a little smirk.

'Ronald,' said Sharkadder in a voice that could curdle milk. 'Get lost.'

'You know, I'm sure I recognise that smell,' said Sourmuddle, sniffing. 'What is it, anyway?'

'Granny Malodour's Wishing Water,' said Pongwiffy. 'I might as well tell you. You'll find out for yourself in the end anyway.'

'Really?' said Sourmuddle with an interested gleam in her eye. 'Granny Malodour's Wishing Water? The real stuff? You're sure?'

She shuffled over to the cauldron and peered in. Snoop, Sharkadder, Pongwiffy and Hugo clustered round and they all stood over it and stroked their chins, examining the unpleasant goo with professional interest.

'Can I see?' asked Ronald, trying to look over their shoulders.

'No,' said Sourmuddle. 'This is Witch Business. Stand back.'

'Go away, Spotty,' said Pongwiffy.

'And write a nice thank-you letter,' suggested Sharkadder in a voice of steel.

157

Ronald flinched and stayed where he was.

'You're right, you know,' said Sourmuddle. 'It *is* Wishing Water. Once smelt, never forgotten.'

'The very same,' nodded Pongwiffy. 'Made to Granny's very own recipe, which I just happened to come across. Look. Here's her Spell Book.'

'Well, well, well,' said Sourmuddle with a little chuckle. 'And I thought Granny Malodour's recipe for Wishing Water was lost for ever.'

'Why? Have you tried it, then, Sourmuddle?' asked Sharkadder curiously.

'Certainly I have. Granny used to send me over a bottle every Hallowe'en. Disgusting taste. But it worked.'

'Why? What did you wish for?' chorused Pongwiffy and Sharkadder together.

'What d'you think? To become Grandwitch, of course. To be Mistress of the Coven and boss everybody about. And my wish came true. Which is why I'm ordering you to hurry up and stick that stuff in a bottle because I'm confiscating it right now.'

'Oh, Sourmuddle, please!' wailed Pongwiffy. '*Please* don't do this! Not until you hear about my plan!'

'Plan? What plan?'

'The plan that's going to benefit all of us. You see, I'm planning to enter Granny's Wishing Water for the Spell of the Year Competition. There are some really good prizes this year. I wanted to share them with all my good friends. And bring honour to the Coven, of course.'

'Really?' said Sourmuddle, perking up. 'What, you'd share the holiday and everything?'

'Oh yes. I thought *you* might like to go on that, Sourmuddle. I know how much you like Sludgehaven-on-Sea. And I thought you could keep the silver cup on your mantelpiece. It'd look really nice up there.'

There was a long pause.

'It would be nice if a Witch won this year,' Sourmuddle said slowly.

'It would, it certainly would,' agreed Pongwiffy eagerly.

'And I am on the jury . . .' Sourmuddle said thoughtfully.

'I know you are,' said Pongwiffy. 'I know I can count on your vote, Sourmuddle.'

'You mean *we*,' Sharkadder reminded her. 'It's a joint entry, remember?'

159

'Of course, rules are rules, Pongwiffy, and you'll have to be punished,' added Sourmuddle.

'But not *too* severely,' coaxed Pongwiffy. 'Concentrate, Sourmuddle. Just hold on to that idea of a Witch win. Beating the Wizards. Just think of it.'

'After that idiot with the pigeons up his jumper . . .' said Sourmuddle reflectively.

'You are so right,' said Pongwiffy, shaking her head sadly. 'He never should have got it. We all said so at the time.'

'I'm tempted,' said Sourmuddle. 'What do you think, Snoop?'

'I say,' said Ronald from somewhere back in the shadows. 'I say, Sourmuddle, look, what about this business of the cloaks and everything? Aren't you going to . . . ?'

He tailed off, as would anyone who was being stared at by three Witches, a Demon and a Hamster.

'Just a moment,' said Sourmuddle. 'I wish to consult with Snoop.'

They went into a conspiratorial huddle in the corner, then made up their minds.

'I tell you what, Pongwiffy,' said Sourmuddle briskly, 'we'll compromise. You stick it in a bottle and I'll confiscate it, but you can have it back in time for the Spell of the Year Competition. How about that?'

'All right,' said Pongwiffy with a little sigh. 'But can't we even try it now? Just one sip? Just to make sure it works?'

'Certainly not. You're supposed to be being punished, not getting wishes. You'll just have to wait.'

At that point, Ronald decided to put up a last protest.

'Just a minute,' he croaked feebly. 'I really must protest.'

He really shouldn't have. All he succeeded in doing was drawing attention to himself. To his horror, he was made to hold a bottle at pitchfork point while the disgustingly smelly brew – Wishing Water, as they called it – was poured in. The bottle was a small green demonade bottle with a very narrow neck. Quite a bit got spilt accidentally on purpose on his robes, he noticed.

'You can go now,' Sourmuddle told him, stoppering the bottle. 'Thank you for your help, young Rodney. Don't want to outstay your welcome, do you? Now, run along, run along. Say goodbye nicely to your aunt. Sharkadder, get rid of him, will you?'

'I'd be delighted,' said Sharkadder. 'Goodbye, Ronald. I'd strongly advise you not to send me another dry-cleaning bill.' She waved her hand casually, and the next thing he knew he was up to his neck in the ornate fountain in the grounds of the Wizards' Clubhouse.

'Very nice, Sharkadder, very neat,' said Sourmuddle approvingly when the blue smoke that had been Ronald cleared. She pocketed the small green bottle. 'Right, I've got the Wishing Water. Don't worry, I'll put it in a safe place. And now, if you'll excuse me, I'm off to get a bit of shut-eye. See you in the morning, Pongwiffy. When you come to clean my boots. Come on, Snoop.'

And with that, she was gone. There wasn't even a puff of smoke.

'See that?' said Sharkadder admiringly. 'Not even any smoke. No wonder she's Grandwitch. Sometimes I think she can see what we're up to from miles away. Hear us talking.'

''Course not,' said Pongwiffy scornfully. 'She's not *that* good. And I wouldn't mind betting she has a swig of that Wishing Water when she gets home.'

162

'I heard that,' said Sourmuddle's disembodied voice.

'You know what I think?' said Pongwiffy hastily. 'I think it's time for bed. Goodnight, Sharky. Let yourself out, will you?'

In she climbed. Her boots were still on the wrong feet, but she didn't even notice. She was so tired that she almost didn't mind that the sheets were clean.

CHAPTER NINETEEN
Spell of the year

'Your Royal Majesty, Honoured Members of the Judging Panel, Witches, Wizards, Skeletons, Spooks, Ghosts, Ghouls, Zombies, Monsters, Mummies, Demons, Trolls, Vampires, Banshees, Werewolves, Gnomes and last and most definitely least, Goblins – welcome, thrice welcome to Witchway Hall!' boomed a rich voice from nowhere.

There was an excited buzz as the house lights dimmed. Conversation died away and was replaced by an expectant hush, during which a lone voice shouted out, 'What about us Fiends?'

The heckler was ignored. Instead, there was a rising drum-roll followed by a clash of cymbals, and suddenly a portly Genie in a gaudy red turban and exotic pants materialised centre stage. He was dramatically lit by a single green spotlight, and he was smiling broadly.

'Friends, my name is Ali Pali and I am your Master Of Ceremonies for the evening,' he announced in oily tones and gave a low, sweeping bow.

Pongwiffy knew this particular Genie of old. She gave a start of recognition and clutched Sharkadder's arm.

'It's him again! That Ali Pali! I don't believe it! That Genie gets everywhere! What a nerve he's got. Oi! You! You've got a nerve, you have, Pali!'

'Ssh,' hissed Sharkadder. 'Do you want to spoil our chances?'

'Tonight, O ladies and gentlemen,' continued Ali Pali, ignoring them, 'tonight we see the return of the ever-popular Spell of the Year Competition, sponsored this year by Genie Enterprises, manufacturers of *Reeka Reeka Roses*, the miracle air-freshener – as used by his gracious Majesty King Futtout.'

Ali Pali beamed approvingly at King Futtout,

who sat miserably in the middle of the Judging Panel. The Judging Panel were arranged in a row behind the very same trestle table that the Witches had used for their Emergency Meeting. Tonight it bristled with scorecards, pencils, notepads, water jugs and glasses. On a high shelf nearby was the coveted silver cup.

The front row of the stalls was taken up by hopeful Witch contestants and their Familiars. The second row contained the competing Wizards, who spent a lot of time laughing confidently and kicking the backs of the seats in front (which we all know is most irritating).

Row Three was occupied by the rest of the contenders who didn't fall into either camp, but who considered themselves no slouches when it came to spell-casting. These consisted mostly of assorted Wise men and women, Palm Readers, Tree Demons, Pixies and the odd Gnome, and they spent most of their time complaining about the double row of tall hats that blocked their view of the stage.

The rest of the seats were occupied by the general public. (Although that's probably too polite a name for them.)

'I trust Your Majesty has no objection to my

mentioning your royal self in connection with this wonderful product?' Ali Pali added smoothly.

'Erm?' said King Futtout, blushing unhappily. 'Erm . . . no, no, of course not . . . erm.'

'I'm sure we're all very grateful that you could spare us some of your very valuable time, Sire. Let's have a big hand for His Majesty the King!'

There was a bit of scattered applause and one or two boos. Opinion was divided as to whether or not King Futtout should be on the Judging Panel. After all, he was hardly an expert on Magic. On the other hand, it didn't hurt to keep the local royalty sweet. As Rory pointed out, you never knew when you might need to use the palace swimming pool.

For his part, King Futtout would never have come. Spell competitions just weren't his thing. All those Witches in the audience gave him the shivers. Brr! He was only there because Beryl and Honeydimple had forced him.

('You tell them,' they had said. 'You tell those Witches they can't get away with it.' And they had said a lot more along the same lines.)

Futtout had rather hoped to forge a sick note and send along his new Wizard to take his place – but unfortunately, Ronald the Magnificent

167

was himself confined to his turret with a sudden mysterious cold.

'And now, without more ado, let me introduce the other six members of our esteemed Judging Panel,' continued Ali Pali.

'Firstly, weighing in at over two hundred years, we have Grandwitch Sourmuddle, Mistress of the Witchway Wood Coven!'

As one, the Witches jumped on the seats, threw their hats in the air, hurled popcorn around and generally misbehaved. Bats zoomed about, stink-bombs were let off, 'Up The Witches' flags were raised, gongs were beaten, Familiars jived in the aisles – it was simply shocking.

'Hooray!'

'Whoopee! You show 'em, Sourmuddle!'

'Attawitch!'

Despite Ali Pali's pleas, Sourmuddle's supporters refused to sit down until their leader put her knitting away, stood up and gave a queenly wave. The non-Witches in the audience sighed and tutted and looked pointedly at their watches.

'And of course, as always, we have the Wizards' representative, the Venerable Harold the Hoodwinker!' announced Ali Pali.

It was now the Wizards' turn to clap and cheer.

'Rah! Rah!' they brayed. 'Good old Harold!'

Nobody else bothered. Harold the Hoodwinker was a permanent fixture on these occasions. The Wizards always wheeled him out because, although he hadn't hoodwinked anyone for years, he was the oldest Club member and entitled to a bit of respect.

'And now, a favourite with all you ladies – Scott Sinister, famous star of stage and screen!'

A tall, thin, pale character in silly sunglasses waved a limp hand, and the audience shouted and clapped enthusiastically. Several of the Banshees in the audience screamed so hard they had to be taken out. A small, bad-tempered Tree Demon brandishing a huge pair of scissors rushed up and menacingly demanded an autograph. Scott Sinister was obviously a popular choice. (Although not with King Futtout, who had at one point nervously asked him to pass the water jug, only to be ignored.)

'Isn't he lovely?' sighed Pongwiffy to Sharkadder. 'Oh, Scott, Scott! Do you think he'll ever forgive me, Sharky? After that Other Business?'

'No,' said Sharkadder shortly. 'And I'd rather not talk about that Other Business if you don't mind, Pongwiffy.'

(In order to understand the above exchange, you should know that Pongwiffy has had dealings with Scott Sinister before – but that, thankfully, is another story.)

'Have you got the Wishing Water safe?' Pongwiffy asked, staring around uneasily at their fellow competitors. Their fellow competitors stared right back, and several made rude faces and poked their tongues out. 'I don't trust this lot, do you? A right bunch of riff-raff.'

'Of course I've got it. It's in my handbag.'

'I think I ought to have it,' insisted Pongwiffy. 'After all, it's my spell. I found the recipe.'

'Nonsense. Sourmuddle gave it to me to look after. Ssh, he's just about to introduce Pierre.'

'Next, our cookery expert, the very popular Pierre de Gingerbeard!' trumpeted Ali Pali, indicating a genial-looking Dwarf sporting a tall chef's hat and a curling ginger beard.

'Pierre! Bongjoor, Cousin Pierre!' shouted Sharkadder. 'Over here! It's me, Sharkadder! He's my cousin, you know,' she informed everyone importantly.

'And now, O ladies and gentlemen, put your hands together for your own, your very own Mr

170

Dunfer Malpractiss, local shopkeeper!' announced Ali Pali, to a chorus of jeers. 'Chosen because of his winning ways and the fact that in the last month he has sold an astonishing *one thousand cans* of *Reeka Reeka Roses*! Congratulations, Dunfer! See me afterwards.'

'I 'ope this won't take long,' grumbled Dunfer Malpractiss. 'I gorra get back to the shop.'

'And last of all,' said Ali Pali, 'we have last year's winner, Batty Bob and his Boring Birds.'

'Booooo!' screamed the audience as a mild little man in a heaving cardigan got to his feet and bowed. 'Boooo! Fix. Loada rubbish!'

'All right, simmer down, simmer down. Well, that's the introductions over, apart from saying a big thank you to the Yeti Brothers for doing the bar snacks. And let's hear it for the Witchway Rhythm Boys – Arthur on piano, O'Brian on the penny whistle, and Filth the Fiend on drums.'

A little burst of tuneless music came from the orchestra pit, followed by a nasty thud as Filth dropped his stick.

'And now,' continued Ali Pali, 'now for the moment you've all been waiting for. Time to get down to the real business of the evening –

the Spells!'

Ali Pali snapped his fingers and a small blue metal waste bin appeared at his feet. It appeared to be full of folded scraps of paper.

'In time-honoured fashion, the running order will be decided by picking names out of the bin. Right, here goes. The first entry for the Spell of the Year Competition is Scurfgo, the Celebrated Miracle Anti-dandruff Shampoo, entered by Witch Scrofula.'

A general sigh went up.

'Oh no, not again!'

'Seen it! Seen it!'

'Every year it's the same! Honestly, you'd think she'd at least change the name or something . . .'

Scrofula shot from her seat and flounced determinedly up to the stage with a foaming bucket in her hand. She always entered her Celebrated Shampoo and made the Judging Panel try and guess which side of her head had been washed in ordinary soap and which had been treated with the special stuff in the bucket. The Judges always got it wrong. Scrofula always retired hurt. It was all very boring and predictable.

In fact if one was honest, the Spell of the Year

Competition as a whole was getting boring and predictable. Every year, the same old spells got dragged out and dusted off, maybe given a new name, but essentially the same as last year's offering.

After the Judging Panel had cast a hasty eye over Scrofula's hair, failed as always to spot the difference and sent the tearful loser scurrying back to cry on Barry's shoulder, it was the turn of a Wizard.

'The next entry is Frank the Foreteller's Astonishing Oracle Tea Bag, without which no soothsayer's kit is complete,' announced Ali Pali.

The audience sat up a little and took a bit more notice. An Oracle Tea Bag didn't sound exactly earth-shattering, but at least it was new.

To Wizardly cheers, Frank the Foreteller strolled onstage and gave a knowing smirk. From one sleeve he produced a kettle and from the other, a cup and saucer. Then from under his hat, he produced a small square tea bag, which he held carefully between thumb and forefinger.

'Ladies and gentlemen, I will now demonstrate this remarkable new fortune-telling Oracle Tea Bag,' said Frank the Foreteller. 'This tea bag is the *only one* of its kind! This tea bag is quick, reliable, and saves all those messy tea leaves. And you can use it

173

again and again. Could I have a volunteer, please?'

Quick as a flash, a small, furry Thing wearing a Moonmad T-shirt was on the stage, hopping about excitedly and waving to its cheering friends in the audience.

'Right, sir, if you'd just like to stand to one side while I concentrate my amazing powers on boiling this kettle,' said Frank the Foreteller, shutting his eyes, holding his breath and going bright red. After a moment or two, steam poured from the spout and the kettle gave a shrill whistle.

The Wizard contingent clapped heartily and shouted encouragement. The rival Witches put in a bit of ostentatious yawning, and several members of the general public began talking amongst themselves.

'Huh. I could do that before I could walk,' remarked Pongwiffy. 'This is so boring. I wish it was our turn next.'

'It won't be,' said Sharkadder. 'We're sure to be on last. We'll have to sit through Sludgegooey's Wart Cream, Gaga's Motorised Rotating Bat Rack, Macabre's Sporran of Invisibility, Ratsnappy's Handy Pocket Wand Set, Greymatter's Dictionary of Useful Magical Terms . . .'

'Stop! Stop!' begged Pongwiffy. 'It's all the same as last year!'

'. . . and that's just us Witches,' finished Sharkadder. 'The Wizards'll be dredging up loads of dreary old stuff, if this act's anything to go by, and so will the rest of 'em.'

'Well, I'm not sitting around watching. It's making me nervous. Shall I get us all an ice cream? There's a bar at the back.'

'Oh, yes please, Pong,' said Sharkadder, surprised. 'That would be lovely. Thank you.'

'The only thing is, I haven't got my purse.'

Sharkadder gave an exasperated sigh.

'Go on, then,' she said. 'Take my handbag. And make sure you check the change. And don't go getting anything too expensive. It's my money, remember.'

'All right. What d'you want?'

'A Bogberry lolly,' said Sharkadder.

'What does Dudley want?'

A growled response from somewhere under Sharkadder's chair indicated that Dudley wanted a Mouse 'n' Vanilla cornet.

'What about you, Hugo?'

Hugo didn't care as long as it had nuts.

CHAPTER TWENTY
An Encounter at the Bar

At the very back of the hall, on a rickety bench, behind a pillar, miles from the stage and in a freezing draught, sat the Goblins. Being Goblins, they had automatically been given the worst seats in the house.

Plugugly sat on the far left. Then came Slopbucket, Eyesore, Stinkwart, Hog, Sproggit and Lardo. They sat with blank, uncomprehending faces, jaws drooping, eyes fixed on the distant stage, watching Frank the Foreteller go through his paces.

Frank the Foreteller had now made his cup of tea,

and was explaining to the Thing in the Moonmad T-shirt that the mystic art of tea-bag reading relied on the accurate, mathematical counting of the exact number of wrinkles in the tea bag and the scientific way it lay in the bottom of the cup, etc.

'Wot's 'e on about?' Plugugly wanted to know.

'Beats me,' said Hog wonderingly. 'Makin' tea, ain't ee?'

'Probably the interval,' said Sproggit knowledgeably. 'You gets tea in the interval, see.'

'Nah, it ain't the interval,' disagreed Hog. 'Issa spell, innit? Issa Spell *Competishun*, innit?'

'Whatever it is, iss rubbish,' observed Plugugly.

The Spell of the Year Competition wasn't for Goblins. Goblins couldn't understand all this Magic business. All those long words and all that finger-wiggling was far too complicated for them. In fact, they had only come in because it was raining.

'Now wot's 'e doin'?' asked Eyesore.

Frank the Foreteller was carefully handing the steaming cup to the Thing in the Moonmad T-shirt, with instructions to sip slowly. The Thing, who had been nodding solemnly throughout, suddenly lost patience, snatched the cup, fished out the Amazing Oracle Tea Bag with hairy fingers and, much to the horror of Frank the Foreteller and the delight of everyone else, swallowed it.

And that was something else Frank the Foreteller failed to predict.

'Rubbish,' repeated Plugugly firmly.

'Lardo's cryin' again,' young Sproggit sniggered unkindly. The other Goblins looked hopefully along the bench. Sure enough, huge tears were welling up in Lardo's eyes, brimming over and splashing down his cheeks. Slowly, unconsciously, his hand crept for the thousandth time to his head and searched in vain for his missing bobble.

''Ee's in mournin' fer 'is bobble,' jeered Slopbucket, and the rest of the Goblins collapsed in fits. This was more like it. This was something they could understand. You could keep your old spells. A nice bit of spiteful teasing, now *that's* what you called entertainment.

'I'm not,' protested Lardo, snatching his hand down. 'I gotta runny eye 'cos I gotta cold. An' I gotta sore throat too. I'm fed up with this old Speller the Year. I'm gonna buy a drink. Oo else wants one?'

'Me! Me! I do!' cried all the Goblins, eagerly shooting their hands in the air.

'Well, 'ard luck, get yer own!' retorted Lardo and

stood up. Plugugly being at the other end, the bench shot up and deposited all the Goblins on the floor.

Blowing his nose, Lardo made his way around the back of the hall to the bar. He cast his eye over the audience, and thought he caught a glimpse of that Tree Demon, the one with the scissors who had made him take his hat off before subjecting him to a humiliating short back and sides. And then his bobble had got stolen and . . . Lardo shivered and hurried on to the bar.

A burly Yeti in a grease-stained waistcoat and gold medallion was leaning on the counter, idly watching the far stage where Witch Gaga was demonstrating her Rotating Bat Rack. In the background, another identical Yeti in a floral pinny, with a knife in its huge hairy paw, was chopping tomatoes. (These were the Yeti Brothers: Spag Yeti and Conf Yeti – Pasta and Weddings a Speciality.)

A couple of Skeletons were propped at the bar, sipping long drinks through straws and sharing a packet of crisps. They looked up as Lardo approached and haughtily turned their backbones on him.

'Yeah? Whata ya wanna?' said the waistcoated Yeti (Spag).

'Demonade, please,' said Lardo.

'You Gobleena?'

'Eh?' asked Lardo, playing for time.

'I aska you Gobleena? Cosa we dona serva no Gobleena. You Gobleena?'

Lardo thought hard. Then, suddenly, in a flash, the right answer came to him. It was clever, it was cunning, and it just might work. 'No,' he said.

'Datsa OK den,' said Spag. 'Justa checkin'. No 'fensa. Demonada, huh? I getta froma de back, OK?'

'Fine,' said Lardo happily. 'Take your time. I'll just wait here.'

Congratulating himself on his clever little bit of subterfuge, he leaned casually on the bar and half turned to watch the stage, where Gaga's Rotating Bat Rack was spinning wildly out of control and showering the audience with dizzy Bats.

It was at this point that Lardo saw Pongwiffy wending her way towards him up the aisle. She was holding a large black handbag which Lardo didn't recognise as hers.

'I bet you stole that handbag, Pongwiffy,' said Lardo as she came up. Just as a pleasant opening conversational remark.

'Go boil your bobble, Lardo,' retorted Pongwiffy,

elbowing past him to the bar. 'Awful haircut, by the way,' she added unkindly.

Lardo desperately tried to think of a fitting insult, but for the life of him he couldn't. All that quick-witted repartee with the Yeti had exhausted him. So he resorted to what he always said in these circumstances. 'Ah shut up,' he said. Feeble, but the best he could do.

'By the way,' said Pongwiffy, standing on his foot. 'Where *is* your disgusting bobble? Didn't it used to live on the top of your horrible hat?'

Tears welled up in Lardo's eyes. He couldn't bear talking about his bobble.

'Someone took it,' he said.

'Is that so? Now, why in the world would anyone do that? Unless, of course, they intended to chop it up and use it in a spell, ha ha. Hey! Spag! Let's have some service here! One small Mouse 'n' Vanilla cone, one stingy-sized Bogberry lolly, something small and cheap with nuts for Hugo and an Extra-Special-Double-Scoop-Mega-Chocko-Jammy Surprise with Extra-Rich Cherry Sauce and Double Cream for me.'

'Letsa see your money firsta, Pongwiffy,' said Spag. 'An' I donna meana dat Magic coin what always go backa to your pursa neither.'

'I don't know, the service these days,' grumbled Pongwiffy, scrabbling in the cavernous depths of Sharkadder's handbag. 'Oh bother, I can't find her purse. And I can't see a thing in this light. Hang on.'

And without more ado, she emptied the contents of Sharkadder's handbag on to the counter. Combs, brushes, mirrors, tweezers, files, pliers, tubes of lipstick, pots of powder and about a thousand hairgrips spilt everywhere. Several tiny, surprised-looking hedgehogs poked their heads out of a frilly sponge bag, climbed out and trotted away. In the midst of the clutter lay Sharkadder's purse.

And, of course, the small green demonade bottle containing the precious Wishing Water.

'Ah!' cried Pongwiffy, seizing upon the purse. 'Here it is. I knew it was in there somewhere. Look, see? I've got loads of money. So I want a small Mouse 'n' Vanilla, a stingy . . .'

'Your drinka, *Signor*. Sorry to keepa you waiting,' said the Yeti in the red waistcoat, returning to the counter with Lardo's drink.

Now, all this time, Lardo had been thinking. Pongwiffy's casual little remark about chopping up his bobble had set him off on a train of thought. It was the sort of train that went very slowly, stopped frequently and invariably arrived late. But it got there in the end.

''Ere,' said Lardo. 'Wachoo mean about my bobble . . . ?'

But he never found out. At exactly that moment, there came an announcement from the stage.

'Ladies and Gentlemen, Witch Gaga's Rotating Bat Rack has been disqualified on safety grounds. So, without more ado we shall move on to the next act, which is a highly secret double entry from Pongwiffy and Sharkadder. Could we have the contestants on stage, please?'

'It's us!' gasped Pongwiffy in a panic. 'Oh bother, why didn't anyone tell me we were next? Wait for me! I'm coming, I'm coming!'

Unceremoniously, she scooped Sharkadder's junk back into her handbag, snatched up the precious bottle of Wishing Water and scuttled back down the aisle. Several legs stuck out to trip her up, but she cunningly avoided them.

She met up with Sharkadder at the foot of the stage. Sharkadder was suffering from stage fright, pacing anxiously up and down with her back to the audience, gnawing on her fingernails.

'Oh, Pong, where have you *been*? It's our *turn*. Have you got the Wishing Water?'

'Yes, yes, of course I have. What d'you take me for? Come on, let's get onstage. The audience are getting restless.'

Indeed, the audience was starting a slow handclap, and a group of Banshees at the back had set up a shrill, impatient screaming. Scrofula and Barry were encouraging some synchronised booing and Agglebag and Bagaggle had come up with a nice line in hissing. Right now, Pongwiffy wasn't the most popular name on everyone's lips.

'Wait a minute, wait a minute, I need my lipstick. I want to look my best for my public. Oh my badness! Whatever have you done to my handbag?'

'Never mind that now!' snapped Pongwiffy crossly. 'It's all your fault anyway! You said we were on last.'

'Oh, do stop going on! There. I've done my lips. Now, just give me the Wishing Water, and we'll get on-stage.'

'What d'you mean, give *you* the Wishing Water? If anyone's carrying the Wishing Water it's me. It's my spell. I found the recipe.'

'Oh, the cheek of it! Who helped you make the

185

brew? Who baked you a sponge when all your other so-called friends deserted you? Eh?'

'Having problems, ladies?' enquired the silky tones of Ali Pali from the stage.

'Certainly not,' snapped Pongwiffy. 'Stand back, Pali, and prepare to be amazed. Me and my assistant are coming up.'

And up they went.

CHAPTER TWENTY-ONE
Wishing Water

'All right, you lot, simmer down! Get lost, Pali, I can do my own announcements, thanks very much. Ladies and gentlemen, I have here, in this perfectly ordinary small green demonade bottle, the most won—'

'What did you mean, "my assistant"?' enquired Sharkadder.

'Eh? Oh, shush, Sharky, now's not the time to get on your high horse. Ahem. As I was saying, ladies and gentlemen . . .'

'No, I'm sorry, but I'd like to get this clear

from the start. What exactly did you mean by "my assistant"?'

Pongwiffy's brain spun madly. If Sharkadder took offence now, everything could be ruined. Luckily, inspiration came.

'Because you're the beautiful one, of course. Haven't you ever noticed? Conjurors' assistants are always very glamorous and dressed in lovely clothes and things. Like you.'

'Oh. Oh, I see what you mean. Yes, I suppose you're right,' admitted Sharkadder, tossing her hair and treating the riotous audience to a sudden, dazzling smile.

'So, can I get on with what I was saying?'

'Yes. Yes, of course,' purred Sharkadder, placing a hand on a hip and striking the sort of showy pose she imagined a glamorous assistant might strike.

'Good. Ladies and gentlemen, as I was saying, before you, in this humble little bottle, you see the winning potion of this year's Spell of the Year Competition. For this little bottle contains a sample of none other than the legendary Wishing Water, made to Granny Malodour's very own recipe!'

There was a surprised pause, followed by some excited whispering and a fair amount of disbelieving laughter. Granny Malodour's famous Wishing Water, eh? A likely story. Why, everyone knew that the recipe had been lost in the mists of time.

'Go ahead, laugh!' Pongwiffy told them. 'You'll be laughing on the other side of your faces in a minute. My lovely assistant, Sharkadder, will now offer each of the Judges a small amount of this amazing potion. A wish each. That's what they get. And if their wishes don't come true, my lovely assistant will personally eat her pointy hat. Sharp end first. That's how confident I am of this spell.'

'Hang on there, just a minute . . .' objected the lovely assistant. But Pongwiffy was in full swing, and there was no stopping her.

'Just to ensure there is no cheating, I will ask the Judges to write down a brief description of their wish. Think carefully, now. This is the chance of a lifetime.'

The Judging Panel thought carefully. One wish. The chance of a lifetime. They mustn't mess this up.

King Futtout thought longingly of becoming a hermit and living in a cave on a mountain, far from the trappings of power; Scott Sinister dreamed of rave reviews of his latest film (*Revenge of the Killer*

189

Poodles); Sourmuddle wished her memory was better, then forgot; the Venerable Harold the Hoodwinker wished he was home in bed; Dunfer Malpractiss had a fleeting vision of thousands of highly successful Malpractiss Magic Ltd Megastores straddling the globe and Pierre de Gingerbeard wished for the thousandth time that Sharkadder wasn't his cousin. Batty Bob and his Boring Birds didn't wish for anything, because they were in the toilet at the time.

And then, as Pongwiffy instructed, the Judges (all except Bob) wrote their wishes down whilst Sharkadder poured out a few drops of the precious liquid into their water glasses.

'Right,' said Pongwiffy after the pouring had been completed and the pieces of paper collected up. 'The wishes are as follows: Cave, Fame, Good Memory, Bed, Money, Not To Be Related To Sharkadder. Could we have a drum-roll, please? Silence, everyone. The Judges are about to sample the Wishing Water. Ready, Judges? All together now . . . *Bottoms Up!*'

The Witchway Rhythm Boys played something vaguely tension-building and the audience held their breath as the panel raised their glasses and drank.

There was a long pause.

'Tastes like demonade to me,' said Scott Sinister with a shrug.

'What?' said Pongwiffy. 'What did you say, Scott?'

'I said it tastes like ordinary demonade. Don't you agree?' he asked his fellow Judges, who chorused their agreement.

'It's nothing like Granny's Wishing Water, Pongwiffy,' said Sourmuddle. 'And I can't remember what I wished for, but I'm pretty sure I haven't got it. Has anybody here got their wish?'

The Judging Panel shook their heads. 'No.' Sadly no one had got their wish.

'I don't understand it,' wailed Pongwiffy, wringing her hands. 'What's happened? I made it to the exact recipe. It's got to be right. Surely *somebody* got their wish?'

Then it happened. Suddenly, without any warning, something soft and green plopped on her head. This was followed by another one, only this time it was blue. Then a tartan one. And then . . . *it began to rain bobbles*! Hundreds of them. Thousands of them. Millions and trillions and zillions of them. All different colours and different sizes. Big bright jolly yellow ones and pretty little pale pink ones. Sensible navy ones and lurid multicoloured ones. It was a bobble blizzard.

Softly fell the bobbles on to the heads and shoulders of the bewildered audience, rolling off and bouncing in the aisles, filling up the orchestra pit, settling in niches and corners, piling up in drifts against the exit doors. In seconds, everyone was ankle-deep in them – and still they kept coming.

'Don't panic! Stay calm!' instructed Ali Pali, before vanishing in a green puff.

People instantly panicked and made for the exits. King Futtout lost his crown, Sourmuddle's corns took a severe bashing, the trestle table was overturned and somebody stole the silver cup. The tide of bobbles rose higher by the second, and several Dwarfs and small Gnomes were already waist-deep and struggling.

Never-ending bobbles. Raining down. Filling up the world.

Now, whoever could have wished for that?

CHAPTER TWENTY-TWO
A Lovely Surprise

'Well, it wasn't my fault,' muttered Pongwiffy for the umpteenth time.

'Yes, it was,' argued Sharkadder. 'Everyone says so, don't they, Hugo? There won't be any Spell of the Year Competitions ever again, and it's all your fault. Why don't you admit it? Pass the frogs, please.'

It was the following day. They were sitting in Pongwiffy's unnaturally clean hovel. Sharkadder had brought over a tin of ginger frogs, and they were morosely dunking them in bogwater whilst raking over recent events in the hope of finding

193

someone to blame.

'You should have noticed it wasn't Wishing Water,' grumbled Pongwiffy. 'You should have noticed when you poured it out. Some assistant you turned out to be.'

'Oh yes? And who got the bottles muddled in the first place? Honestly, the ingratitude of it! That's the last time I lend you my handbag, Pongwiffy. And the last time I help you out with your rotten old spells.'

'Hugo should have noticed, then,' sulked Pongwiffy. 'What's the point of having a Familiar if he doesn't notice things?'

'I did,' objected Hugo. 'I shout from ze stalls. I shout, "Mistress, you got ze wrong bottle." But you no hear.'

There was a long pause. Then, 'It's the waste,' Pongwiffy said gloomily. 'That's what I can't get over. The waste of a perfectly good bottle of Wishing Water. And for what? So some stupid Goblin can have a lifetime's supply of bobbles. *Bobbles!* I ask you.'

'That's Goblins for you,' agreed Sharkadder.

'All that trouble, and I didn't even get to taste it.'

There was an even longer pause.

'I think I'm going to cry,' said Pongwiffy.

'Oh, cheer up, Pong, do,' said Sharkadder, giving her a little pat on the shoulder. 'You've still got the recipe. You can always make some more.'

'What, after all the trouble I went to the first time? Not likely. It was all for nothing and I nearly killed myself getting all those ingredients. And nobody likes me any more.'

'I do,' said Sharkadder kindly.

'Me too,' said Hugo.

'No, you don't. You were right. It was all my fault. It was all my fault that the audience stampeded and the cup got stolen and everything. Everyone hates me now. I'm the most unpopular Witch in the Coven.'

'W-e-ll – yes,' admitted Sharkadder. 'Yes, you are. But that's nothing new. And you're still my best friend,' she added loyally.

'And mine,' nodded Hugo.

'Really? You mean it?' sniffed Pongwiffy.

'Certainly we do. And just to prove it, we've got something for you, haven't we, Hugo?'

Sharkadder reached for her handbag and took something out. She handed it to Pongwiffy with an air of triumph.

195

'There. For you. It's the bottle of Wishing Water. Hugo took it from Lardo before he could finish it. We saved it for you. There's just enough drops left in there for a wish, I'd say.'

'He did? You did? There is? You mean, I'm going to sample Granny's Wishing Water after all?' Pongwiffy took the bottle with trembling fingers. 'But why didn't you tell me? Why wait till now?'

'We were waiting to hear you say it was all your fault,' explained Sharkadder. 'We wanted to see you grovel before springing this lovely surprise on you. Are you pleased?'

'Pleased? I'll say I'm pleased. Thanks, you two. Right, here goes. I'm going to make my wish. But first, Granny's Magic words . . . *Bottoms Up!*'

Eagerly, she raised the almost empty demonade bottle and drained it. Sharkadder and Hugo watched, eyes popping, as she lowered it and made a face.

'Yuck,' said Pongwiffy. 'Yep. That's Wishing Water all right. Pass me a ginger frog, Hugo. I need it to take the taste away.'

'Vat you vish for, Mistress?' asked Hugo eagerly.

'Wait. Be patient. You'll find out.'

They waited. And waited. Sharkadder was just

about to remark that Wishing Water didn't appear to be all that it was cracked up to be, when finally, something happened.

A sudden wind blew up.

At the same time, a low rumbling noise came from outside. There were crashings and slitherings, clankings and clatterings, tinklings and jinglings. There was also a very nasty smell in the air.

The hovel door exploded open – and in flowed a mighty river of rubbish! It was like a dam bursting. Everything that Hugo and the Broom had worked so hard to get rid of came pouring back in, bringing with it a lot of extra dirt and debris that hadn't even been there in the first place.

Sharkadder shrieked, snatched up her skirts and leapt on the table for safety. Pongwiffy and Hugo hastily joined her, and all three of them huddled together and watched in amazement as the sea of rubbish slowly reclaimed the hovel.

All Pongwiffy's cast-offs were there – the old socks, the broken glasses, the bits of cheese, the maggot collection, the cauldron, the teddy, the hot-water bottle, the . . . well, you know. All of it.

After oozing around all over the floor for a bit, the rubbish began to separate out into

197

recognisable bits. The various components made for their old, familiar nooks and crannies where they settled comfortably, obviously pleased to be back home again.

The old newspapers flapped their pages and flew clumsily up to a high shelf, where they formed themselves into untidy piles. The hot-water bottle gave a little leap and hung itself on a nail in the wall.

Sharkadder, Pongwiffy and Hugo ducked as crumbling old spell books with half the pages missing whizzed past their ears and hurled themselves back into the bookcase any old how.

The sofa came crashing back in, broken springs waving jauntily, and settled in its old place with a proprietorial air. Drawers slid open, waiting for the dozens of odd socks and old cardigans to crawl back into them. A disgracefully filthy sheet spread itself on the bed (over the nice clean one), tucked itself in (badly) and waited for its coating of biscuit crumbs to arrive.

All the pieces of broken, dirty china made for the sink, and soon the draining board was piled high. While all this was going on, the window cracked and dirtied itself, cobwebs sneaked back over the ceiling and dust rained down in a steady shower.

198

Outside, weeds grew up the walls and all the fresh paint peeled off the door. At the same time, a party of starved-looking Spiders came wandering up the garden path, crying, 'How about this, Ma. It looks even worse than the last place. Oh, my legs, it *is* the last place! How come?'

The Broom, aware that there was some sort of emergency, came whizzing in from outside, took one look at the state of the floor and promptly passed out.

When the dust had finally settled and the Spiders had unpacked and the last dead plant had finished arranging itself tastefully on the window sill, Sharkadder, Pongwiffy and Hugo slowly climbed down from the table.

'So,' said Sharkadder, tutting and looking around. 'This is your wish, is it, Pongwiffy? To live in squalor.'

'It certainly is,' said Pongwiffy, eyes glowing. 'It suits my personality, don't you think? I've been very unhappy these last two weeks. It just wasn't my own little hovel any more, not since it was spring-cleaned. I'm sorry, Hugo. After all your hard work.' Hugo gave a little shrug.

'Is OK. After all, you vitch of dirty 'abits. I should

199

know better. Besides, I sorta missed ze Spiders, you know?'

Up above, lots of little legs clapped together approvingly, and Gerald, the smallest Spider, took a dive into Hugo's bedside glass of water, out of sheer high spirits.

Turn the page for another
Pongwiffy adventure!

more
Pongwiffy
stories

The Holiday of Doom

PROLOGUE

I n Witchway Wood, there is no noise. Only the faint hissing of rain falling lightly on to waterlogged leaves and sodden branches. No noise at all except . . .

Except the rhythmic sound of bicycle wheels sloshing through mud, accompanied by some enthusiastic bell dinging and a burst of cheerily horrible singing. And through the trees comes a small, furry Thing in a Moonmad T-shirt, sporting a bright yellow baseball cap and with a large bag slung over its shoulder.

It is the Paper Thing.

The Paper Thing really loves its job. It has taken ages to master all the necessary skills and subtle tricks of the trade, such as the art of Balancing the Bike, the art of Stopping, the art of Steering, the art of Fiddling the Takings and so on – but my goodness, it was worth it. Not only did it get paid to zoom around like a maniac all day, IT GOT A FREE YELLOW CAP! The Thing adores its cap. It wears it to bed sometimes.

The Thing sings cheerily to itself as it cycles on, splattering mud all over a couple of glum rabbits who have unwisely decided to eat out this wet morning. 'Ha, caught you on the hop there, carrot crunchers! Yahoo!'

It rounds the corner, screeches to a halt, dismounts and throws its bike in a puddle (not yet having mastered the art of Propping). It rummages in its bag and brings out a cellophane-wrapped magazine. Or is it? No, in fact closer inspection reveals it to be a brightly coloured holiday brochure! It is addressed to The Occupier, The Hovel, Number One, Dump Edge, Witchway Wood. The Paper Thing stares in puzzlement at the front cover on which a group of grinning Banshees in bathing costumes are leaping in an azure blue sea. Splashed across the top, in a great sunburst, are the words:

SLUDGEHAVEN-ON-SEA
Where Fun, Excitement and Olde Worlde
Charm Combine to Create that
Special Holiday Magic!

The Thing is puzzled because exotic holiday brochures are seldom seen in Witchway Wood. Newspapers, yes. Spell catalogues, yes. Badly wrapped newspaper parcels full of soggy herbs, yes. Final reminders, definitely. But *holiday brochures?*

After a long inspection, the Paper Thing gives a shrug, rummages deep in its bag and brings out a stout wooden clothes peg which it proceeds to clip on to its nose. It has delivered to this particular Occupier before.

It is prepared

CHAPTER ONE
Cooped Up

In Number One, Dump Edge, a heavy silence reigned. It was the sort of silence that descends after Sharp Words have been spoken – which, indeed, they had. Witch Pongwiffy had let the fire go out, and Hugo (her Hamster Familiar) was not amused.

It was very depressing in the hovel. Not only was the fire out, the roof was leaking. Big drips gathered on the blackened rafters and fell with dull *thunks* into the army of old saucepans and cracked basins littering the floor. Hugo was picking his way between them, armed with twigs and little pieces of screwed-up newspaper. He was wearing his HAMSTERS ARE ANGRY T-shirt, and right now you could believe it.

'Anyway, it wasn't my fault,' muttered Pongwiffy after a bit. She was slumped in her favourite rocking chair, sulking. 'It's not my job to see to the fire.'

'Oh no?' snapped Hugo. 'Whose job is it, zen?'

'The Broom's. Always has been.'

'Ze Broom is off vork, remember?' Hugo reminded her.

It was true. The Broom was down with a severe cold and had taken to its sick bucket (which was the same as its usual bucket with the addition of a spoonful of honey dissolved in warm water).

'Well, in that case, it's your job,' said Pongwiffy firmly. 'I'm the Witch around here, remember? I do all the important, Magical stuff. You're just my helper. If the Broom's off, the fire's up to you.'

'Oh ya? Along viz ze shoppink and ze cookink and ze cleanink, I s'pose? I only got two pairs of paws, you know. Who you sink I am? Superhamster?'

Pongwiffy considered. It was true. Hugo was a treasure and it was all her fault that the fire had gone out. Now would be a perfect moment to admit it gracefully and apologise. On the other hand . . .

'Ah, go drown in an egg cup, shorty!' she snarled, and the perfect moment was gone.

We have to forgive her. It was the rain, you see. It had been raining incessantly for weeks, driving Pongwiffy slowly but surely round the bend. She was a Witch of Action, who hated being cooped up. The sort of Witch who liked to be out and about, swapping gossip and recipes, popping in on people unexpectedly and inviting herself to tea. That sort of Witch.

It had been ages since anyone had invited her to tea. It seemed that the entire Coven had taken to their beds and were refusing to answer their doors, despite her plaintive cries and loud bangings.

Hugo sat back from arranging his twigs with an exasperated little sigh. One more day of Pongwiffy mooning about the place starting arguments was more than he could bear.

'Vy you not make some Magic?' he suggested. 'Little bit of cackling, hmm? Mix up a brew? All zis rain, plenty of frogs about. Turn some into princes or sumsink.'

'Don't you think I'd *like* to? There's nothing I'd like better. But we've run out of all the basic ingredients. There isn't a speck of newt vomit left, and all the recipes call for that. I tried to get some from Malpractiss Magic, but as usual he didn't have any. "Call yourself a Magic Shop," I said.'

'And vot he say?' asked Hugo, struggling with a box of matches that was bigger than he was.

'He said he didn't call himself a Magic Shop, he called himself an Umbrella Shop. And he took me outside, and there it was. Malpractiss Umbrellas Ltd, right across the shop front. Trust him to cash in on the bad weather.'

'Did you buy umbrella?' enquired Hugo.

'Of course I did. It was raining.'

'Zere you are, zen! Take it and go visit a friend!' cried Hugo.

'No one wants me,' explained Pongwiffy with a hurt little sniff. 'Everyone's got colds. No one's answering their door, even Sharkadder. Yesterday I took her round a lovely Get Well card and Dudley scratched me and wouldn't let me in. Huh! And she calls herself my best friend.'

'Does she?' asked Hugo doubtfully.

'Certainly she does. And she was mine. Until yesterday. Now she's my worst enemy, and I'm never speaking to her again. I'm going to tear up the

213

card I bought her. On second thoughts, I'll cross out the "Well" and write "Knotted" instead. Where's a pencil?'

She sprang from her chair, marched to the kitchen table, pulled out the drawer and upended it on the floor. Hugo shook his head resignedly as she scrabbled about on hands and knees, hurling things over her shoulder and muttering, 'A pencil, a pencil, where's a flipping pencil?'

Then, all of a sudden, she stopped, sat back and rubbed her eyes.

'Oh, Hugo,' she said weakly. 'Just listen to me. I've done nothing but shout at you all morning. You, my very own little Familiar who's been so good to me. And now I'm about to send my very best friend a Get Knotted card. Whatever is happening to me? I'm changing personality.'

'Is because you cooped up. You bored, zat's all.'

'I am, I am, you're absolutely right. I need a change of scene.'

'Vell, tonight you get ze chance. It ze monthly Meetink in Vitchvay Hall, seven-thirty sharp, remember? See all your friends. Have little chat, ya?'

'I don't mean *that* sort of change. Who wants to turn out on a rainy night to go to a boring old

Coven Meeting? Half of them probably won't turn up anyway, specially as it's Gaga's turn to bring the sandwiches. If I wasn't Treasurer this month, I don't think I'd bother to go. But Sourmuddle says I've got to take along the Coven savings.'

She glanced at her bed, under which the official Coven money box (labelled COVEN FUNDS – DO NOT TOUCH) was hidden, in case of burglars. And a very good place it was too. Any burglar who would remove something from under Pongwiffy's bed would have to be *really* keen.

'She wants to check and make sure I haven't spent any,' continued Pongwiffy, sounding slightly miffed. 'I don't think she trusts me – can't think why. No, I mean a *real* change. Just go away for a few days, get away from all this rain . . .'

Right on cue, there came an interruption. The letter box flapped, and something flopped on to the mat. From outside, there came the sound of receding footsteps and the faint strains of tuneless singing, which soon mercifully died away to nothing.

'Oh, goody!' cried Pongwiffy, leaping to her feet. '*The Daily Miracle*'s arrived. At least I can do the crossword puzzle!'

215

And she scurried across to pick it up. But it wasn't the paper. It was something much more interesting than that. There it lay, all glossy and gleaming, contrasting strangely with the surrounding Wilderness Where No Broom Dare Go (Pongwiffy's floor). A small, square, sunny, bright blue island of paradise amidst a sea of squalor.

'Well now,' said Pongwiffy, a gleam in her eye. 'Here's an interesting thing! Look what's just arrived, Hugo.'

Excitedly, she held it up.

'"*Sludgehaven-on-Sea — Where Fun, Excitement and Olde Worlde Charm Combine to Create that Special Holiday Magic!*" Oh, Hugo. Doesn't it look lovely? Look at the colour of that sky! Not a cloud to be seen. Just think of it. Kippers for breakfast. Strolls along the prom. Sunshine. Sea breezes. That'd blow the cobwebs away.'

'It take more zan sea breeze to blow *zose* cobvebs avay,' observed Hugo, glancing grimly up at the shadowy ceiling, where dozens of cheeky spiders were currently running around with thimbles, trying to prevent their rafter from flooding. 'It take typhoon to shift zat lot.'

'I meant the cobwebs in our *brains*, silly. Oh,

216

imagine going to the seaside, Hugo, you and me. Better still, what if we could all go! The whole Coven. Familiars, Brooms, everybody! Wouldn't it be fun?'

She scuttled across to the kitchen table and settled herself down, thumbing through the glossy pages.

'There's even a pier, Hugo. I've always wanted to visit a pier. There's a Hall of Mirrors and a Haunted House – and it says here *"Star-studded entertainment in the Pier Pavilion"*. Oh my! Do you know what I think, Hugo? I think I'm going to suggest it. I shall take this along to the Meeting tonight and persuade Sourmuddle that what everyone needs is a holiday.'

'You never do it,' said Hugo flatly. ''Olidays cost money. You know Sourmuddle. She don't like to part viz ze money.'

'Ah,' said Pongwiffy. It was a meaningful sort of ah. 'Ah. But she hasn't *got* the money, has she? I'm Treasurer this month, remember? And what's done can't be undone, *if you know what I mean*.'

Hugo looked up sharply. His eyes widened.

'You vouldn't dare! Not vizout Sourmuddle's permission!'

'Why not? There's loads in the money box.'

'But zat not ours! It ze official Coven savinks!'

'So? What are we saving it for?'

'A rainy day. So Sourmuddle say.'

'Well, there you are, then!' cried Pongwiffy triumphantly. 'You couldn't get a rainier day than this, could you? No, Hugo, I've made up my mind. I'm going to go right ahead and book it. I'll spring it on them as a lovely surprise. "Pongwiffy," they'll say, "trust you to come up with yet another brilliant idea . . ."'

'Are you sure?' asked Hugo doubtfully.

'No, actually,' admitted Pongwiffy. 'But I'm doing it anyway.'

CHAPTER TWO
The Meeting

'All right,' called Grandwitch Sourmuddle, Mistress of the Witchway Coven, banging her Wand sharply on the long trestle table. 'Stop coughing, everyone, I'm about to take the register. The sooner I get it done the sooner I can deliver my summing-up moan and we can all go home. Pass me the register, Snoop.'

The small Demon sitting next to her obediently began to rummage around in a large bin liner.

'How can we stop coughing?' Witch Scrofula wanted to know. 'You can't stop coughing just like that.'

To prove her point, she coughed all over Witch Ratsnappy, who was sitting next to her. Ratsnappy retaliated by blowing her nose in Scrofula's face, but Scrofula by now had moved on into a fit of sneezing and didn't appear to notice.

'Excuse me, Sourmuddle,' interrupted Witch Greymatter, looking up from the poem she was currently co-writing with Speks (her Owl Familiar). It was entitled 'Ode to Rain' and Greymatter was rather hoping to read it out. 'There are only six of us here. You, me, Scrofula, Macabre, Ratsnappy and Sharkadder. Everyone else is at home in bed. It's hardly worth calling the register. It's just a process of simple deduction.'

'Hmm. All right, then. Who's missing?'

'Agglebag and Bagaggle, Bendyshanks, Bonidle, Gaga and Sludgegooey. Oh, and Pongwiffy. They've dictated a general sick note which they've all signed, except Pongwiffy. Shall I read it out?'

'Go ahead,' nodded Sourmuddle.

'"We the undersigned are all very poorly and can't come to the Meeting."'

'Well, that's a bit of a cheek,' complained Scrofula. 'Barry and I succeeded in struggling along, though

220

I don't know how we managed it, do you, Barry? With our bad backs.'

The bald Vulture hunched mournfully on the back of her chair confirmed that no, he didn't know how they had managed it either.

'Bad back? Is that all?' sneered Witch Sharkadder, who was sitting on Scrofula's right. She was dabbing delicately at her long red nose, which had developed a very nasty cold sore. 'You wait till you've got 'flu, like me. And Duddles has it too, don't you, darling?'

Dead Eye Dudley, the one-eyed tomcat, looked up from her bony lap and leered.

'What aboot me, then?' chimed in Witch Macabre from the depths of a large tartan hanky. 'Ah've got bronchitis, a sore throat, gout an' a frozen shoulder. And Ah've got Rory at home wi' foot an' mouth disease. Plus mah bagpipes have got the mange . . .'

But Macabre was unable to complete her catalogue of disasters. She was drowned out in a chorus of jeers.

'Is that all? That's nothing! I've got all that, and funny little red spots besides!'

'Ah, but I've got all that *and* athlete's foot!'

'I've got a runny eye! Has anyone else here got a runny eye? Tell me that!'

Sourmuddle banged her gavel, and gradually the pathetic outcry died down, finally fizzling out in a sickly chorus of snuffles and sneezes and eye-wipings from Ratsnappy, who did indeed have a runny eye.

'Order, order! Well, all right, so none of us is well, we all know that. It's this dratted rain, gets into your bones.'

'Talking about rain,' said Greymatter, 'I've got a poem here which I'd like to read out. It's called "Ode to Rain".

'Rain, rain, you run down the pane.
Rain, rain, you go down the drain.
Rain, rain, you give me a pain.
Rain, rain, you're hurting my brain.
Rain, rain, I wish you'd refrain.
Rain, rain, you make a worse noise than a train . . .'

'I don't think that last bit was very good,' observed Ratsnappy.

Greymatter paused and gave her a steely glare.

'Sorry,' muttered Ratsnappy. 'Do go on.'

'Rain, rain, you'll drive me insane.

222

Rain, rain, I wish you were champagne.
Or maybe chow mein.
And then I'd catch you in a bucket and eat you.'

'That's the end. Thank you.'

She sat down to a thin sprinkling of applause.

'Thank you, Greymatter, that was very nice,' said Sourmuddle. 'And now I think we'd better move on to the main business of the evening. We'll keep it short, because I for one am keen on getting home to a nice lemon drink.'

'I don't know why *you're* complaining, Sourmuddle,' sniffed Sharkadder. 'You tell us all we mustn't use Magic to interfere with the weather, but I notice you've got your own private bubble of dry air around you whenever you go out. I don't think you've got wet once.'

'That's because I'm Grandwitch,' said Sourmuddle. 'And Grandwitches do what they like. And right now I'd like to have a sharp word with our missing Treasurer. She's supposed to be bringing along the Coven funds for me to count. Anyone seen Pongwiffy recently?'

Everyone looked at Sharkadder, who was Pongwiffy's best friend. Sometimes.

'Don't look at me,' said Sharkadder with a shrug. 'I've been in bed, remember?'

'Anybody else had a sighting?' enquired Sourmuddle.

It transpired that no one had seen Pongwiffy for a day or two. That was funny, because usually everybody saw a great deal too much of her, particularly at mealtimes.

'Hmm,' said Sourmuddle. 'That's worrying. Let's hope our savings are safe. All right, let's move on. Anybody got anything they want to discuss? No new spells? Recipes? Knitting patterns? Cold remedies? Anyone whacked any Goblins into next week? No? Deary me, it *has* been a slow month. What's got into you lot? Call yourself Witches or what?'

'Well, I don't know about anybody else, but Barry and I have been much too ill to think about a thing,' said Scrofula huffily.

'That's right, Sourmuddle,' agreed Macabre. 'None of us ha been up to it. There's noo point in going on. We're all run doon. Ye can't make Magic when ye're run doon. Apart from anything else, your nose keeps drippin' in the brew . . .'

But she didn't get the chance to finish, for the door suddenly blew open, admitting a squally shower of rain, a blast of chill air and a very familiar smell. Several candles flickered out and Sourmuddle's register blew off the table. Barry the Vulture lost his grip on the chair-back and dropped to the floor, banging his head quite badly.

'Sorry I'm late, everyone!' cried a cheery voice. 'Go ahead, start the Meeting, Sourmuddle, don't wait for me. Hugo, you can come out now. We're here.'

And in marched Pongwiffy, rain dripping from her rags, trailing muddy footprints behind her. Two pink paws appeared over the edge of her pocket and Hugo's small furry head poked out. He spotted Dudley and immediately stuck his tongue out. Dudley stiffened and dug his claws into Sharkadder's thighs.

'Don't do that, Dudley, darling,' said Sharkadder with a little wince. 'It hurts Mummy.'

'I don't know what you think you're doing, turning up now, Pongwiffy,' Sourmuddle said sharply as Pongwiffy pulled up a chair. 'I particularly asked you to be early so that I could count the Coven funds.'

'Ah,' said Pongwiffy. 'Ah yes. The funds.'

'The funds. I take it you've brought them?'

'Ah,' hedged Pongwiffy. 'Well, actually, Sourmuddle, there is a slight problem with that.'

'What d'you mean, problem? You don't mean to tell me you've forgotten?'

'Not exactly forgotten.'

'*Lost?* You haven't *lost* them, have you?'

'Not exactly. More kind of – spent,' admitted Pongwiffy, adding hastily, 'But don't panic, Sourmuddle, it wasn't on myself. This will benefit everybody. The whole Coven.'

'Spent?' quavered Sourmuddle weakly, hand over her heart. '*Spent?* All our *money?*'

'Yes, actually. But you'll be thrilled when you hear what I spent it on. Look at this! This'll cheer you up no end.'

And with a dramatic flourish, she took the brochure out from beneath her cardigan and slapped it triumphantly on the table, right under Sourmuddle's nose.

'We,' she announced, 'are going on holiday!'

CHAPTER THREE
plans

"Sludgehaven-on-Sea,"' read Sourmuddle slowly, peering over her half-glasses at the glossy brochure, on which the Banshee bathers cavorted. '"*Where Fun, Excitement and Olde Worlde Charm Combine to Create that Special Holiday Magic!*" What's this all about, Pongwiffy?'

'That's it,' said Pongwiffy. 'That's where we're going. I've booked us seven carefree, sun-soaked days in glorious Sludgehaven. It's all organised. I've done everything. I've even ordered a luxury motor coach to take us there. And yes, I used the Coven

227

savings and I know I should have asked you first, Sourmuddle, but I knew you'd all thank me. I mean, look at us. I've never seen such a sickly bunch. If there's one thing we all need, it's a holiday. Don't you agree?' She appealed to the room in general.

The sickly bunch stared back at her. For the moment, even the coughing had been shocked into submission.

'Holiday?' said Greymatter, rolling the word experimentally around her mouth. 'What, us?'

'Us,' said Pongwiffy firmly. 'A lovely holiday in the sun.'

'But we're Witches. We're noo supposed tae like sun. We're supposed tae like blasted heaths and drippy caves,' objected Macabre, who was a strong traditionalist.

'Ah, but you like ice cream though, don't you?' asked Pongwiffy slyly. Macabre had to agree that yes, she liked ice cream. Especially porridge-flavoured.

'Well, sea air would certainly be efficacious in removing the possibility of further infection,' said Greymatter, who never used a short, simple word where a long, complicated one would do.

'Absolutely!' cried Pongwiffy, who hadn't

understood a word but had a feeling that Greymatter was on her side.

'It says here there are lots of rock pools full of jelly-like things with legs,' observed Ratsnappy, craning over Sourmuddle's shoulder and pointing at the brochure.

'There you are, you see, it's educational as well!' cried Pongwiffy enthusiastically. 'I knew you'd like that, Ratsnappy, with your interest in disgusting life forms. And there's a pier with a Hall of Mirrors and a Haunted House and stuff. And Punch and Judy and clock golf and – oh, all sorts of things. So – er – what d'you say, Sourmuddle?'

All this time, Sourmuddle had been flipping over the pages of the brochure. Now she looked up.

'I say you're a rotten Treasurer, Pongwiffy,' she said sternly. 'You had no right to use our savings. We're supposed to take a vote before we spend any money and then I overrule everyone and spend it on what I like. It's in the Rule Book. I've a good mind to expel you from the Coven. For misappropriation of funds.'

There was a concerted gasp. Expulsion from the Coven! That was the worst punishment anyone could think of. Dudley sat up, looking hopeful. If

Pongwiffy was expelled, that would mean at long last he would see the back of that cocky Hamster and regain his rightful place as leader of the Familiars. Oh joy! Oh fish heads and crab sticks, could it *be*?

'On the other hand . . .' Sourmuddle paused, 'on the other hand, I *am* over two hundred years old. It's time I had a break. We'll take a vote on it. All those in favour of a holiday say "Aye".'

'Aye!' came the thunderous response.

'The ayes have it. Pongwiffy, you're off the hook.'

'One moment,' said Greymatter. 'What about our poor sick friends?'

'What about them?' asked Sourmuddle.

'Well, they haven't voted, and this is supposed to be a democratic Coven.'

'Only when I say so,' said Sourmuddle firmly. 'And I say we're going on holiday.'

A great cheer went up. Disgustedly, Dudley jumped from Sharkadder's lap and went to sulk under the table.

'I dinnae like the sound o' this motor coach business, though,' complained Macabre. 'What's wrong wi' going by Broomstick in a proper manner?'

'It wouldn't be like going on holiday then, would

it?' argued Pongwiffy. 'Whoever heard of going on holiday by Broomstick? We'd be a laughing stock. Anyway, it'll be a bit different, won't it? Going by coach. We can sing songs and eat sandwiches.'

'Where will we stay?' Ratsnappy wanted to know.

'I've booked us into a charming family-run guest house with lovely sea views. Mrs Molotoff, Ocean View.'

There was a murmur of excitement. Just imagine, staying in a proper guest house!

'One last thing!' called Pongwiffy over the general clamour. 'I think I'd better mention it now. We're not allowed to use Magic. Sludgehaven is strictly a No Magic resort.'

There was a gasp of dismay. What? No *Magic*?

'What, not even *little* spells? In the privacy of our own bedroom?' wailed Ratsnappy.

''Fraid not. The Council's very fussy about it, apparently,' explained Pongwiffy. 'It's a law. Look in the brochure, Sourmuddle. It says so on the last page.'

Sourmuddle turned to the last page, and read:

WARNING

**Visitors are respectfully reminded that
Sludgehaven-on-Sea is a holiday resort and
THE USE OF MAGIC IS STRICTLY FORBIDDEN.
Anyone not complying with this rule faces a heavy
fine followed by instant banishment.
By order of the Council.**

There was a short silence while everyone
wrestled with the novel idea of doing without Magic
for a whole week. Witches' lives revolve almost
entirely around making Magic. On the other hand, if
it meant going without a holiday . . .

'I suppose they've got to do that,' said Scrofula
doubtfully. 'You've got to have rules. I mean,
everyone can't just go around using Magic
willy-nilly. Not in a respectable holiday resort, I
suppose.'

'Absolutely!' cried Pongwiffy cheerfully. 'It
won't hurt us to hang up our Wands for a week,
will it? It'll be a bit like cowboys hanging up their
holsters when they ride into town. What do you
think, Sourmuddle? You're Grandwitch. It's

your decision.'

'I think . . .' said Sourmuddle, and paused while everyone hung on her words. 'I think if cowboys can do it, so can Witches,' she finished, and a second cheer went up. Everyone leapt to their feet and clustered around, trying to look over her shoulder at the brochure and talk at the same time.

Everyone, that is, except Sharkadder, who was dabbing at her cold sore, looking hurt.

'I do think you could have told me what you were planning, Pongwiffy,' she said. 'I thought we were best friends.'

'You've been in bed all week, remember?' Pongwiffy reminded her. 'I came calling, but you wouldn't answer the door. I was bringing you round a Get Well card too.'

'Oh. Really? Well, that was very thoughtful of you. I'm sorry, Pong. I haven't been myself these last few weeks.'

'That's all right, Sharky,' said Pongwiffy nobly. 'None of us has, which is why we all need a holiday. What d'you think of the idea anyway? Isn't it wonderful?'

Sharkadder thought.

'Did you say something about a Hall of

233

Mirrors?' she asked.

'I did,' said Pongwiffy.

'Would those be *full-length* mirrors, do you suppose?'

'Sure to be. You can spend all day looking at yourself if you want.'

'I think it's a wonderful idea,' said Sharkadder.

CHAPTER FOUR
The Goblins are entertained

If the weather was bad in Witchway Wood, you should have seen it in Goblin Territory!

Goblin Territory. What a dump. Imagine a stony mountainside with lots of sharp rocks and clumps of stinging nettles and the odd stunted thorn bush. Include a snake or two, some biting insects, maybe a bad-tempered eagle. And a bog.

Next, imagine a damp, dark cave. At the cave's entrance, stick an abandoned pram, a rusty old shopping trolley and a huge pile of burnt-out pots and pans. Fill the cave with seven unbelievably

235

stupid Goblins called Plugugly, Stinkwart, Hog, Slopbucket, Lardo, Eyesore and Sproggit.

Now add rain. Lots and lots and lots of it.

Plugugly, Stinkwart, Hog, Slopbucket, Lardo, Eyesore and Sproggit, however, were used to rain. It almost always rained in Goblin Territory, so this was nothing new. Right now, actually, things were looking up a little, because for once, they had ENTERTAINMENT. Something to eat would have been better, but ENTERTAINMENT came a close second. (Or was it third? Difficult to say – the Goblins got mixed up after one.)

They had managed to capture a small Gnome called GNorman who, because of the awful weather, had rashly decided to take a short cut back from the paper shop. The short cut consisted of a little path which bordered the southern edge of Goblin Territory. GNorman was aware of this, but had assumed (wrongly) that the Goblins would be safely tucked away in their damp cave, eating nettle soup or whatever it was they did all day.

Instead, they jumped out at him from behind a rock, laughed at his pointy ears, threw his hat around, bent his fishing rod, put both him and his *Daily Miracle* in a big sack and bore him home in

236

triumph. Once there, they set him on a rock and made him do a song-and-dance act. Some Gnomes wouldn't have minded this, but GNorman was one of those rare things – a tone-deaf Gnome with absolutely no sense of rhythm. His efforts at the traditional Gnome Fishing Song caused no end of hilarity and reduced him to a sulky, scarlet-cheeked figure of fun.

'More! More!' begged the Goblins, clutching on to each other and wiping their eyes. 'Do it again! Please!'

'No,' said GNorman through tight lips. 'I won't.'

'Just de chorus,' pleaded the big dopey one they called Plugugly. 'Go on, go on. Just de bit about bein' king o' de pond. Where you wave your fishin' rod and do dat funny jumpin' fing an' make us larf.'

GNorman kept his lips firmly buttoned.

'Poke 'im wiv a stick,' suggested young Sproggit. This provoked a chorus of agreement. Goblins know a good suggestion when they hear one.

'Yeah, yeah! Go on, Plugugly, poke 'im wiv a stick!'

'Can't,' said Plugugly. ' Ain't got one. Anyone got a stick?'

No one had a stick. Young Sproggit nearly

volunteered to go out and get one, then remembered the rain and kept his mouth shut. The Goblins all looked disappointed. They shuffled their feet and stared at each other.

'What shall we get 'im to do then?' enquired Hog. 'No point in gettin' a Gnome in unless we gets 'im to *do* somethin'.'

'We didn't just get a Gnome in,' pointed out Slopbucket. 'We got a noozpaper too.'

The Goblins stared at the crumpled copy of *The Daily Miracle*, lying forgotten in a dark corner.

'Not much we can do wi' that,' observed Lardo.

'Anyone know 'ow to make a paper aeroplane?' asked Eyesore, not very hopefully.

Nobody did.

'We could tear it up,' suggested young Sproggit, who had a very destructive streak. 'Tear it up before 'is very eyes. Unless 'e sings us that funny song again.'

'I'm not singing again,' GNorman told him firmly. 'Do what you will.'

'Pity we can't read,' remarked Lardo, eyeing the newspaper with a slightly wistful air. 'Then we'd know wot wuz goin' on in the world. Fer once.'

Hog nodded. 'There might be somethin' about

Goblins in there. And we wouldn't know, 'cos we can't read.'

'De Gnome can, though, can't 'e?' Plugugly suddenly burst out. 'We could get 'im to read de paper to us. See?'

This suggestion stunned the Goblins by its sheer simplicity. Of course! There was today's paper, and there was a Gnome who could read! All you had to do was put the two together! What a brilliant idea!

'Cor!'

'Fabutastic!'

'Nice one, Plug!'

Plugugly glowed with pride. There was no doubt about it. These days, he was coming up with some real brainwaves!

'What about it, Gnome? Are you gonna read us the paper or what?' demanded Hog, pushing his face unpleasantly close to GNorman.

'Oh – all right,' said GNorman with a little sigh. 'If I must.'

GNorman couldn't sing or dance, but he could read all right. He sat down cross-legged on the rock and held his hand out. 'Give it here then. Everybody sit down quietly. You're supposed to sit quietly when you're being read to.'

Obediently, the Goblins sat. This was novel. This was different. They watched in wonderment as GNorman took out his reading glasses and placed them on his nose. They nudged each other excitedly as he straightened out *The Daily Miracle* and gave it a professional little shake.

'Are you sitting comfortably? Then I'll begin. *Witches To Go On Holiday! Witchway Wood will be a quiet place next week when the Witchway Coven departs for a holiday in sunny Sludgehaven-on-Sea. The holiday is the brainchild of Witch Pongwiffy. "The girls were feeling a bit down in the dumps," she said. "I thought they needed cheering up."'*

'Wot?' interrupted young Sproggit suddenly.

'Beg yer parsnips?' said Eyesore, cleaning out his ear with a dirty fingernail.

'Eh?' said Lardo.

'Did 'e say wot I thort 'e juss said?' enquired Hog.

'Read dat again,' Plugugly instructed. 'And slower dis time. Last time, you went too fast. You got to wait for our brains to catch up, see.'

GNorman began again, a shade irritably.

'"*Witches To Go On Holiday! Witchway Wood will be a quiet place . . .*"'

This time, there was instant outrage.

''E did, 'e did! *'E did say* wot I thort 'e did!'

'Well I never! Them flippin' Witches! They're goin' on 'oliday!'

'*I* wanna go on 'oliday! 'Ow come them old Witches get to go on 'oliday an' I don't? I ain't never been on 'oliday . . .'

''S not fair! 'S not fair!'

There was a great deal more of this sort of thing, accompanied by much angry teeth-gnashing, eye-rolling, heavy pacing about and the thumping of frustrated fists into palms. At one point, Slopbucket paced heavily on Stinkwart's foot. Seconds later, Stinkwart's frustrated fist somehow missed his palm and connected with Slopbucket's rolling eye. This was the signal for everyone to wade in with fists flailing. For the next few minutes, pandemonium reigned.

GNorman tutted disapprovingly, turned to the back page of the *Miracle*, settled more comfortably on his rock and began to get involved with the crossword puzzle. One Across was tricky. The clue said, *Words spoken by backward giant (3,2,2,3)*. Hmm.

Meanwhile, the fight raged about him. If Goblins could write (which they can't) and were asked to compile a list of popular Goblin activities, it

241

would go like this:

    2. Eeet
    3. Get entertayned
    1. Fite

Being mind-bogglingly stupid, Goblins really enjoy a good punch-up, particularly when they've got something special to get upset about. Ten minutes later, dizzy and bruised, they all lay groaning on the floor, sucking their skinned knuckles and trying to get their breath back.

'That were a good one, weren't it?' gasped young Sproggit, dabbing at his cut lip.

'One o' the best we've ever 'ad,' agreed Hog, clutching his throbbing ear.

Everyone agreed that it had, indeed, been a fight to remember. Then Plugugly climbed painfully to his feet, lumbered over to where GNorman was still poring over the crossword, sat down expectantly in front of him and said, 'Go on, den.'

'Mmmmmmm?' said GNorman, nibbling his pencil, lost in his little square world.

'Go on wid de paper. But not dat bit about de

Witches goin' on 'oliday. We don't like dat bit, do we, boys?'

'No,' agreed the others, clutching at various injured bits of themselves as they came limping back to sit once again in a semicircle at GNorman's pointy-toed feet.

'Well, what, then?' asked GNorman, impatiently riffling through. 'What d'you want to hear? The Skeleton Raffle was cancelled because of the rain. Luscious Lulu Lamarre is starring in a summer show somewhere on the coast. The Yeti Brothers are opening another spaghetti restaurant in Wizard Territory. There's a letter here from some Werewolf complaining about being short-changed in Malpractiss Magic Ltd . . .'

'No, no!' howled the Goblins. 'We don't wanna hear 'bout that! We wanna hear 'bout Goblins!'

'Goblins, eh? Well, I don't suppose there's anything in the paper about Goblins because, quite frankly, you're not newsworthy,' said GNorman, enjoying getting his own back.

The Goblins' faces fell.

'Nuffin' at all?' asked Eyesore sadly.

'Nope. 'Fraid not,' smirked GNorman, leafing through the pages without really looking.

'Oh well. I suppose we might as well juss tear it up, then,' said young Sproggit, reaching out with a malevolent glitter in his eye.

GNorman snatched his paper away in alarm and clutched it protectively to his breast. He didn't want to lose the crossword puzzle. *Words spoken by backward giant (3,2,2,3).* Intriguing.

'Oh, wait a minute,' cried GNorman. 'I've just noticed. Here's something that might interest you, tucked away right at the bottom of page three. It's an advertisement for somewhere called Gobboworld. Something called a Theme Park, whatever that might be. *"A whole world of spectacularly idiotic fun,"* it says here. *"A Goblin's paradise, opening shortly. Attractions will include lots of terrifying and stupidly dangerous rides, regular punch-ups, wet bobble hat competitions, overpriced junk food . . ."'*

He broke off, becoming suddenly aware of a strange silence. He looked up from the paper to find all the Goblins staring at him with their jaws dropping open. It was most unnerving.

'What?' said GNorman uncomfortably. 'What's the matter? Why are you looking like that?'

And in hushed tones, Hog said, 'Gobboworld.'

'Junk food,' breathed Lardo.

'Punch-ups,' drooled Slopbucket.

'Stupidly dangerous rides,' hissed young Sproggit, eyes rolling.

And Eyesore and Stinkwart simply put their arms around each other and burst into silent, heaving sobs.

Plugugly's little red piggy eyes shone. He let out a long, shaky breath and spoke for all of them.

'I wanna go dere,' he said.

CHAPTER FIVE
The wizards get a shock

'Well, I'll be frazzled with a lightning bolt! If that doesn't beat all!'

It was Frank the Foreteller who spotted it first. He was sitting in the lounge of the Wizards' Clubhouse at the time, idly thumbing through a copy of *The Daily Miracle*. One or two of his colleagues looked up from their armchairs with mild interest at his startled cry – but most carried on with what they were doing. Dozing, mainly, after a large cooked breakfast featuring far too many greasy sausages.

'What?' enquired Ronald the Magnificent,

turning away from the rain-streaked window, where he had been following the dreary adventures of three little drips with his finger. 'What beats all?'

He could have kicked himself as soon as he said it. If he had just kept his mouth shut and carried on playing with his drips, Frank the Foreteller might not have noticed him. As it was, he came down on Ronald like a wolf on the fold.

'Well, well, well, if it isn't young Ronald. What are you doing standing up, lad? Don't tell me they still haven't got you a chair?'

Ronald flushed and said nothing. That was the trouble with being the youngest Wizard. You got picked on a lot. And you never got a chair.

Or a locker to put your sandwiches in.

'Dearie dearie me,' said Frank the Foreteller sadly, shaking his head. 'Still no chair. No beard yet either, I notice.'

This caused a ripple of appreciative titters from the assembled company, the majority of whom were not so much bearded as *buried* in beard. There was not a Wizard present who didn't have every part of his face above the shoulders colonised by some sort of jungly growth. Everyone except Ronald, who had three flimsy little hairs on his chin which simply refused to grow despite being talked to encouragingly every night before he went to bed.

'What beats all, anyway?' asked a short, tubby Wizard by the name of Dave the Druid.

'Eh?' said Frank the Foreteller.

'What beats all? You said something beats all.'

'Oh – right.'

Frank the Foreteller suddenly remembered what he'd been going to talk about, before he got sidetracked with Ronald. He pointed to the paper.

'See the headlines? "*Witches To Go On Holiday!*" Seems the Witchway mob are off on a vacation to Sludgehaven-on-Sea. That's your aunt's Coven, isn't it, young Ronald? Nice Auntie Sharkadder, who makes you your favourite fungus sponge. Hmm?'

Ronald blushed scarlet. It wasn't done in Wizard circles to admit you had a Witch auntie.

'I went to Sludgehaven once,' said a disembodied voice from an empty chair, making everyone jump. Alf the Invisible had forgotten to take his reversing pills again. 'Delightful little place. Quiet. Completely unspoilt. Delicious local delicacy, I remember. Jelly-like things with legs. Used to buy 'em off stalls. And then we'd take a nice little stroll along the prom. Ah me!'

'Imagine it overrun with Witches,' said somebody else with a shudder.

'Yes, it makes you sick, doesn't it?' agreed Frank the Foreteller. 'That lot running amok in a respectable seaside resort. Witches shouldn't be allowed to go on holiday. They should stay in their revolting caves, where they belong.'

There were a few cries of 'Hear hear!' and 'Back to the cauldron with 'em, I say!'

'Actually, not all Witches live in caves,' observed a thin, hawk-nosed Wizard, peering over his half-glasses and taking a sip from a small glass containing something green and smoking. His name was Gerald the Just and he had a reputation for being fair-minded. 'And everybody needs an occasional break. Even Witches.'

'Shouldn't be allowed,' insisted Frank the Foreteller. 'They'll lower the tone, you mark my words.'

'Sure to be some truth in that as well,' nodded Gerald the Just fairly.

'Actually, I've heard that Sludgehaven's not the place it once was,' observed a short, pipe-smoking Wizard with a large burn hole in his sleeve. His name was Fred the Flameraiser. His

249

speciality was setting fire to things. 'A lot of riff-raff there these days. And someone told me they're about to open some sort of ghastly Theme Park for Goblins just along the coast. Gobboworld or something. The Sludgehaven Council's been trying to get it stopped, and quite right too.'

Just then, a thin, tremulous sound quavered up from the scrawny throat of the Venerable Harold the Hoodwinker, the oldest Wizard of all. It was quite unusual for the Venerable Harold to wake up between meals, let alone contribute to the conversation, so everybody paid attention.

'Shludgehaven? Ishn't that where our Convention ish being held thish year?' enquired the Venerable Harold in his reedy little voice.

There was a long silence, heavy with anxiety, while the Wizards tried to remember.

'He could be right, you know,' said Dave the Druid at last. 'I'm pretty sure it began with an S. And it's on the coast.'

'Might be Spittlesands,' came the voice of Alf the Invisible, providing a little flicker of hope in the all-pervading gloom. 'Spittlesands is on the coast. Yes, I'm pretty sure it's Spittlesands. Find the letter about it, Dave – it'll be behind the clock. I'd do it

250

myself, but you know . . .'

Dave the Druid hurried over to the mantelpiece and dragged a yellowing pile of old postcards, unpaid bills and ancient circulars from behind the clock. It was a large clock, ornately carved and covered in meaningful astrological symbols. It had a massive key for winding and a big, slow-moving pendulum. It showed the rainfall on Oz, the humidity in Never Land and the current time and temperature in Narnia. Its face was a mass of tiny dials and gauges and little spinning hands. None of the Wizards could work out how to tell the time from it, but it had a solemn sort of tick, which suited the lounge, and was useful for stuffing junk mail behind.

'Now, what have we got here? Spell circulars, *Fly Me Carpets* cards, the sausage bill – ah, here we are. Oh dearie dearie me. Harold's right. What a disaster. It *is* Sludgehaven.'

The small flicker of hope provided by Alf died.

'In fact, I remember now. Brenda booked us the top-floor suite at the Magician's Retreat. That's where the Convention is being held.'

There was an even heavier silence.

'On the other hand,' said Gerald the Just, 'we

should look on the bright side. It'd be pretty bad luck if the Witches are there the same time as us. And even if they are, they won't bother us. After all, we spend all our time in the hotel, don't we? Having our Convention.'

Ronald had been listening to all this with interest. He had only been a proper Wizard for a short time, and still had a lot to learn. This was the first time he had heard of any Convention.

'What, you mean we go away?' he asked. 'Have a Convention, you mean? At the seaside? In a proper hotel and everything? And meet other Magicians and Sorcerers and Soothsayers and have intelligent conversations and – and – read out learned papers and stuff? Really?'

'All that, and a sea view as well,' Gerald the Just told him. 'You can't say fairer than that,' he added fairly.

'Could *I* read out a paper?' enquired Ronald breathlessly.

'Well, yes. Anyone can.'

'Wow!' said Ronald. He couldn't wait to find a pen and paper and get started. But first he had another burning question to ask.

'Do – er – do we get to paddle?'

He tried to sound casual, but deep down he was very excited. He had never paddled. In fact, if the truth be known, he had never even been to the seaside.

This brought forth a chorus of disapproval.

'Certainly not! The very idea!'

'I didn't get where I am today through paddling!'

'Wizards paddling indeed! Mixing on the beach with the plebs! Where's your sense of dignity, boy?'

'This isn't a holiday, you know!'

'Sorry,' said Ronald, quite humbly for him. 'Do go on. About the Convention.'

But someone heard the distant rattling of cups and saucers, which meant that elevenses were on their way.

And with Wizards, elevenses always come first.

CHAPTER SIX
Scott Sinister – Has-Been!

In the curling grey mists of dawn, a forlorn, wind-whipped figure stood by the rail at the end of the Sludgehaven pier, staring out to sea. This was Scott Sinister, once Famous Star of Stage and Screen. His cape flapped wildly about him and his sunglasses were flattened against his pale, thin face, making his eyes water.

Apart from Scott and a couple of large Yetis busily setting up a hot-dog stand, the pier was deserted. The Ice-Cream Parlour, the Rifle Range, the Coconut Shy, the Hall of Mirrors, the Haunted

House, the Fortune Teller's booth and the Souvenir Stall – all lay empty.

Above him, mewling seagulls circled in the grey sky. Below, between the planks, scummy waves sploshed against the barnacled supports. Behind him rose the Pier Pavilion – a crumbling dome of flaky paintwork and cracked plaster cherubs with missing noses. A broad flight of steps led up to the main doors, to the right of which hung a billboard. It said, in whacking great letters:

OPENING SOON!
summer spektacular
starrinG
Luscious Lulu Lamarre
and
spot Snitser

Not only was he bottom of the bill, they had even spelt his name wrong. Scott couldn't look at it without bursting into tears – which, if the truth be known, was why his eyes were watering, and nothing at all to do with wind or sunglasses.

Poor Scott. The world of show business is fickle

255

and things hadn't been going at all well for him lately. His last film, *Return of the Avenging Killer Poodles IV*, had flopped horribly. The punters had stayed away in droves, and the film had broken all box office records with the lowest ever takings in history (£5.25, and that was from his mum).

Since then, he had been what is commonly referred to in show business circles as 'resting', which in all other circles means out of a job. His pathetic spot in the Summer Spektacular was the first bit of work he had been offered in over six months.

The Yeti Brothers finished setting up their stall and the smell of frying onions drifted towards Scott, making his empty stomach churn. He turned from the rail and walked back along the pier.

The Yetis stared at him as he approached. Their names were Spag Yeti and Conf Yeti, and they had a monopoly of fast food in these parts. Greasy-spoon cafes, pizza parlours, burger bars – they owned them all and ran them all, Spag taking the orders, Conf doing the cooking. They did wedding receptions and birthday parties too. They seemed to work in a hundred places simultaneously. Nobody knew how they did it. Maybe they cloned

256

themselves in some mysterious Yeti way. Or maybe they were just very fast runners.

'Yeah?' said Spag, who was cleaning his claws with a fork. His brother sat in the background, sullenly slicing tomatoes.

'A hot dog, if you please, my good man,' said Scott, counting out coins.

'You gotta wait,' said Spag, staring at him. 'Onions ain't-a burnt-a yet.'

Scott tutted irritably. He wasn't used to waiting for food. One click of the fingers, that's all it used to take. But that was when he was rich and famous and able to afford posh meals in fancy restaurants. Now he was poor and desperate, at the mercy of hairy oafs in greasy waistcoats.

'Mamma mia! I know you!' cried Spag suddenly. 'You're Scott-a Seenister, the feelm-a star!'

'Well – yes, actually,' Scott admitted, smoothing his hair back.

'Hey, Conf, look-a here!' Spag gave his brother a prod with his fork. 'Ees-a Scott-a Seenister! Hey, Scott! Our mama used to love-a your feelms.'

'Oh, really?' said Scott, reaching into his pocket for pad and paper so that he could graciously give his autograph.

257

'She theenk-a you rubbish now,' Spag informed him.

Scott bit his lip, made out he was looking for a hanky and said nothing. This sort of thing was always happening. One slap in the face after another.

'Een-a the show, then?' enquired Spag, jerking his head towards the Pier Pavilion.

'Yes,' agreed Scott. Well, he was. Just.

'Must-a remember not-a to come,' said Spag, adding with a leer, 'Mind you, that-a Lulu Lamarre, she a corker, she ees. Dona you theenk so?'

'No,' said Scott stiffly. 'I don't.'

He clenched his fists and turned away so that Spag couldn't see the black rage welling up inside him. Lulu Lamarre indeed! The very sound of her name was enough.

All right, so once she had been his girlfriend. That was back in the good old days, when she had been a humble starlet and his career was at an all-time high. Then had come the unpleasant incident at a Witch Talent Contest when a certain smelly old Witch – what was her revolting name again? – had taken exception to his beloved, called her a stuck-up hussy and, in a fit of jealous pique, had made her vanish in a puff of smoke!

Lulu hadn't reappeared for days. When she did, they had had a blazing row, after which she had stormed out, vowing never to return.

He wouldn't have minded – well, not that much – except that she had become a star overnight, calling herself Luscious Lulu Lamarre and taking top billing over him! In the blink of an eye she had become a household name, while he became a nobody. He had never felt so mortified in his life.

'What hotel-a you staying at?' enquired Spag, breaking into his thoughts.

Scott pulled himself together.

'The Ritz, naturally,' he lied with a haughty air. 'Where all the stars stay.'

He wasn't really, of course. He couldn't even afford bed and breakfast, let alone a posh hotel like the Ritz. In fact, it was as much as he could do to scrape together enough money for breakfast. The truth was, he was camping out in his dressing room in the Pier Pavilion. Well, it wasn't so much a dressing room. More a broom cupboard really. A broom cupboard-cum-junk room, lit by a single bare bulb, stuffed with buckets and mops and bits of old scenery and smelling of mice. He had complained to the management, of course – but it hadn't got

259

him very far.

Lulu had the big, proper dressing room – the one with the star on the door and the little lights around the mirror and the huge wardrobe for all her costume changes. And the one and only coffee machine.

'Here's your hot-a dog,' said Spag, handing it over.

Ah! Food at last. Scott's spirits rose a little. Eagerly, he bit into it.

As you might expect, it tasted awful.

CHAPTER SEVEN
Mrs Molotoff Prepares

'Cyril! Have you got the keys to the larder?'

'No, my love,' came a worried bleat from the kitchen.

'Well, where are they, then? You know I don't like them lying around, particularly with a party of Witches about to descend on us.'

The door to the dining room opened and Mrs Molotoff, landlady of Ocean View, strode into the room. She stood, arms akimbo, glaring around. A tiny curved beak of a nose jutted out of her big, cross red face. She had hard beady eyes and a sour

261

little mouth painted a fearsome shade of vermilion. Her clashing red hair was arranged in a complicated series of nests on top of her head.

Her eagle eye alighted on a huge bunch of keys lying on the table.

'Aha! Here they are. You left them on the table, Cyril! I said, you left them on the table! That was very foolish, Cyril, very foolish indeed.'

She swooped upon the keys, dropped them into her apron pocket and gave it a satisfied little pat.

'Sorry, my love.'

'I should think so. I dread to think what might happen if that lot get at the larder, simply dread to think. You know what Witches are like. What are you doing *now*, Cyril?'

'Counting the tea leaves, my love.'

'Well, be quick about it. The beds haven't been made yet. And what about the breakfast menus? Have you done those?'

'Not yet, my love.'

'Well, get a move on. And don't forget what I told you. A boiled egg *or* a piece of toast, not both. We're trying to run a business here. And, Cyril–'

'Yes, my love?'

'Don't use the best sheets. Only one piece of

262

soap in the bathroom. And half a candle each to light them to bed. Half, mind, not three-quarters. And don't forget what I told you. Three to a room, four wherever possible. And no Familiars in the bathroom. If there's one thing I can't abide, it's bats in a bathroom. And if they try to sneak in any Magical equipment, it's to be surrendered to me upon arrival. If you see anything suspicious, you're to tell me. I'm not having any cackling around cauldrons nonsense in *this* house.'

'My love, I don't think Witches will take too kindly . . .'

'Witches? Ha! They don't frighten me. I've seen 'em all, I have. Skeletons, Zombies, Trolls, the lot. Witches are no different. They'll obey the House Rules, same as anyone else!'

Mrs Molotoff straightened the copy of the House Rules, which hung in a prominent position by the mantelpiece, cast a steely eye over the table, moved a fork half a millimetre to the left and went off to water down the orange juice.

CHAPTER EIGHT
The Coach

'Well, this is nice, isn't it? Come on, Sharky, admit it's nice. Bowling along in a luxury air-conditioned motor coach on our way to the seaside. And all thanks to me,' said Pongwiffy, settling back in her seat with a pleased sigh. Up on her hat, Hugo (wearing a tiny pair of shorts and a jaunty straw hat) made himself comfortable and began to draw little Hamster faces on the dirty glass of the window.

'If this filthy old wreck is a luxury air-conditioned motor coach, I'm the Sugarplum Fairy,' grumbled

Sharkadder, in a bad mood because Pongwiffy had pinched the window seat.

'Oh, don't be such an old fusspot. It's a nice little coach. Homely. I think it's quite clever, the way it's all held together with string. I loved it when the exhaust pipe fell off on the driver's foot when he was loading the Brooms into the boot. It's got character, this coach. It could have been a touch bigger, mind. We are a bit squashed.'

It could. They were. Fitting thirteen argumentative Witches and their assorted Familiars, Brooms and luggage into one saggy, old, fit-for-the-scrap-heap coach had been no easy task. However, after a good deal of squabbling, everyone had finally managed to find a seat (except Gaga, who had elected to hang from the luggage rack with her Bats). And now the holiday spirit was back with a vengeance as they trundled, creaking and backfiring, along the winding road that led away from dripping Witchway Wood towards the as yet unknown delights of the sunny seaside.

Everyone was really beginning to get the hang of things. There are certain traditional things you *do* on a coach, and the Witches were determined to get their money's worth. There were sweets to be passed and maps to be consulted. There was scenery to be admired. There were sandwiches to be eaten. There were passing wayfarers to make rude faces at. There were songs to be sung.

'*Ten green Lizards wiggling down the road!*' started up the Witches in the back seat, led by Sourmuddle.

> '*Ten green Lizards*
> *Wiggling down the road,*
> *And if one green Lizard*
> *Should suddenly explode . . .*'

'What a vulgar racket,' tutted Sharkadder, clutching her head. 'You'd think Sourmuddle would tell them, wouldn't you?'

'You would,' agreed Pongwiffy, looking around to see where Sourmuddle was. She located her slap in the middle of the back seat, about to commence a solo. 'On second thoughts, maybe you wouldn't. After all, it *is* a holiday. We're supposed to be letting our hair down.'

'Mine's down already,' said Sharkadder, taking out a mirror and examining her tortured curls with satisfaction. 'This is my holiday style. It's called

Matted Mermaid. I think it rather suits me.'

In honour of the occasion, she had twined a bright green length of material printed with little anchors around her tall hat. Her hair was dyed to match and huge, unnerving octopus earrings dangled from her ears. A kind of Sea Theme, as she explained to anybody who would listen. The Theme apparently extended to Dudley, who was kitted out with a matching scarf which he wore rakishly over one ear.

'Oh, it does. It's lovely. I must say you look very stylish, Sharky. Very holidayish. I really like the Sea Theme.'

'Why, thank you, Pong.' Sharkadder brightened up a bit and fumbled in her handbag for her sea-green lipstick. 'I like to look my best. I don't like to let the Coven down. Not like *some* people.'

She stared pointedly at Pongwiffy's holey cardigan.

'Do you mind? These are my holiday rags,' said Pongwiffy, slightly hurt.

'What d'you mean? They're what you always wear.'

'No, they're not.' Pongwiffy pointed proudly at some new red blobs. 'I've painted flowers on, see?

Nice flowery print, very suitable for the seaside.'

Sharkadder opened her mouth to speak, then decided not to. Conversations about Pongwiffy's clothing never got anywhere. She knew. She'd tried.

'What's in the chest, then?' Pongwiffy pointed to the huge receptacle blocking Sharkadder's bit of aisle.

'My make-up, if you must know,' Sharkadder said defensively. 'And Dudley's things. His cushion and his catnip mouse. And his fish heads.'

She smiled fondly down at Dead Eye Dudley, who was crouched on her lap, glaring up at Hugo with an expression of feline menace that would curdle cheese. Hugo was retaliating with a Hamster version which would strip paint.

'You should have been like me. Just brought the one bag,' said Pongwiffy, holding up a particularly tatty plastic one from Swallow and Riskitt that looked as though it had been used to strain curry.

'I wouldn't even put Dudley's fish heads in there,' said Sharkadder with scorn. 'Yuck!'

'Why can't you get fish heads in Sludgehaven-on-Sea?' Pongwiffy wanted to know. 'You're daft, you are. I'll bet you can buy any amount

269

of fish heads there.'

'Not the sort he likes,' said Sharkadder firmly.

Just then, the coach went into a deep pothole. Things came clattering down from the luggage racks. Everyone lurched and fell about. Greymatter made a mistake on her crossword puzzle. Macabre's bagpipes went off with a wild cry. Bonidle almost woke up. Sludgegooey dropped a bag of sherbet all over Ratsnappy and Gaga's bats flapped wildly.

'Bother!' said Sharkadder, who now had a trail of sea-green lipstick going up her nose. 'Now look!'

Ribald jeers and the jolly strains of 'For He's a Jolly Bad Driver' rose from the back seat. The driver (a bad-tempered Dwarf called George) tightened his grip on the wheel and did some terrible gear-clashing.

'Told you so!' grumbled Macabre from across the aisle. She was squashed uncomfortably between her bagpipes and Rory. 'Gi' me a Broomstick any day!'

'When do we stop for lunch?' bawled Bendyshanks. 'Oi! Driver! When do we stop for lunch?'

'There's no stops,' said George firmly.

There was immediate consternation. No stops? All the way from Witchway Wood, over the Misty

Mountains to Sludgehaven with *no stops*? After all those cups of bogwater?

'What d'you mean, no stops?' enquired Sourmuddle dangerously.

'Not on my schedule,' George informed her smugly. He wrenched the wheel, purposely swerving in order to drive through a big puddle, thereby spattering with mud a Gaggle of rainsoaked Goblins who, for some strange reason, were trudging slowly in single file along the middle of the road.

'I don't do stops on this run.'

'Oh yes you do,' said Sourmuddle briskly, and twiddled her fingers. Much to everyone's delight, George's cap immediately rose from his head and sailed gaily out of the window.

Muttering under his breath, George slammed on the brakes and the coach juddered to a halt. To a chorus of loud jeers he dismounted and stumped back to pick up his cap from where it had landed – in the large, muddy puddle he had just driven through. He bent down to retrieve it – then became aware that he was being watched by seven pairs of accusing eyes. They belonged to the rainsoaked Goblins he had just splashed with mud.

(Of course, they weren't just any old Goblins. They were Plugugly, Slopbucket, Hog, Eyesore, Stinkwart, Sproggit and Lardo, who were on their way to Gobboworld with packs on their backs, sticks in their hands and a dream in their hearts.)

And now they had mud on their faces as well.

'I suppose you enjoyed dat,' said Plugugly. 'Splatterin' us wiv mud like dat. I suppose dat gave you a great big larf.'

'Yep,' said George. 'As a matter o' fact, it did.'

'Let's do 'im over, Plug,' urged young Sproggit, jumping up and down and waving his fists. 'Come on, come on, let's scrag 'im! Let's roll 'im in the mud and throw 'is 'at in a bush!'

'Oh yeah?' said George smugly, jerking a thumb towards the coach, where the Witches had started up a hearty rendition of 'Why are We Waiting?' 'An' leave that lot without a driver? I don't fink so, some'ow.'

And with a confident air, he clapped his cap on his head and turned his back. The Goblins watched helplessly as he climbed in and the coach pulled away, belching exhaust fumes. The last thing they saw as it hurtled off around the corner was Agglebag and Bagaggle in the back seat, laughing merrily while making identical rude gestures.

''Ow come nuffin' ever goes right for us, Plug?' asked Lardo sadly when they had all finished choking.

'I dunno,' said Plugugly with a sigh. 'But it'll be all right when we get to Gobboworld,' he added more cheerfully. 'Come on, lads. We gotta long way ter go. Best foot backward.'

'There's somethin' wrong wiv that,' pondered Hog with a little frown. 'But I'm blowed if I can fink wot.'

And with great heavings and sighs and doleful head-shakings, the Goblins picked up their sticks and followed in Plugugly's wake.

CHAPTER NINE
A Tent in the Garden

'Cyril! They're here! Have you hidden the silver?'

'Yes, my love.'

'Did you spread the newspaper in the hall? I don't want them treading on my carpets.'

'All done, my love.'

'What are you doing now, Cyril?'

'Halving the candles like you told me, my love.'

Outside, as dusk fell, the parched, hungry, weary travellers clustered at the gate and peered nerv-ously up the path of Ocean View. There was something very forbidding about the scrubbed white doorstep, the thick lace curtains and the various signs reading NO HAWKERS, NO CIRCULARS, NO GOBLINS and POSITIVELY NO MAGIC.

'I don't like the look of it,' whispered Pongwiffy to Sharkadder, who was redoing her lipstick. 'Too clean by half.'

'I don't know why it's called Ocean View, do you?' asked Sharkadder. 'I can't see a glimpse of the ocean from here.'

'You might if you climbed on the chimney,' said Pongwiffy doubtfully. 'And had a very strong telescope.'

'Quiet over there!' commanded Sourmuddle. 'Gather round, everyone – I'm about to give a pep talk. Now, this is a charming family-run guest house, and we've never stayed in one of those before. The landlady's name is . . . What is it, Snoop?'

'Mrs Molotoff,' Snoop told her.

'That's it. So it's Yes, Mrs Molotoff, No, Mrs Molotoff, Thank you very much, Mrs Molotoff. Understand? You've got to obey the House Rules. Be polite at all times.'

Sourmuddle was a great one for rules. Even other people's, provided they didn't conflict in any major

275

way with her own.

'Polite?' protested Macabre. 'Ah've never been polite in ma life. Witches dinnae have tae be polite.'

'They do when they're staying in guest houses,' said Sourmuddle firmly. 'I'm not having it said that Witches don't know how things are Done. I want all of you to say "Please" and "Thank you" and "Could I trouble you to pass the spiderspread?" and things like that. Of course, they might not have spiderspread. That's another thing. There might be all sorts of strange food. If in doubt, take your cue from me. I'm not Grandwitch for nothing. I'll show you how it's Done. Right. Put your best faces on – I'm going to ring the bell.'

But she didn't have to, for at that moment the front door opened and Mrs Molotoff, brandishing a large feather duster like a whip, strode out on to the top step and gave them a Look. It was the sort of Look that people wear when they discover something nasty living in their salad. The Witches' best Sunday-go-visiting smiles started up, tried to get going, then dwindled away to nothing. All except Sourmuddle, who glowed away like a beacon in a fog, showing them all how it was Done.

'Are you the Witchway party?' demanded Mrs

Molotoff. 'You're late. I hope you're not expecting any supper. Who's in charge here?'

'Me,' beamed Sourmuddle, all sweetness and light. 'Grandwitch Sourmuddle, Mistress of the Witchway Coven. *Soooo* pleased to meet you. What a delightful place you have here. So – scrubbed.'

'Hmm. What have you got in the way of Familiars?'

'Three Cats, a Vulture, an Owl, a Demon, a Fiend, a Sloth, a Rat, a Haggis, a Snake, some Bats and a Hamster,' obliged Sourmuddle helpfully. 'All completely guest-house-trained, of course.'

'Well, they're banned from the bathroom. And I'll thank you to keep them in order. This is a respectable household and I don't want any carryings-on. That applies to all of you.'

'Carryings-on? What, my girls? Never!' cried Sourmuddle, hand on her heart.

'Hmm. Well, we'll see. In you go, wipe your feet, straight upstairs, four to a room, no bouncing on the furniture, no snakes on the bed, Brooms in the shed, no noise after sundown, breakfast at seven sharp. And may I remind you that a strict No Magic Rule is in force here. Any Magical equipment you may have about your person is to be locked away in my cupboard, to be signed for and returned upon your departure.'

'Lovely, lovely, whatever you say, that'll be just fine,' cooed Sourmuddle. 'No problem at all. I'm sure our valuables will be quite safe in your delightful cupboard. I, of course, will be keeping my Wand with me. Official purposes, you understand. You heard our charming hostess, ladies. In you go.'

And everyone picked up their cases and trooped in, meek as lambs, under Mrs Molotoff's steely gaze.

'Not you,' said Mrs Molotoff, barring Pongwiffy's way. 'You with the pet Hamster and the horrible smell. I've just polished.'

Dudley broke into a delighted grin. Up on Pongwiffy's shoulder, Hugo began to bristle as he always does when anyone mentions the three-letter 'P' word.

'Oh, but she has to come in! She's sharing with me and Dudley,' cried Sharkadder loyally. 'In fact, the whole holiday was her idea. Don't scratch Mummy, Dudley. It's not nice. Pongwiffy's our friend. I refuse to be parted from her.'

'Well, she'll have to sleep in a tent in the garden. I'm not having her indoors.'

Pongwiffy opened her mouth to argue, caught

Sourmuddle's warning look and decided against it.

'Will you come with me, Sharky?' she asked.

'Er – no, actually,' said Sharkadder, not so loyally.

'What, you mean you'll desert me in my hour of need?' wailed Pongwiffy.

'Dudley and I are not sleeping in a tent for anyone,' said Sharkadder firmly. 'Not without a proper dressing table.'

'But you promised you'd share! You promised!'

'Oh, stop all this nonsense, Pongwiffy dear,' said Sourmuddle, smiling, with a threatening glint in her eye. 'In you go, Sharkadder. Thank Mrs Molotoff for the tent, Pongwiffy. Where are your manners?'

'Oh lovely!' said Pongwiffy between clenched teeth. 'Thanks very much. A tent in the garden, you say? What could be nicer?'

'A tent in ze garden, eh? Vot could be nicer?' mocked Hugo as they huddled under canvas later that night. A fine sea mist coiled and curled around the tiny tent erected on the minute patch of lawn which was the garden.

Over in the garden shed the Brooms could be heard rustling around, sweeping their own little bit of floor space and squabbling with a couple of resident deckchairs in Wood (by all accounts a very difficult language to master).

Flickering lights shone from the bedroom windows of Ocean View as the subdued guests tiptoed around with their half-candles, trying to unpack and arguing over the sleeping arrangements in whispers. Every so often, the stern voice of Mrs Molotoff would ring out, reminding them of the Rule about NO NOISE AFTER SUNDOWN.

'Oh, stop complaining,' said Pongwiffy with a yawn. 'I'd sooner sleep out here anyway. I don't like the look of it in old Molotoff's. Much too strict. And did you see how *clean* it looked? Ugh! And who wants to share a room with rotten old Sharkadder anyway? No, it's nice out here under the stars. Come on, let's get to sleep. We must be up bright and early tomorrow. We've got a busy day before us.'

'Vot ve do first? Go svimmink?' asked Hugo, eyes round with excitement.

'What, in all that water? Not likely. No, tomorrow morning first thing, we're going to hit the pier. That's where all the action is. It says so in the brochure. Now, go to sleep.'

'OK,' said Hugo, curling up with a little sigh. 'But

280

your smell has a lot to answer for.'

'I'm a Witch of Dirty Habits. We must all suffer for what we believe in. Oh my badness! Whatever is that noise?'

From far away, further along the coast, borne on the night breeze, came a hideous sound. It was a combination of nails scraping on blackboards, burglar alarms and dustbin lids blowing down the road. Yes. It was the unmistakable sound of Goblin music.

Gobboworld had opened.

GOBLIN NEWSFLASH 1

We interrupt this story to bring you news of the Goblins. For the past twenty-four hours, they have walked a long, hard trail beset with difficulty and danger. Sproggit has a thorn in his toe, Stinkwart has a piece of grit in his eye and both Slopbucket and Hog have horrible blisters. Eyesore has come out quite badly in a fight with a baby rabbit and has a scratch on his arm. Lardo has lost his hat. Plugugly's knees have swollen up like balloons.

Sadly, the long, hard trail has turned out to be in a circle, and right now they are back where they started, sleeping in an exhausted heap, worn out by blaming each other as much as anything.

That is the end of the Newsflash.

CHAPTER TEN
The Beach

'Come to the pier with me, Sharky? Please?' begged Pongwiffy for the thousandth time. She was sitting fully clothed, drumming her feet restlessly on a small rock. Nearby, Hugo waded about in a miniature rock pool, thrashing about with a lollipop stick, hoping for piranhas.

'No,' said Sharkadder, who was sunbathing. She lay on a large purple towel, surrounded by dozens of little bottles containing home-brewed sun preparations. She wore a startling yellow and black striped woolly bathing suit and a large cucumber lay

283

across her forehead (she had read somewhere that cucumber was cooling to the eyes). She looked like a greasy hornet with a touch of vegetable and a lot of stick insect in its ancestry.

'But what about the Hall of Mirrors? You said you wanted to go there,' protested Pongwiffy.

'I'm saving that for later, when I've acquired a glorious tan. Anyway, I'm all comfy. I'd be even comfier if those two hadn't pinched the only available sunbeds.'

She removed her cucumber and glared a short way along the beach to where two Mummies were busily rubbing embalming lotion into their bandages. Their names were Xotindis and Xstufitu. They had been Pharaohs once, in pre-bandaged times, and considered it their divine right to commandeer the sunbeds.

The beach was filling up. A family of Trolls in Hawaiian shirts had collected up a pile of rocks and were marking out their territory. Down by the water's edge, a group of screeching Banshees were chasing each other with a rubber shark. Nearby, a gang of Zombies were shuffling around with a beach ball and over by the breakwater a gang of grinning Skeletons were posing for photos.

'You're going all pink,' Pongwiffy warned her. 'You'll burn.'

'Nonsense. My skin has nothing to fear from the sun's rays. I'm using my own personal range of suncreams,' Sharkadder explained. 'You can borrow some if you like,' she added generously.

'No thanks,' said Pongwiffy hastily. 'My dirt protects me from the sun. Oh, DO come to the pier with me.'

'I said no. Besides, Dudley won't know where I am when he comes back from his inspection of the boat yard. He was a seafaring cat in his youth, bless him. I think he feels the call of the salt, or something. He was singing shanties in his sleep last night. I had a terrible night, what with him and that awful Goblin music. And I'm sharing a room with Sludgegooey. She snores and eats treacle sandwiches in bed.'

There was a short silence.

'What was the breakfast like, by the way? At Ocean View?' Pongwiffy asked casually. She didn't really want to seem interested. She still hadn't quite forgiven Sharkadder for deserting her in her hour of need.

'Awful. Boiled eggs and weak tea. We all hoped

Sourmuddle would say something, but she didn't. Some of us think she's taking this politeness business too far,' said Sharkadder darkly.

'You should have come out to my tent,' said Pongwiffy smugly. 'Hugo and I cooked ourselves a lovely little fishy each over an open fire. Delicious it was.'

Indeed, they had very much enjoyed their breakfast. Particularly Pongwiffy, who hadn't done any of the work.

'I wish I had,' confessed Sharkadder enviously. 'But I wasn't sure I'd be welcome after the tent business. It was a hard decision, believe me, but I keep telling you, there wasn't enough room. Not for all four of us and my make-up.'

There was another short silence.

'I expect you'd like a big ice cream, then,' Pongwiffy said at last. 'If you haven't had any breakfast. I bet there's ice cream on the pier.'

'I don't want ice cream. I'm sunbathing. Go on your own if you want.'

'All right then, I will,' said Pongwiffy crossly. 'Come on, Hugo, hop in my bucket. We're off to find the action!'

And off they set, taking care to kick a lot of

pebbles in the laps of Xotindis and Xstufitu.

Far away in the distance, the twin Witches Agglebag and Bagaggle, armed with jam jars and fishing nets, were climbing over the slippery rocks and peering into rock pools, looking either for some new pets or, possibly, lunch.

'Yoo-hoo, Pongwiffy!' they cried. 'Come and help us fish!'

'No thanks,' shouted Pongwiffy. 'We're off to the pier!'

Down by the water's edge, Sludgegooey and Bendyshanks had removed their boots and stockings and were having a jolly water fight with buckets.

'Hey there, Pongwiffy!' cried Sludgegooey and Bendyshanks in unison. 'Come and have a paddle with us.'

'Not likely,' called Pongwiffy with a shudder. 'I'm not much of a water Witch really.'

And on she went.

A bit further along, a surly-looking Tree Demon had just finished setting up a rickety Punch and Judy show. Scrofula, Macabre and Ratsnappy had joined an expectant crowd and were seated in the front row.

'Hey! Pongwiffy! Come and join us – the show's just starting!' shouted Scrofula excitedly.

'Well – only for a minute,' said Pongwiffy, who was a sucker for puppet shows.

The tiny curtains jerked open and Mr Punch bobbed up. He was a particularly battered, creased Mr Punch, who looked as though he had been used at some point to clean somebody's bicycle.

'Hello, boys and girls,' he squeaked. 'I'm Mr Punch, I am. Will you be my friend?'

'Not likely,' shouted Ratsnappy rudely. 'Catch me being friends with a moth-eaten old glove puppet!'

'And this is my wife, Judy,' squeaked Mr Punch, ignoring the interruption. 'Say hello to the boys and girls, Judy.'

Up bobbed Judy with a tiny bundle of rags in her stiff arms.

'Hello, everybody!' she squealed. 'I'm Judy and this is my baby. Mr Punch is going to look after it for me while I go fishing. Will you help look after the baby, boys and girls?'

'We certainly will!' cried Ratsnappy, Scrofula and Macabre, sitting up and looking important. It wasn't often they got asked to look after people's children.

Judy tossed the ragged bundle to Punch, who

288

dropped it. Immediately a high-pitched squalling rent the air.

'Naughty baby,' scolded Punch, picking up the bundle and giving it a rough shake. 'I'm going to have to smack you, I am!'

'Did ye see that? He dropped it!' howled Macabre, unable to believe her eyes. 'You leave that wee babby alone, you tyrant you!'

'Smack, smack, smack,' carried on Punch blithely, bashing the small bundle on the edge of the stage. 'That's what I do to naughty babies. Smack, smack, smack. And now I'm going to throw you in the dustbin, that's what I'm going to do. I'm going to thr—'

But he didn't get any further. The outraged babysitters leapt to their feet and charged the booth. It collapsed on top of the Tree Demon, who gave a small, surprised yelp. Still wearing his puppets, he crawled out from beneath the wreckage. The watching audience cheered and clapped as Ratsnappy and Scrofula sat on him. Macabre seized Mr Punch, ripped his nose off and held it up in triumph. This was better than a puppet show.

'Come on, Pong!' shouted Scrofula cheerfully. 'Pass over that seaweed and help us slime him!'

'Not just now, thanks. Hugo and I are off to check out the pier,' Pongwiffy told her. Sliming the Tree Demon would indeed be fun, but right now the delights of the pier called and her Magic coin – the one that always came back to her – the one she didn't hand in to Mrs Molotoff – was burning a hole in her pocket.

CHAPTER ELEVEN
The Pier

To get to the pier, Pongwiffy and Hugo had to walk along the promenade, which was lined with posh hotels and the better class of guest house. Every so often, benches were placed beneath shady trees for the convenience of visitors who preferred to view the pebbly beach from a safe distance. One such bench contained Witch Greymatter, seated next to a huge pile of dictionaries. Both she and Speks were frowning over an old copy of *The Daily Miracle*. They had been stuck for days on One Across, *Words spoken by backward giant (3,2,2,3)*. They

291

didn't even look up as Pongwiffy and Hugo went by.

At the entrance to the pier, they came across Sourmuddle and Snoop, who were busily buying up the best part of the Souvenir stand. Both sported Kiss Me Quick hats and were dripping with keyrings, plastic sharks' teeth necklaces and small rubber octopuses on elastic.

'Hello there, Pongwiffy!' called Sourmuddle, waving excitedly. 'Come and see what we've bought! This is the life, eh? I'm jolly glad I came up with the idea of a holiday. Are you walking along the pier? We'll join you. You can buy me a hot dog. It's the only thing I haven't tried yet.'

'I shall be delighted, Sourmuddle,' said Pongwiffy. And they linked arms and, with Snoop and Hugo in tow, set out along the decking.

The pier, just as Pongwiffy thought, was indeed where the action was. Merry crowds of holidaymakers thronged its length, busily scoffing candyfloss and ice cream and toffee apples and sampling the various attractions.

There was the Haunted House, which Sourmuddle insisted on visiting. That proved a disappointment, mainly because all the Ghosts fled

292

the minute they walked in. Witches are Witches, even on holiday, and Ghosts know when they're beaten.

'I've seen scarier things under my sofa,' observed Pongwiffy, and everyone agreed.

Mystic GNoreen, Fortune Teller, was the next attraction. She turned out to be a lipsticky Gnome in big earrings whom Pongwiffy thought she recognised.

'I know you,' said Pongwiffy accusingly. 'You're the same one that turned my shed into a Fortune-Telling Booth that time at Hallowe'en, when the riff-raff came and raided my Dump!'

'No I'm not,' lied Mystic GNoreen, who was. 'That was my identical twin, Mystic GNorma. I'm Mystic GNoreen. Either cross my palm with silver or get out of my tent, Pongwiffy.'

'Shall I do it?' said Pongwiffy to Sourmuddle, flexing her fingers dangerously. 'I've got a nasty spell just dying to get out. Just say the word, Sourmuddle, and I'll zap her!'

'Certainly not. No Magic while we're on holiday, remember?' scolded Sourmuddle. Fuming, Pongwiffy had to follow her out. However, in doing so, she managed accidentally-on-purpose to trip over one of the guy ropes, bringing the booth crashing down on top of the unfortunate GNoreen, who said quite a few unmystic things. So that was all right.

On they went to the Rifle Range, where Sourmuddle won seventeen goldfish, a china wildebeest, a cuddly squid and a scale model of a Transylvanian castle.

'And I didn't even have to fire it!' she boasted, beaming at the white-faced stallholder. 'All I did was wave the rifle in his face and he gave me all these prizes!'

Next came the Hall of Mirrors.

'Funny,' said Pongwiffy, standing before one that made her look like a sack suspended on scaffolding poles. 'I don't remember looking like this. When did my legs go like this, Hugo?'

But Hugo wasn't listening. He had found a mirror to his liking. It made him look every bit as big and fierce as he felt himself to be on the inside.

'Look, mistress!' he squealed, sticking his chest out, sucking in his stomach and flexing his pea-sized biceps. 'Zis is 'ow an 'Amster look to a snail! Scary, huh?'

'Hmm,' said Pongwiffy, still worried about her

294

legs. 'Actually, I've had enough of mirrors. Come on, Sourmuddle. Let's get that hot dog.'

But Sourmuddle and Snoop were speechless with laughter, falling about and pointing at each other's reflections. Sourmuddle was all chin and knees and Snoop's horns were five times bigger than his body.

'Come on, Hugo,' said Pongwiffy restlessly. 'Let's see what else there is.'

But Hugo was busy posing. They were all having a wonderful time, so Pongwiffy left them to it and wandered back out into the sunshine.

Outside the Pier Pavilion, a crowd had gathered around the billboard advertising the Summer Spektacular.

'Who's starring?' Pongwiffy asked a large Zombie, who was shuffling away after having stared at the poster for a good half-hour.

'How should I know?' said the Zombie rudely. 'Think I can read or something? Go and see for yerself.'

There was nothing else for it. Pongwiffy took a deep breath, stuck out her bony elbows and began to force her way to the front of the crowd. Summer Spektacular, eh? This sounded interesting.

CHAPTER TWELVE
The Convention

'Disgusting, I call it,' remarked Frank the Foreteller, his telescope trained on the beach below. 'Shouldn't be allowed. Ought to be a law against it. There ought to be signs. NO WITCHES ON THE BEACH. The place is crawling with them. You should see what they're doing to the Punch and Judy Demon!'

'Let's have a look,' said Fred the Flameraiser, holding out his hand.

The Wizards were stretched out on sunbeds on the balcony of the Magician's Retreat – a lurid pink, turreted, teetering-on-the-edge-of-the-cliff

297

edifice of the type that Wizards go for. They had taken over the entire top-floor suite, where they proceeded to make themselves as comfortable as they would have been in the Clubhouse back home. In fact, they could almost have *been* in the Clubhouse back home. The only difference was that here they tended to lie on sunbeds on the balcony rather than just sit in overstuffed armchairs indoors.

The Wizards loved the balcony. It was just up their street. Not only did they have a bird's-eye view of the disgraceful goings-on on the beach below, but it also provided the perfect place to snatch forty winks. Dozing on the balcony came after a disgracefully late, gargantuan breakfast served on silver platters in the grand dining room on the ground floor.

Also on the ground floor was the Conference Room, where the Convention was taking place – but the Wizards studiously ignored that. After the huge breakfast, they would wipe their beards, collect their daily papers and troop back to the lift, stonily ignoring the queue of keen, brainy-looking Convention-goers from elsewhere, who took everything seriously. Not so the Wizards. Let others read out learned papers and discuss the relative properties of invisibility and the ins and outs of a pentagram. Their balcony called, and to the balcony they must go.

All except Ronald. Ronald was bitterly disappointed. He had spent long days and nights working on a paper entitled 'Are Pointy Hats a Good Thing?' He had hoped to read it out. In fact, he had been as good as *promised* he would be able to read it out – but so far, to his great dismay, none of the Wizards had shown any desire to even stick their noses inside the Conference Room, let alone listen to Ronald read his paper.

All they did was lie about on the balcony all day, snoozing and looking through telescopes and demanding room service and complaining about their fellow guests (whom they considered themselves a cut above) and the shocking behaviour of the merry holidaymakers on the beach. And then shuffle off to bed at nightfall, when all the fun was beginning. Or, at least, Ronald imagined that there would be some fun beginning somewhere, outside the constraints of the stultifyingly boring Magician's Retreat. At night, when the lights began to twinkle, the faraway pier looked quite festive.

'What's the matter, young Ronald? Haven't you

299

got a sunbed?' asked Frank the Foreteller slyly.

'No,' said Ronald sulkily. 'They keep forgetting to bring another one up.'

That was another thing. He didn't have a sunbed. It was just like in the Clubhouse back home, where nobody had bothered to provide him with a chair.

Or a locker.

'Shouldn't we go down to the Conference Room?' he asked desperately. 'I was rather hoping I might read my paper this morning . . .'

'All in good time, young Ronald, all in good time,' smirked Frank the Foreteller. 'Ah me, the keenness of youth, eh? Ah well, he'll learn, he'll learn.'

'But I thought we were supposed to be here to work. I thought that was the idea of a Convention. That's what you said. You said we would mingle with learned people and have intelligent discussions.'

'Did we?' said Fred the Flameraiser. 'I don't remember saying that. I thought we were here for the food.'

'What about a stroll, then?' persisted Ronald. 'We could at least have a dignified saunter along the pier, couldn't we? Get a bit of exercise?'

'What, with all those Witches crawling around?

300

Talk sense, boy,' scoffed Frank the Foreteller. 'I'll have that telescope back now, Fred.'

'I rather think I'll ring for room service, you know,' said Dave the Druid lazily. 'I fancy another platter of those sausages before lunch. Apart from that, I don't feel up to doing another thing today. Did you hear that awful Goblin music coming from over the headland last night? Quite ruined my night's sleep.'

With a sigh, Ronald turned and leaned on the balcony railing. The sea looked particularly tempting this morning. Far out on the horizon, a tiny, wild figure with bats flapping around her head went zooming along on the end of a long rope attached to a small red boat which was going much too fast for its own good. (Gaga had discovered the joys of water sports.)

Jolly, distant cries rang up from the beach below where a couple of Witches were paddling at the water's edge. Paddling! Something he'd never done. Sun glinted on the frothy little waves caressing the pebbles. Further along the beach there was some sort of interesting incident going on involving, as far as he could make out, several Witches, some seaweed and a Punch and Judy Demon. And here he was, muffled up in itchy, uncomfortably hot robes, stuck on a stifling balcony without so much as a sunbed.

'Could I borrow your telescope for a moment?' Ronald asked Frank the Foreteller.

'No,' said Frank the Foreteller.

It was all too much.

GOBLIN NEWSFLASH 2

We interrupt this story again to bring you the latest Goblin news. Against all odds, the Gaggle have at last reached the lower reaches of the Misty Mountains and have begun to toil up the first slope. So far, they have managed to fall down three ravines. A short while ago, Sproggit slipped between the slats of a rope bridge and fell into the raging torrent below, where he survived by hanging on to the tail of a beaver. Plugugly has stubbed his toe badly on a BEWARE OF AVALANCHES sign. There is a storm threatening, and they have run out of nettle sandwiches. There is now some doubt whether they will ever reach their goal.

That is the end of the Newsflash.

CHAPTER THIRTEEN
A Chance Meeting

Scott Sinister (or Spot Snitser as he was now known) had spent a rotten night in the stifling cupboard the theatre management called a dressing room. Groaning, he unfolded creaking limbs and hauled himself up from the musty pile of old stage curtains which served for a bed.

Blearily, he examined his haggard features in a small, cracked mirror hanging on the wall. He looked terrible. This was no life for a superstar. He felt quite faint. Food, that was what he needed. Glumly he reached into his cloak and carefully counted the few small coins that were all that remained of his vast fortune. Just enough for one more hot dog. After that, there would be no more food until his first pay cheque at the end of the week. If he survived that long.

Not like Lulu, who was rolling in money. Lulu, who right now was most probably tucking into a hugely overpriced breakfast in her suite at the Ritz.

It wasn't fair! It simply wasn't fair! He had more talent in his little toenail than she had in her whole body. If only he had the chance to prove himself, just once more. He'd show them! He could pull himself back up again, he knew he could. If only . . .

But this wasn't getting him anywhere. First things first. If he was going to make it to opening night, he had to keep his strength up.

With a sigh, he opened his battered case and took out a large red false beard. This morning, he was in no fit state to face his public. Better to go unrecognised than to have to run the gauntlet of the sneers and put-downs he had recently had to endure. He pulled the beard elastic over his head and tugged the hood of his cape well down over his head. There. What a master of disguise he was. His best friend wouldn't recognise him now. Not that he had any

305

friends these days.

He cautiously opened the door, peered to left and right, scurried down the dark corridor that led to the stage door – and stepped out, blinking, into bright sunshine.

The pier was crowded. It must be later than he thought. A party of Skeletons in shorts nudged each other and pointed with sticks of bright pink candyfloss as he emerged from the stage door.

'Look at that scruffy old tramp. Whatever is Sludgehaven coming to?' he heard one of them say sniffily as he scurried past.

Out of the corner of his eye, he noticed by the main entrance to the theatre a tall, pointy hat sticking out from the crowd who had gathered around the poster on which his misspelt name appeared in such disgracefully small letters. Scott kept his head well down and hurried by. Tall pointy hats meant Witches. He didn't like Witches. Witches meant trouble. It had been a Witch who had caused all the trouble between him and Lulu that time. What was her name again? Wiffsmelly? Fugstinky?

He headed straight for the hot-dog stand.

'A hot dog with honions, please,' said Scott, in a high, nasal, disguised voice. He felt quite pleased with himself. This was where the actor in him came out.

'Right away, *meester* Seenister,' said Spag with a leer. 'By the way, I like-a the beard.'

'Just hurry it up, will you?' growled Scott. A queue was forming behind. It made him feel uncomfortable. He couldn't cope with crowds these days. He just wanted to get his breakfast and scuttle off back to the sanctuary of his broom cupboard.

He turned to face the sea with a huge sigh – and at that moment a mischievous little sea breeze swooped down and snatched at his false beard. The sudden air pressure proved too much for the flimsy elastic, and the beard flipped off his face and blew away. It rolled a short way along the decking, then stopped. In a panic, Scott ran after it.

'Oi!' came Spag's voice behind him. 'You wanna hot dog, you give-a me the dough, huh?'

'Be right with you!' called Scott, making a grab for the beard. He almost had it but it took off again, this time rolling towards the railing! Another gust, and it would be over the edge and into the sea below. Scott gave a little sob and threw himself full-length on the decking in a final, desperate attempt at recovery, knowing as he did so that he

307

would be too late . . .

But fate intervened. The escaped beard was brought up short by a pair of disreputable boots. Suddenly, he became aware of a certain smell. A smell he recognised.

'Well, badness me!' said a familiar voice. 'A runaway beard. Whatever next?'

Slowly, Scott looked up and found himself staring into the face of . . .

'P-Pongwiffy?' he said weakly.

'The very same,' twittered Pongwiffy, coming over all fluttery. 'Scott, dearest, we meet again! What a lovely surprise!'

'PONGWIFFY! AAAAAAH!' screamed Scott. And bolted.

CHAPTER FOURTEEN
Talk about Red

'Sharky! Wake up! You'll never believe who I've just seen on the pier! Scott! Scott Sinister!'

'Mmm? Wha—?'

With a struggle, Sharkadder awoke from a terrible dream in which she was lying on a bed of coals being blasted by hairdryer-wielding Goblins in a cave that was heated by a thousand furnaces.

'I said you'll never believe who ... oh my badness, Sharky! Look at your nose. Talk about red. Good thing I came back when I did.'

'Really?' mumbled Sharkadder. 'Must have dozed

309

off there for a minute or two. Is it really that bad?'

She sat up groggily and crossed her eyes in an effort to inspect the offending appendage – which had, indeed, caught the sun. That's the trouble with long sharp noses like Sharkadder's. They catch things. The sun. Colds. Even flies sometimes.

'It's sort of pulsing,' Pongwiffy told her. 'Redly pulsing. That's the best way I can describe it. I'd say that if Rudolph ever retires, you're in with a fighting chance, wouldn't you, Hugo?'

Sharkadder scrabbled frantically for her mirror.

'I wouldn't look. You won't like it,' Pongwiffy warned her.

Sharkadder found her mirror and anxiously inspected her reflection. She gave a horrified little wail.

'She doesn't like it,' Pongwiffy told Hugo.

'Does it 'urt?' Hugo wanted to know.

Gently, ever so gently, Sharkadder touched the very tip of her nose with a finger. With a howl of agony, she leapt to her feet and fled to the nearest rock pool.

'It hurts,' chorused Pongwiffy and Hugo.

They stood and watched as Sharkadder lowered her unfortunate appendage into the water. There was a hiss and a cloud of steam. Small crabs and fish fled in panic as the water began to bubble.

'Ahhh. Thad's bedder,' said Sharkadder, speaking with difficulty because her nose was in the water. 'Whad was id you were sayig, Pogwiffy? Aboud Scod Sidister?'

'He's here! In Sludgehaven! I saw him on the pier! But, oh Sharky, it wasn't *my* Scott. He's but a shadow of his former self. You'd weep to see how he's come down in the world. I knew him right away, of course, being his biggest fan. Even before his beard blew away.'

'Beard? Whad beard? Whad are you talking aboud?' bubbled Sharkadder.

'He was in disguise, Sharky! He can't bear to face his public. He's too ashamed. That's why he ran away from me, of course.'

'Whad d'you mead, id disguise? Whad's Scod Sidister doig id Sludgehaved id disguise?'

'He's in the Summer Spektacular. I saw the poster. Bottom of the bill, with his precious name spelt wrong. And guess who's starring?'

'Who?' asked Sharkadder, coming up for air.

'That stuck-up starlet Lulu Lamarre, that's who! The one who was hanging around Scott the time he came to judge our Talent Contest, remember? I got rid of her pretty quick. I said to Scott, "You don't want to go hanging around with her sort," I said. "You can do better for yourself than that."'

'Meaning you, I suppose. I think I'll go back to the guest house now, Pongwiffy. I'm not feeling too well,' said poor Sharkadder, soaking her towel in the rock pool and draping it over her nose.

'I'll come with you,' said Pongwiffy, putting her arm around her. 'I'll buy you an ice cream cone on the way. You can stick your nose in it.'

On the promenade, a crowd had formed at the foot of the steps leading up to the Ritz. Word had got round that Luscious Lulu Lamarre, dazzling star of stage and screen, was about to emerge for her first photocall of the day, and all her admirers had turned out in force, armed with cameras and autograph books. Several of the Skeletons were wearing WE LUV LULU T-shirts and a large Troll was sheepishly clutching a bunch of pansies.

'Look,' said Pongwiffy, grabbing Sharkadder's arm and pointing. 'What's happening over there? Somebody important must be staying at the Ritz.

Let's go and see who it is.'

'I don't want to. I don't care. My nose hurts. I feel dizzy. I want to lie down in a darkened igloo,' moaned Sharkadder.

Just at that moment, a cheer went up from the assembled crowd, and flashlights exploded as Lulu Lamarre stepped out from the doors and greeted her public with a toss of her curls and a cry of 'Dahlings!'

Hot on her heels came a short, portly Genie wearing a rather odd ensemble of too-small suit, red turban and traditional curly-toed Genie-type slippers. On his left lapel he sported a large badge. It said ALI PALI – BUSINESS MANAGER TO THE STARS.

'Luscious Lulu Lamarre, ladies and gentlemen!' he cried, waving his arm at Lulu, who was fluttering her eyelashes and blowing kisses to her cheering fans. 'Opening tomorrow night in the Summer Spektacular! Get your tickets today!'

'I don't believe it!' gasped Pongwiffy. 'It's her! It's that Lulu! Look at her showing off – it's disgraceful! And if that sneaky Ali Pali hasn't gone and made himself her manager! Isn't it possible to go *anywhere* these days without that Genie turning up?'

(It should be mentioned here that Pongwiffy has had dealings with Ali Pali before. Unpleasant dealings, involving treachery and double-crossing and loss of face. Suffice it to say that, where Ali Pali is concerned, Pongwiffy is not keen.)

'Let's go,' begged Sharkadder miserably. 'Take me home, Pong, please. I've got sunstroke.'

'All right. I can't take any more of this anyway. That ought to be Scott up there. He's the real star. It shouldn't be allowed. Somebody ought to do something about it. And I know just the right person.'

'Do you? Who?' asked Sharkadder.

'Somebody who cares about him. Somebody who still believes in his great talent. Somebody with enough brains to come up with a brilliant plan to save his career and put his name back up in lights, where it belongs.'

'Who?'

'Me,' said Pongwiffy.

'I was horribly afraid you were going to say that,' sighed Sharkadder.

CHAPTER FIFTEEN
Breakfasts

Breakfast in Ocean View was a subdued affair. Everyone sat in uncomfortable silence, chipping away at rock-hard boiled eggs under the stony gaze of Mrs Molotoff, who stalked up and down like a prison wardress, pouring cups of weak tea from a large brown teapot.

The only time anyone spoke was when she left the room to shout at Cyril in the kitchen. That was the signal for a bitter chorus of complaints.

'Is this all we get?' hissed Scrofula. 'We should complain, Sourmuddle. We really should.'

'Nonsense,' said Sourmuddle, sipping her tea and smacking her lips with appreciation. 'Lovely cup of tea, that. Eat your egg, Scrofula, and stop your moaning.'

'I think I've broken a tooth,' complained Sludgegooey. 'It was my last one too,' she added sadly.

'Barry doesn't like eggs,' insisted Scrofula. 'It's a very offensive breakfast to birds. Isn't it, Barry?'

'Ah wanted porridge,' grumbled Macabre. 'Ah *need* porridge. She said it wasnae on the menu. Noo on the menu! *Porridge!*'

'Neither's molten lava,' moaned Snoop. Sourmuddle gave him a sharp glance. 'Sorry, Mistress,' he mumbled, 'but you know what I'm like if I don't get my cup of lava in the mornings.'

'Tell me about it,' moaned Filth the Fiend, another great lava-drinker. 'Lava gives me rhythm, man.'

'Well, I don't know about anybody else, but I'm starving!' announced Ratsnappy crossly. 'In fact, I'm going to ask for toast. I'm going to say, "Please, Marm, I want some toast." Like that Gulliver Twine.'

'Oliver Twist,' corrected Greymatter, who

was well read.

'You wouldn't dare, Ratsnappy!' gasped Bendyshanks, eyes round with excitement. 'You rebel, you.'

'Yes, I would,' argued Ratsnappy. 'Can I, Sourmuddle? Can I ask for some more?'

'Certainly not,' said Sourmuddle briskly. 'The menu says egg *or* toast. Not both. It's not Done to ask for toast.'

There was a united sigh. Once Sourmuddle got a bee in her bonnet there was no budging her.

'I wish I was having breakfast with Pongwiffy out in her tent,' mourned Sludgegooey. 'Sharkadder is. They're having sausages. I smelt them. Now, that's what you call a breakfast.'

'And what *do* you call a breakfast, pray?' enquired a steely voice, making everyone jump. Mrs Molotoff stood in the doorway.

'A nice, exceedingly hard-boiled egg,' said Sourmuddle firmly. 'Absolutely delicious, and so filling. Isn't it, everyone?'

Glumly, everyone agreed it was delicious.

Out in the tent, Sharkadder paused with a

sausage halfway to her lips. Her poor nose was a sorry sight after the excesses of the day before. Even a night spent submerged in a bowl of ice cubes had done little to dim its ruddy glow. Luckily, you don't eat with your nose, and Sharkadder still had her appetite.

'You're joking!' she gasped.

'No, I'm not,' said Pongwiffy. 'I told you I'd think of a brilliant plan. We were up all night talking about it and making preparations, weren't we, Hugo?'

'Ve vere,' agreed Hugo with a yawn, adding, 'Vell, you did all ze talkink. I did all ze vork. See my eyes? Zey gone all peenk.'

'They're always pink,' growled Dudley, looking up from a corner where he was worrying a sausage. 'Nasty little pink eyes. All 'Amsters 'ave got 'em.'

'Oh ya?' bristled Hugo. 'Since ven does a vun-eyed fleabag become optical expert, huh?'

'Pet,' retaliated Dudley with venom.

'Who you callink pet?'

'You. Pet, pet, pet.'

'Hear zat, Mistress? 'E call me pet!'

'Be quiet, you two,' ordered Pongwiffy. 'This is no time for petty squabbles. Sharky and I are

318

discussing my brilliant plan.'

'You'll never get away with it,' scoffed Sharkadder.

'We, you mean,' said Pongwiffy.

'Oh no,' said Sharkadder. 'Not me. You're not involving me. Not this time.'

'Oh, but Sharky, you've got to help! We're doing this for Scott, remember. I'll buy you a lifetime's supply of make-up! There, I can't say fairer than that.'

'No,' said Sharkadder.

'I'll clean your boots for the rest of the year.'

'No,' said Sharkadder.

'I'll let you have the window seat on the way home.'

'No,' said Sharkadder.

'I'll have that sausage back, then,' said Pongwiffy slyly, holding her hand out.

'Oh – all right,' said Sharkadder sullenly. 'I suppose I'll help. If I must.'

Everyone has their price.

In the Magician's Retreat, the Wizards were also getting stuck into sausages. Great, heaped, greasy platters of them, served by creaking waiters. There

319

was healthy muesli as an alternative, but the Wizards ignored that. Well, Gerald the Just had tried a small bowlful once, just to give it a fair try – but everyone noticed he went back to sausages the next day.

'Anyone seen young Ronald this morning?' asked Frank the Foreteller, chewing away. Teasing Ronald was a popular breakfast sport. It went with the sausages. It got the day off to a good start.

'Can't say I have,' said Dave the Druid, sucking his fingers.

'Probably in his room working on his paper,' suggested Fred the Flameraiser, tapping his pipe out on his napkin, which immediately caught fire. Everyone gave a little chuckle. Ronald's paper was a constant source of amusement.

'Perhaps he's not feeling well,' said the voice of Alf the Invisible. A sausage floated off his plate, hovered a moment, then vanished into thin air. 'Perhaps one of us should go and look.'

'Mmm,' said everyone vaguely. But nobody did.

GOBLIN NEWSFLASH 3

We interrupt this story again to bring you the latest news on the Goblins. They too are currently eating breakfast. Hog, Eyesore and Stinkwart have lit a small fire and are heating up a lovely bowlful of nice, appetising moss. Slopbucket and Lardo are arguing over a small spray of berries, which both claim to have seen first. Sproggit has wrested a nut from a passing squirrel and is vainly attempting to crack it by jumping up and down on it while Hog holds it steady. Plugugly has found a toadstool and is nibbling at it delicately, trying to make it last.

But things could be worse. They have successfully weathered the storm and the avalanche. They have made it to the very top of the Misty Mountains. From now on, it's downhill all the way. On the horizon, they can see the clear blue sweep of the sea – and last night, Plugugly swore he could almost see the faraway lights of Gobboworld.

The dream is within their grasp.

That is the end of the Newsflash.

CHAPTER SIXTEEN
Ronald's Paddle

Ronald wasn't working on his paper. Neither was he in bed sick. Ronald, in fact, was about to fulfil a lifetime's ambition. He was standing at the water's edge on the deserted beach, about to have his first-ever paddle.

Things had really been getting on his nerves back at the hotel. The constant round of the three Bs (breakfast, balcony and bed) was more than he could take. His paper on pointy hats still languished in his bedside drawer, unread. He hadn't set foot in the Conference Room because nobody would go with him and he didn't like to go in on his own. As far as Ronald was concerned, the Convention he had been so looking forward to was a complete washout.

All this made him even more determined to paddle. All right, so it wasn't a Wizardly sort of activity – but if he was careful and sneaked out early and did it when nobody else was about, who was going to know? Anyway, he was past caring. He was going to defy everybody and dip his big, pink, flapping feet in the briny if it killed him. Even if it was flying in the face of tradition.

He had risen at sunrise, sneaked out the back way through the kitchens and hurried down the steep cliff path which led from the Magician's Retreat to the empty beach. Heart pitter-pattering with guilty excitement, he had hidden behind the breakwater and furtively removed his Hat of Knowledge, his Robe of Mystery and his Cloak of Darkness, hiding them carefully under a large stone. This, of course, was against the rules – for, as everyone knows, *A Wizard and His Gear are Never Parted*, on the grounds that once you lose the clobber you lose the dignity.

Some while later he had emerged self-consciously clad in a pair of large, bright yellow shorts which

323

he had secretly purchased from a souvenir shop the day before (under the pretext of popping out for a pencil sharpener). He had loved the look of them in the window, but now he had them on, he wasn't so sure. He had a niggling feeling they didn't do a lot for his knees. Draped around his neck was a towel emblazoned with the words HOTEL PROPERTY – DO NOT REMOVE. He felt horribly naked.

The sea was a long way out, and it had taken him ages to pick his way over the millions of excruciatingly sharp pebbles and acres of smelly, slippery seaweed that lay between him and the water's edge. There was a chilly wind too, which blew up his shorts most unpleasantly.

But at last, he made it. Arms clutched across his skinny chest, he balanced stork-like on one thin white leg and dipped an experimental toe in the water.

Brrr! It was freezing. Still, he had set out to paddle – and paddle he jolly well would. At least he'd have one happy memory to take home with him at the end of it all.

Shivering, he took a deep breath and waded out into the cold grey water.

Far behind him, on the beach, unobserved by

324

Ronald, two small Troll children overturned the large stone and made off with his clothes, just for a laugh.

And that was only the first bad thing that happened.

CHAPTER SEVENTEEN
Getting Rid of Lulu

Lulu Lamarre was seated before her dressing table mirror, trying to decide which wig to wear. She had risen late, after a luxurious breakfast in bed. That's one of the advantages of being a superstar and staying in the top hotels. You can have breakfast in bed any time you like. You can order what you like too and nobody will bat an eyelid. Lulu had chosen chips, tuna fish, chocolate cake and a cherry float with a side order of chutney. And very nice it had been too.

Now then. Which wig? After a bit of thought,

Lulu decided on the long, blonde curly one. She pulled it on, fluffed it up, batted her eyelashes and smiled complacently at her reflection.

Lulu had been doing a lot of complacent smiling recently. She had come a long way since the early days when she was a mere extra, hanging around the edges of show business. Her career was really beginning to take off. Lulu Lamarre was fast becoming a household name. Just one more well-paid film, that's all it would take, and she would be able to buy herself that rather nice holiday retreat on the other side of Witchway Wood. The one that used to be owned by Scott Sinister, her ex-boyfriend.

Ha! That'd show him.

There came a discreet tap at the bedroom door.

'Come in,' purred Lulu huskily, fluffing up her frilly robe and adopting a glamorous pose.

The door opened, and in came a creaking old waiter, bearing a grubby envelope on a silver tray.

'A letter for you, Miss Lamarre. Handed in at reception early this morning.'

'For me? Oh, how adorable!' cried Lulu, snatching it up. 'I wonder who can be writing to me? One of my many fans, I suppose. All right, servant, you can clear off now.'

Eagerly she tore it open, and read:

Dear Miss Lamarre,

It has come to my attenshun that you are starring in the Summer Spektacular at the Pavillion. i am a Millyonair film prodooser and rite now i am holydaying on my fabulus lukshoory ~~yachght yoght~~ yot in the next bay. i wood very much lik you to star in my neckst blokbuster. i will pay you a lot. you will be sucksessfull beyond yore wildest dreems. plees cum to the old jetty in the Bote Yard at ten o'clock sharp. you will be piked up by my trusty old boteman who will row you out to my ~~yaucht yahat~~ yot and we can diskus a skreen test over a glass of ~~champayn shampagn~~ shampain wine.

Yores sinseeerly

Sebastian B. Jetsetter (millyonair)

P.S. Cum alone. Don't tel anywun.

She should have been suspicious, of course. The spellings alone should have told her something, as should the crossings-out, fingermarks and general disgustingly grubby state of the thing. But being a superstar doesn't necessarily mean you have to be intelligent.

With a little squeal of excitement, Lulu leapt to

her feet and launched herself at her wardrobe.

'This isn't going to work, I tell you!' said Sharkadder nervously. She was standing on the jetty with Pongwiffy and Dudley, casting dark glances at the small rowing boat bobbing about at the foot of a flight of slippery steps.

Sharkadder was wearing a long black oilskin, matching sou'wester and a pair of thick-soled rubber boots, all of which had been hired by Pongwiffy at great personal expense. (Well, it would have been, if she hadn't used her Magic coin.) Dudley was crouched on the top of a nearby lobster pot, chewing on a fish head and growling every time anyone came near.

'Of course it'll work. You make a very convincing boatman. Your nose in particular has got a real weatherbeaten look about it.'

'Why can't *you* be the boatman?' cried Sharkadder, stamping her rubber-booted foot. 'I don't know anything about boats! Why does it have to be me?'

'Because she knows me and she doesn't know you, that's why. Look, it'll be fine. Just talk about

329

port and starboard and say Arrr and Avast and Belay and things like that. Spit in the wind. Get Dudley to sing one of his sea shanties. On second thoughts, I should only use that in an emergency.'

'Which is port?' asked Sharkadder, all flustered.

'I don't know. The sharp end. Who cares? She won't know the difference anyway. The most important thing is to get her into the boat and away from the harbour. Once we're into the open sea, we can all relax. Me and Hugo will come out from hiding under the tarpaulin and take over the oars.'

'Which are the oars?' enquired Sharkadder.

'They're the long stick-type things you put in the water,' explained Pongwiffy a touch impatiently. 'There's nothing to it. Just dip 'em in and splash 'em about a bit, and the boat'll move.'

'Yes, but which way?' said Sharkadder worriedly.

'Forward, hopefully.'

'As long as it's not down. Look, Pong, I really don't think this is a good idea.'

'Yes it is. It's brilliant. We simply row out to sea and maroon her on a rock for a few days. Just to keep her out of the way long enough for Scott to have his chance. He'll take over the show at a minute's notice and get rave reviews. It's bound to work. It always does in books.'

'We're not in a book,' said Sharkadder. 'This is real. That's real wet water down there and I'm not at all sure that boat's seaworthy.'

'Of course it's seaworthy. Trust you to pick holes in my plan.'

'It's holes in the boat I'm worried about.'

'Nonsense. It'll work like a dream. We'll go back and pick Lulu up later, when Scott's a star again and everyone's forgotten about her. You know how it is in the world of show business. Out of sight, out of mind. Here today, gone tomorrow. Easy come, easy g—'

'Mistress!' Hugo emerged from a dark alley where he had been posted as lookout and came running towards them across the cobbles, eyes bulging. 'It her! She comink!'

'Right, this is it. Come on, Hugo, down into the boat. It's all up to you now, Sharky. Don't let me down.'

The two of them hurried down the steps and climbed into the rocking boat. They lay down and pulled the tarpaulin over themselves just as Lulu emerged from the alley and stood looking about her hesitantly. She was wearing her most

331

glamorous gown, her most glittery jewellery and highly unsuitable high-heeled gold sandals. This was her big chance and she was obviously intent on making an impression.

Sharkadder cleared her throat nervously. 'Step this way, lady,' she called. 'All aboard for Mr Jetsetter's luxury yacht. Arrr.'

'Are you the boatman?' demanded Lulu imperiously, teetering unsteadily along the jetty.

'Avast and belay, I certainly am,' agreed Sharkadder. 'That's me. Just a salty old seadog who knows all about port and starboard and things. And this is my trusty ship's cat. Excuse me while I spit in the wind. Step right down into the boat, and sit down the blunt end, well away from the tarpaulin. There's a whole pile of dead fish under there and I don't want 'em disturbed. Arrr.'

Lulu gathered up her gown, gingerly picked her way down the slippery steps and clambered into the boat, which wobbled alarmingly.

'I see what you mean about the fish,' she said, wrinkling her nose and staring about her disdainfully. 'It's very smelly in this boat. And why isn't there a cushion? I must say I'm very surprised a millionaire like Mr Jetsetter can't afford something a bit better for his guests.'

'Nothing wrong with my boat,' protested Sharkadder with a heartiness she didn't feel. She climbed in and groped her way unsteadily to the helm. 'All right, Dudley, you can cast off now. No, there's nothing wrong with the good old *Saucy Sal.* Arrr.'

'*Saucy Sal?* I thought it said *Bouncing Billy* on the side,' said Lulu suspiciously.

'Oh, do it?' said Sharkadder, affecting vague surprise. 'I wonder who changed that, then. Hurry up, Dudley, leave that fish head and untie the rope. We have to catch the tide, remember?'

The rope tethering the boat slithered down with a thump, closely followed by Dudley. Sharkadder picked up an oar and pushed with all her might against the jetty. Rocking wildly, the boat shot out across the water, surprising everyone. Sharkadder wobbled and flailed her arms wildly, letting go of the oar, which fell over the side with a splash and floated away in the opposite direction. With a little shriek, Sharkadder fell over backwards into the bottom of the boat, where she lay with her legs kicking feebly in the air in a most unboatman-like manner. Lulu gave a sharp scream and clutched at the sides.

'What's happening?' she squealed as the boat got caught in an eddy and began to spin in circles.

'Don't panic!' cried Sharkadder, picking herself up and grabbing for the one remaining oar. 'Everything's under control. I'll just steady us up a bit. Arrr.'

'Let me off this minute!' demanded Lulu. 'I don't believe you're Mr Jetsetter's boatman at all. In fact, I don't believe there *is* a Mr Jetsetter! I think this is all a *trick*!'

And she attempted to stand up. At the same time, Sharkadder made a great, despairing dig at the water. The boat spun wildly. Sharkadder lost her balance for the second time, this time falling forward on to the heaped tarpaulin in the bottom of the boat. There was a muffled cry of pain and the tarpaulin gave a convulsive heave.

'Ahhhha!' screamed Lulu, pointing with a trembling finger. 'The fish! The fish! They're coming alive! They're . . .'

'Oh, stop your blithering!' said an irritable voice. 'Honestly, Sharky, can't you do *anything*? Give me that oar and get out of the way before you have us over.'

334

And to Lulu's horror, she found herself staring into the dreaded countenance of her old enemy.

CHAPTER EIGHTEEN
All at sea

'I thought you said you could row,' taunted Sharkadder as the current swirled the boat out to sea. ' "Nothing to it," you said. "I'll come out of hiding and take over the oars," you said. I distinctly heard you say it.'

'Help!' screeched Lulu in her ear. 'Help! Help me, someone!'

'Well, I can hardly row with only one oar, can I?' objected Pongwiffy. 'And we all know whose fault *that* is.'

'Help!' bawled Lulu. 'Call the coastguards! Boxing

Day! Boxing Day!'

'I think it's Mayday, actually,' Pongwiffy told her. 'And shut up,' she added as an afterthought.

'I said all along I didn't want to be boatman,' said Sharkadder crossly. 'Don't blame me. It's all your fault that we're lost at sea. This is the last time I go along with any of your half-baked ideas.'

'Half-baked idea? You're talking about an ingenious plan, worked out to the last detail. Or it was, until you mucked it up. Anyway, we're not lost at sea. We're merely temporarily caught in a fast-moving current.'

'Which is hurtling us to our doom,' said Sharkadder darkly.

'HELP! HELP! HEEEEELP!'

'Of course it's not,' scoffed Pongwiffy. 'Now see what you've done. You've set her off again with all your talk of doom.'

'I don't care, it's true. In fact, this whole holiday was doomed from the outset. That's because it was your idea.'

'Oh, don't be such an old grouch! Anyway, we're only just out of the harbour. You can see the beach from here. Besides, Hugo knows what to do, don't you, Hugo? He's been shipwrecked off Cape Horn, he told me. Haven't you, Hugo?'

But Hugo had gone pale green and didn't answer.

'Not much help there,' said Sharkadder cuttingly, adding, 'But then, what do you expect from a Hamster? It's lucky we have my Dudley. He can share his seafaring knowledge with us. What do we do next, Duddles, darling? Tell Mummy.'

But Dudley had his head over the side and was groaning.

'Well, that's just terrific,' said Pongwiffy, disgusted. 'Perhaps we are hurtling to our doom after all.'

'HEEEEEEELLLLLP! HELLLLPPPP!'

'I thought I told you to shut up,' she told Lulu.

'Why should I? You're just a couple of spiteful old Witches out to get me. You've always had it in for me. What have I ever done to you?'

'You've ruined Scott's career, that's what,' snapped Pongwiffy. 'You've taken his rightful place at The Top. But you reckoned without us. We're going to dump you on a deserted rock for a day or two. That'll teach you to steal his thunder.'

'You can't do that! What about my public? It's opening night and I'm the star!'

'Not any more you're not. Scott's going to Save

The Show and after that you'll be lucky if you get a walk-on part. So there.'

'I hate to be a spoilsport, Pong, but I don't actually see any deserted rocks,' pointed out Sharkadder. 'And even if I did, we'd probably swish right past. We seem to be rather at the mercy of the current, don't you know.'

'Well, that's just where you're wrong, because look what's ahead!' Pongwiffy pointed triumphantly. 'If that's not a rock, what is it? That tall, thin, greyish thing sticking up out of the water.'

'It's a person,' said Sharkadder, squinting. 'A person stranded on a sandbank, by the look of it. In fact, unless I'm very much mistaken, I do believe it's my nephew Ronald.'

'Oh botheration,' said Pongwiffy, who didn't like Sharkadder's nephew Ronald. 'That's all we need.'

'Ssh! I think he's shouting something. It sounds like . . .'

'HEEEEELLLLPPPP!' screeched Lulu, getting a second wind.

'That's it,' agreed Sharkadder. 'Cooeee! Ronald! What are you doing on that sandbank? And wearing those hideous yellow shorts? Have you no fashion sense?'

'I'm stranded!' came the faint cry. 'Help me, Aunt Sharkadder!'

'Shall we? What do you think?' Sharkadder asked Pongwiffy.

'No,' said Pongwiffy firmly. 'Anyone who wears shorts like that doesn't deserve to be rescued.'

'Mmm. You have a point. But perhaps I better had. After all, he is Family. All right, Ronald, we're coming. Be ready to grab the oar as we go past! Hold out the oar, Pongwiffy – we're going to rescue Ronald.'

'Why?' asked Pongwiffy, stubbornly clutching the oar to herself. 'He calls himself a Wizard, doesn't he? Why can't he rescue himself?'

'Oh, give it to me, I'll do it! Come on, before it's too late.'

She held out her hand. Reluctantly Pongwiffy surrendered the oar and Sharkadder stuck it out over the side of the boat at arm's length as the boat came level with Ronald. He reached out desperately clutching fingers and caught it. The boat slowed just long enough for Sharkadder to grab a handful of shorts and haul him in over the side. He toppled in and fell to the bottom, white, wheezing, whimpering and extremely wet.

'Ugh!' said Lulu, hastily drawing her feet away. 'He's all soggy. What have we got to have *him* for?'

'My sentiments entirely,' Pongwiffy agreed. 'That's the first sensible thing I've ever heard you say. You're just an old softie, Sharkadder. It's too crowded in this boat. Look how we're shipping water.'

'Sit up, Ronald,' Sharkadder instructed him severely. 'I have a few questions to ask you, and I want some straight answers. I asked you what you think you're doing, stranded on a sandbank in the middle of the ocean.'

Ronald rolled over, sat up and mumbled something.

'What? Speak up – I didn't quite hear.'

'I said I was paddling,' muttered Ronald, wringing out his shorts.

'Paddling? Not a very Wizardly occupation, is it? What are you doing in Sludgehaven anyway? And where are your lovely robes? And most important, who told you you could wear shorts with *those* knees?'

But Ronald wasn't listening. He had just noticed Lulu. His jaw went slack and a silly look came over his face.

'I say,' he said. 'I say, aren't you Luscious Lulu Lamarre, the superstar?'

'Well, yes,' admitted Lulu, patting her wig and preening a bit. 'I am, actually.'

'Gosh,' said Ronald, quite overcome. 'Gosh. I'm a big fan of yours. Can I have your autograph?'

'Well, yes of course, I . . .'

'No you can't,' broke in Pongwiffy crossly. 'Let's throw him overboard, Sharkadder. He's getting on my nerves.'

'He's my nephew, Pongwiffy. If there's any throwing overboard to be done, I'll decide. I asked you what you're doing in Sludgehaven, Ronald. Apart from drowning.'

'Having a Convention,' mumbled Ronald sheepishly, shivering and crossing his arms over his puny chest. 'We're all staying up at the Magician's Retreat. It's a very serious sort of thing. I – er – just slipped out for a quick paddle and the tide sort of came in when I wasn't looking. You – er – you won't tell the others, will you, Auntie?'

'*I* will,' promised Pongwiffy with relish. 'I'm going to tell everybody, the minute we land.'

'If we ever do land,' remarked Sharkadder, and Lulu burst into loud sobs.

Indeed, the possibility of landing was becoming ever more remote. The current was fairly zipping along, and the beach was now out of sight. They had rounded the headland, and the coastline was an unfamiliar vista of craggy, towering cliffs and sharp rocks, wet with crashing surf.

'Listen,' said Sharkadder, cupping her ear. 'I think I can hear something.'

She could. Across the waves came a ghastly drone, interspersed with various tinklings and crashings.

'Goblin music,' said Pongwiffy grimly. 'We must be getting near to Gobboworld. What a racket. I can't stand this. There's nothing else for it. We'll have to use Magic.'

'We're not allowed,' Sharkadder reminded her. 'No Magic in Sludgehaven, remember? Anyway, we haven't got our Wands.'

'Ah, but we're not exactly *in* Sludgehaven, are we? We're at sea. That's different,' argued Pongwiffy. 'And I don't need a Wand,' she added. 'I'll just do a tiny little landing spell, off the top of my head, and get the boat to take us to a suitable rock. Then we can drop off Lulu and get back in time to see Scott's moment of glorious triumph.'

'Oh no!' cried Sharkadder. 'You're not using one

343

of those wonky old spells of yours. Don't! You know they never wor—'

But she was too late. Pongwiffy had already started. She flexed her fingers and screwed her eyes tight shut, concentrating.

'Wind and waves, now hear my cry!
Take us to a rock nearby.
O'er the sea now let us float
In this little rowing-boat.'

'There. That should do it. What's happening?'

'We're sinking,' Sharkadder told her sadly. And indeed, they were.

CHAPTER NINETEEN
Gobboworld!

'Gobboworld! We made it!' gasped Lardo. And he burst into tears.

The Goblins stood in a swaying huddle, staring up in awe at the towering gates with their huge, neon-lit sign. In true Goblin fashion, neither of the Bs that spelt out the name were working, turning the name into Gooworld – but Goblins can't read, so it hardly mattered. From within came the sound of wildly pumping music, wailing sirens and thin, high-pitched screaming.

'Well,' said Plugugly. 'Dis is it, boys. End o' de

345

line. De answer to all our wassits. Dem pichers you get when you sleeps.'

'Dreams,' said Slopbucket, excelling himself.

'Mine 'ave always got alligators in,' remarked Eyesore vaguely.

'So what are we waiting for?' squawked Sproggit, jumping up and down, beside himself with excitement. 'Come on, come on, less go!'

Hearts hammering with anticipation, they once again picked up their sore feet and limped to the turnstile, which barred their entrance.

There was a small, dark ticket booth set to one side. Sticking out of it and effectively barring their way was a huge, muscular, hairy arm. The Arm bore a tattoo of a heart. Across the heart was the word MUDDER. It was the sort of arm you wouldn't want to argue with. The sort of arm only a mudder could love.

'Ticket, please,' said a gravelly voice from the depths within. And the sausage-like fingers flapped with sluggish impatience.

'Derrrr . . . eh?' said Plugugly, taken aback.

'I said ticket, please,' repeated the Arm's owner impatiently.

'Derrrrr . . . tick what? I don't get yer,' said

Plugugly, confused, looking around for something to tick.

'You got to have a ticket,' explained the Arm. 'To get in.'

'No one ever said nuffin' about no tickets,' complained Plugugly, finally seeing the light. 'Did dey?' he appealed to the Goblins behind.

Everyone agreed that nobody had said anything about tickets. There was an anxious silence.

'So are you lettin' us in, den, or what?' asked Plugugly after a bit.

'Got any money?' asked the Arm.

A hasty trawl of the Goblins' pockets and backpacks produced quite a pile of interesting things. Ancient sweet wrappers. Crisp socks. A short, heavily knotted piece of old bootlace. A fossilized apple core. A safety pin. The exhaust pipe off a motorbike. Part of an old mangle. Unpleasant handkerchiefs. Three rusty keys. A photograph of Sproggit's mum. Enough fluff to stuff a mattress. But money, sadly, was conspicuous by its absence.

'Can't we owe you?' asked Plugugly desperately.

'Nope,' said the Arm. 'You gotta have a ticket or gimme some dosh.'

The Goblins simply couldn't take it in. They

stared at the Arm blocking their way in slack-jawed disbelief. To suffer all that hardship, walk all those miles and then to be told to clear off? It was just too ghastly to contemplate.

It was Hog who finally broke the silence. He gave a shrill howl, threw himself full-length on the ground and began to pummel the grass with his fists. This was the cue for Slopbucket to stuff his knuckles in his eyes and start up a horrible wailing. Eyesore, Lardo and Stinkwart formed a circle and began to perform a dance which is known in Goblin circles as the Fed Up Stomp, and consists of stamping as hard as you can on someone else's foot while simultaneously pulling your hair, beating your breast and gnashing your teeth. (Ideally, it should be performed at full moon, but this was an emergency.)

Sproggit, with a shrill scream of frustration, ran at the tall fence which bordered Gobboworld and thumped it as hard as he could.

To his surprise, his arm went through.

"Ere!' hissed Sproggit. 'Over 'ere! Dis fence musta bin built by Goblins. Look, me arm's gone in! There's an 'ole!'

Sure enough, there was. A neat, fist-shaped one.

Eagerly, Sproggit applied his eye to it. And oh, what sights he saw inside! It was enough to make a Goblin weep.

He saw the Bobble Hat of Doom – a great swing in the shape of an upturned bobble hat, full to the brim with laughing thrill-seekers. Even as he watched, it turned in a full circle, sending its shrieking passengers plummeting head first into a large pool of warm, bubbling mud, which had been thoughtfully placed below.

He saw bungee-jumping with elastic that was just that bit too long. He saw a roller coaster with an interesting gap right at the top. He saw a helter-skelter which had been made even more exciting with the addition of a wall at the bottom. He saw . . .

'Less 'ave a decko, then,' complained Slopbucket, pulling at Sproggit's jumper. 'You've 'ad long enough, Sproggit. It's my turn now.'

'No it ain't, it's mine,' protested Hog. 'I was 'ere first.'

'No you wasn't! I was!' insisted Slopbucket, raising his voice.

'Oi!' boomed the voice of the Arm from the booth. 'You get away from that fence, you lot!

349

Think I can't see you? Go on, clear orf. Shan't tell you again.'

'I wuz only looking,' whined Sproggit piteously, tearing his eye away with great reluctance. 'It's a free country.'

'Not in Gobboworld, it ain't. See this arm?'

The fingers closed in a great, tight fist and the muscles wriggled ominously.

'Yeah?' said Plugugly, Hog, Lardo, Eyesore, Stinkwart, Slopbucket and Sproggit.

'Wanna see what it's attached to?'

The Goblins shook their heads. No. They didn't. They tore themselves away from the hole in the fence and stood in a subdued little cluster.

'Now what do we do?' Hog enquired brokenly.

'Go 'ome, I suppose,' said Lardo, kicking dully at a stone, which flipped up and hit Eyesore in the eye. Eyesore was so depressed he couldn't even be bothered to make a thing of it.

'I suppose we oughter look at de sea while we're here,' said Plugugly with a huge sigh.

'Why?' asked Slopbucket uninterestedly. 'What's so special about the sea? Nasty, big, grey, wet, sloppy thing, the sea. What we wanna look at that for?'

'I dunno,' said Plugugly with a shrug. 'Traditional,

innit? Come to de seaside, gotta look at de sea. Anyway, you got any better idears?'

Nobody had. So, muttering miserably, they trailed off towards the edge of the cliff.

And there they stood, hands in pockets, beside themselves with grief and disappointment, looking out over the heaving waves . . .

On which bobbed a little boat. Or, rather, on which *sank* a little boat. Even as the Goblins watched, it gave up the unequal struggle and vanished beneath the surface, depositing its six passengers into the water.

But not before the Goblins recognised them. Oh dear me. They knew those passengers all right.

'Boys,' said Plugugly, 'I reckon our luck's just turned.'

'Oh yeah? 'Ow's that, then, Plug?' asked Hog, watching the tragedy at sea with interest.

'Because,' said Plugugly slowly, 'because I got an idear.'

CHAPTER TWENTY
Captured!

A short while later, the Goblins once again stood at the ticket booth.

'You again,' said the Arm.

'Yep,' said Plugugly.

'Got yer tickets this time?' demanded the Arm with a sneer.

'Nope,' said Plugugly cheerfully. He had been through this little ritual before. He knew what to expect. He had all the right answers ready.

'Got any money?'

'Nope. We got summink better, ain't we, boys?'

'Yer!'

'Too right we 'ave!'

Excitedly, the Goblins agreed that they had indeed got something better. Something much, much better.

'Oh yeah? And what might that be?' the Arm asked with a sneer.

This was Plugugly's big moment.

'Step back, boys,' he commanded in ringing tones. 'Let 'im see de new Main Attraction!'

And the Goblins stood aside and the Arm got his first eyeful of the bedraggled, sorry-looking bunch that stood in an exhausted, dripping huddle behind them.

The captives glared back sullenly. It had been a long, hard swim to shore after the boat had capsized. Waves had buffeted them. Fish had nibbled them. Sharp rocks had grazed their knees. It was only due to the pockets of air trapped in Ronald's shorts (thus keeping them afloat) that they had made it at all.

Then, to add insult to injury, the minute they crawled thankfully on to dry land, they had fallen into enemy hands! To their great surprise and eternal shame, they had been pounced

353

on by none other than Plugugly and Co, and tied up with a long, improvised rope consisting of Slopbucket's scarf, Lardo's braces and a heavily knotted fragment of Hog's old boot-lace.

Pounced on! Tied up! By Goblins, of all things!

'It's embarrassing, that's what it is,' hissed Pongwiffy to Sharkadder through clenched teeth. She only normally took one bath a year, and her sudden enforced dip in the briny had put her in a very bad mood indeed.

Sharkadder, busily squeezing water from her ruined hair, said nothing. But she glowered a great deal.

Lulu, who had quite spoiled her dress as well as losing her wig and one of her gold shoes, was weeping noisily – a sort of horrible lead singer caterwauling to which Ronald's chattering teeth provided a kind of castanet rhythm section.

Poor Ronald. Of all of them, he had suffered the most. Being, as you might expect, an abysmally poor swimmer, he had swallowed a great deal of sea water and looked as though he was shortly about to be very poorly indeed.

Both Hugo and Dudley were past caring. Their

fur was plastered to their backs. Despite their tales of past daring exploits on the high seas, neither had proved to be a good swimmer. They were both so exhausted, they couldn't even lick themselves dry.

The sight of the sodden party obviously had an effect on the Arm. There came a startled gasp from the booth.

'Well, boil my bobble 'at! What you got there, then?'

'Told you,' said Plugugly with pride. 'Amazin' what de sea washes up. Two Witches, a Wizard in shorts, a Superstar an' a coupla cut-price Familiars. Not a bad catch, eh?'

It wasn't. For Goblins, who traditionally never caught anything, it was nothing short of miraculous.

''Old it right there,' said the Arm excitedly. 'I'll 'ave ter consult wiv my colleagues.'

And there came the sound of a door slamming, followed by the sound of rapidly disappearing footsteps.

The Goblins exchanged satisfied beams. Things really were looking up.

'D'you know what I could go for now?' remarked Hog. 'A nice, big, greasy plate o' chips. To celebrate.'

At this point, the sea water in Ronald's stomach made a noisy reappearance.

'I'll get you for this, Plugugly,' snarled Pongwiffy, baring her teeth most unpleasantly. 'Just see if I don't.'

'Why? What you gonna do? Squelch us?' taunted Sproggit – a brilliantly witty remark which set the Goblins rocking with laughter.

'You can't put spells on us this time,' Slopbucket reminded her sneeringly. 'We ain't at 'ome now. There's a NO MAGIC rule in Sludgehaven, an' if you break it, we'll tell. So na, na, na, na, na!'

And he poked his tongue out and waggled his fingers on his nose, which was typical.

'I s-s-s-say!' said Ronald, who had suddenly found his voice. It had been lost for ages somewhere deep down in his stomach, along with the sea water. And now, like the sea water, it was back again! 'I say! You'd b-better jolly well loosen these b-b-bonds and let me go this minute. I'll have you know I'm a W-Wizard. I demand to be let go at once.'

'You're our 'ostage. You ain't going nowhere,' Hog told him cheerfully.

'That's right. We got plans fer you. Anyway, you can't do a fing wivout yer silly ole Wizard robes, can yer?' taunted Lardo.

'A Wizard always needs 'is kit,
Or else 'e can't do doodly-squit,'

chanted Sproggit. It was an old Goblin rhyme which all Goblins learn at their mothers' knees. Unlike most old Goblin rhymes, it rang true.

'Is that true, Ronald? Can't you?' demanded Sharkadder.

Ronald flushed and bit his chattering lip. It was true. He couldn't. Wizardry depends on the paraphernalia. Without his Cloak of Darkness and his Hat of Knowledge and his Robe of Mystery and his Staff of Wisdom and whatnot, he was helpless. Cold, too.

'Well, I must say, I'm very disappointed in you, after all that education,' said Sharkadder cuttingly. 'Just think. A nephew of mine. Can't even summon up a bit of lightning without his trousers on. Tut tut. What *do* they teach in Wizard school these days?'

'Well, it's more the *theory* side of things ...' Ronald began desperately, but Pongwiffy stood on his foot and after a short squawk he went quiet.

'Oi! Wizard! Let's see yer do a spell in them

357

shorts!' jeered Hog, enjoying the comic potential of Ronald and not wishing to let it go.

''Ere! 'E could do a spell that makes everyone 'oo sees 'im laugh at 'im!' suggested Eyesore, adding, ''Ere! It's workin'!'

This made the Goblins so helpless with laughter that Pongwiffy almost considered suggesting they make a run for it. But she decided against it. After all, they were still tied up. In their current weakened state, they wouldn't get more than two paces without someone tripping up, and then they'd all fall down and be an even bigger laughing stock than they were already.

'I fink we should apologise to de lady, though,' said Plugugly with a sudden show of gallantry. Lulu stopped bawling, and gave a hopeful sniff. 'Dat's Luscious Lulu Lamarre de Superstar, dat is. I seen 'er picture. 'Course, she ain't too luscious right now, but dat's 'cos she's all wet.'

Lulu began to snivel again.

'Dere, dere, don't you go gettin' all upset,' Plugugly said, patting her on the shoulder. 'We hasn't got nuffin' against you. Come on, boys, show de lady dat Goblins got manners. Line up an take yer 'ats off an' say yer sorry.'

Obediently, the Goblins lined up and solemnly said they were sorry. Lulu fluffed her hair and cheered up a bit, especially when Slopbucket confessed sheepishly that he was a big fan. 'But we can't let you go,' Plugugly explained sadly. 'You're part of de Main Attraction, see.'

'I'll give you Main Attraction!' snarled Pongwiffy, nearly bursting with fury. 'I'll zap you into next week, I will! I'll . . .'

'Naughty, naughty!' jeered Lardo, waggling his finger. 'The Rule. Remember?'

'I'll give you Rule . . .' began Pongwiffy recklessly.

But luckily – or unluckily, as it turned out for some – at that moment, something happened. The music which had been continuously droning on in the background suddenly ceased. There was a silence – then a rumbling noise. Everyone turned to look at the great gates of Gobboworld, which gave a little shudder, opened a bit, stuck, then slowly, dramatically, drew apart.

'In yer go, then, sir,' said the Arm from the booth. 'I got instructions ter let yer pass.'

'Dis is it, den,' said Plugugly, swelling with pride. He'd never been called 'sir' before. 'Our big moment. Straighten up, you 'ostages. We're goin' in.

Quick march. Er – 'ow's it go again?'

'Summink about right an' left, ain't it?' said Hog, scratching his head.

'Dat's it! Right, 'ere we go. Right, right, left, right, right, left, er – left . . .'

And – somehow – in they went.

CHAPTER TWENTY-ONE
postcards

Back in Sludgehaven, blissfully unaware of the plight of their friends, the Witches were having the time of their lives. Bendyshanks, Ratsnappy and Sludgegooey were reclining in deckchairs on the promenade, busily writing postcards.

'Dear Great-Aunt Grimelda,' wrote Sludgegooey. 'Well, here we all are on our hols. It's all go. Yesterday we slimed a Punch and Judy Demon, which was a right lark. Gaga's learnt to waterski. Filth is getting quite a tan. Wish you were here.

All the best, your loving niece, Sludgegooey.'

'How d'you spell "disgusting"?' enquired Ratsnappy, sucking her pencil. 'I want to tell my cousin Catnippy about Old Molotoff's breakfasts,' she explained.

'How should I know? Ask Greymatter,' suggested Sludgegooey, sticking a stamp on.

'I daren't. She's still stuck on One Across. Here come the twins, look. Hey, you two! What's that you've caught?'

'Minnows,' said Agglebag proudly, showing her jam jar. 'Two of them. Twins, we think. We're taking them home, aren't we, Ag? To live happily ever after on our mantelpiece. We're calling them Minnie and Manfred.'

'How d'you know which is Manfred?' asked Sludgegooey doubtfully.

'We don't yet,' confessed Bagaggle. 'But when we get home, Ag's going to knit him a little waterproof tie.'

'And Bag's going to make a little bow for Minnie,' agreed Bagaggle. 'We're good with our hands.'

This interesting conversation was interrupted by a further arrival. Scrofula and Macabre turned up with Barry and Rory in tow. They were all

362

very excited, having found a little shop that sold sandwiches with decent, Witch-friendly fillings, including porridge.

'This is more like it,' said Macabre, parking herself in a deckchair and taking a huge bite of her porridge sandwich. 'This'll help make up for breakfast – or the lack of it. Anyone seen Bonidle?'

'Still in bed,' sighed Ratsnappy. She had the misfortune to be sharing a room with Bonidle, whose life was one long lie-in. 'I can't get her up. Cyril had to hoover under her this morning. Old Molotoff's quite put out about it.'

'What about Gaga?' someone else wanted to know.

'Scuba-diving,' said Scrofula.

There was a short silence. Nobody quite knew what scubas were, or why anyone should want to dive for them – but it sounded a Gaga-ish sort of thing to do.

'Pongwiffy and Sharkadder still missing?' enquired Scrofula. A general nodding of heads signified that this was indeed the case. Nobody had seen them since breakfast.

'Ah well. Probably got tied up somewhere,' said Ratsnappy.

'Here comes Sourmuddle,' announced Macabre, pointing to an excited figure hurrying towards them with Snoop hard on her heels.

'Ah! There you are! We've been looking for you,' puffed Sourmuddle, waving a handful of little pink slips. 'I've got a lovely surprise for us all. My friend at the Rifle Range gave me all these free seats for this afternoon's Mystery Tour!'

Joyous cries greeted this announcement. Everyone wanted to know what a Mystery Tour was.

'We all get on a coach and it takes us somewhere mysterious,' explained Sourmuddle.

'Where?' asked Macabre.

'If we knew that, Macabre, there wouldn't be a mystery, would there?'

'Supposing we don't like it when we get there?' objected Ratsnappy, who liked to be awkward.

'I shall demand a refund,' said Sourmuddle airily.

'I thought you said the seats were free?'

'So?' said Sourmuddle. 'I shall still demand a refund. I'm Grandwitch. I know my rights.'

So that was all right.

Meanwhile, up at the Magician's Retreat . . .

'I'm not at all sure about this Mystery Tour business, you know,' Fred the Flameraiser was saying. 'On a coach, do you say? Sounds a bit too adventurous for my liking. Will I be allowed to set fire to anything, do you think?'

'Oh, I should think so,' said Dave the Druid, helping himself to another scone. 'We're Wizards, aren't we? Nobody tells us what to do.'

The Wizards were sitting in the lounge, tucking into lunch. Lunch, by popular request, was a cream tea set out on hostess trolleys. There were mountains of scones, vats of jam and great jugs of cream. There was much rattling of teacups and licking of fingers and greedy spooning of jam, which almost drowned out the sound of voices droning on drily in the Conference Room next door.

'Does it mean mixing with the riff-raff, though? That's what I want to know,' enquired Alf the Invisible anxiously. A scone laden with jam and cream rose from his plate, hovered a moment, then vanished in a puff of crumbs. Several of the crumbs remained hanging in mid-air, obviously caught on his invisible beard.

'Certainly not. I've spoken to the driver and

arranged for us to be picked up first. We get the plum choice of seats,' explained Dave the Druid.

'That sounds very fair,' nodded Gerald the Just. But Alf the Invisible wasn't reassured.

'Why do we have to go anywhere? What's wrong with sitting on our balcony?'

'The maid wants to clean it,' explained Dave the Druid.

'But I thought we could start a little fire up there today,' mourned Fred the Flameraiser. 'I've got my magnifying glass all ready.'

'I just thought we should perhaps get out and about a little,' explained Dave the Druid. 'We don't have to move or anything. Just sit in a coach and watch the scenery go by. And I've arranged for the hotel to pack us a hamper. Just a light snack. Couple of sides of ham, a cold chicken or two, some sandwiches, tomatoes, a few eggs, pork pies, sausage rolls, a big cake, fizzy lemonade – that sort of thing. Just to keep us going until supper.'

'Oh well,' said Alf the Invisible, sounding relieved. 'If there's going to be a *hamper . . .*'

'I suppose we should let young Ronald read out his paper at some point,' said Frank the Foreteller, helping himself to his fourth scone. 'I could do with a good laugh.'

'Did anyone check his room, by the way?' asked Fred the Flameraiser. 'I don't think I've seen him all day, come to think of it.'

'Sulking, I shouldn't wonder,' said Frank the Foreteller with satisfaction, spooning on lashings of cream.

'Well, somebody had better tell him about the Mystery Tour,' said Dave the Druid. 'He wouldn't want to miss that. He's been complaining the whole time that we never do anything. Go on, Fred. Pop up and give the lad his ticket.'

'Mmm,' said Fred vaguely. 'Later. After lunch. Er – does anyone want that last scone?' Everyone did. So they ordered some more.

CHAPTER TWENTY-TWO
Scott Gets His Chance

Scott Sinister was in his dressing room. In fact, he hadn't dared move from it since the previous day when he had run into Pongwiffy, of all people! Whatever was she doing in Sludgehaven? Wherever Pongwiffy went, trouble followed, He knew that. So what if she was the one remaining loyal fan he had left in the whole world? She was the sort of fan he could do without. Even on a hot day.

Scott gave a little shudder as he recalled that heart-stopping moment of the day before when they had come face to face. Luckily, he had escaped before she could engage him in conversation – or even worse – aaaah – kiss him!! One look at her dazzling smile of greeting had been enough for instinct to take over. He had uttered a low, rising, wobbling wail, taken to his heels and fled to the safety of his broom cupboard, where he spent the rest of the day and the whole of the night quaking under a pile of curtains, convinced she would seek him out.

But she hadn't. And now it was morning – and tonight was opening night. Scott was nothing if not a trouper. The theatre was in his veins. As his mum always boasted, his very first baby sentence (announced imperiously from the potty) had not been the usual 'I want my eggy.' It had been the far more impressive utterance, 'The show must go on.'

There was something about being in a theatre that aroused all the ancient actorly feelings. The smell of greasepaint, combined with the distant sounds of an orchestra tuning up, revived him as effectively as smelling salts. Right now, he was sitting before his cracked mirror applying the finishing touches to his make-up. When he had finally got it to his satisfaction, he carefully combed his hair, took his sunglasses from his pocket and put them on.

There. That was an improvement. Time now for some soothing deep breathing. In – out – in – out.

The breathing helped a lot. In fact, he was beginning to feel much better. So much so that he felt ready to attempt his voice exercises.

'Mee mee meeeeeeee,' sang Scott. 'Mee mee mee ma mee moo may!'

There came the sound of pattering footsteps, followed by an urgent knock on the door.

'Who's in there, please?' came the voice of the call boy.

'Meeeeeeeee!' trilled Scott.

'Is that you, Mr Sinister?'

'Of course it is,' snapped Scott. 'I'm trying to do my voice exercises. What do you want? I'm not receiving any visitors, mind.'

'You haven't got any, Mr Sinister. It's not that. It's Miss Lamarre. She's gone missing. Not in there with you, is she?'

'Of course not,' growled Scott. 'How can she be with me? There's only enough oxygen in here for one.'

'It's just that she's late for rehearsal. She was due here hours ago and she hasn't shown up. The orchestra's threatening to pack up and go home.'

370

'Well, what do you expect when you engage amateurs?' said Scott coldly. 'Kindly go away and leave me in peace. There are only a few hours to curtain-up. I want to be alone. I need to get into role.'

There was a short pause, and the footsteps pattered away.

Scott felt *much* better. Telling off the call boy had made him feel more important, somehow. He could feel his old confidence flowing back. Perhaps he would go over his act one more time. He needed to be word perfect. His was only a small spot, but at least he'd give it all he'd got.

He fished inside his cloak, and brought out a sheaf of well-thumbed paper. He glanced briefly at the topmost sheet, mouthed a few words under his breath, then deliberately placed the script to one side, leaned back in his chair, closed his eyes and began.

'Thank you very much, ladies and gentlemen, thank you very much! Hey! It's great to be back in good old Sludgehaven again.' (Pause for applause. Hopefully.) 'I love the seaside, don't you? Talking of the sea, have you heard the one about the haddock who robbed a fish bar and was done for

371

salt and battery? And what about the mermaid who . . .'

'Mr Sinister, sir!'

The call boy was back again.

'What! What is it!' roared Scott. 'Can't an artiste be left to go over his lines in peace!'

'It's Miss Lamarre, sir. They still can't find her. The Stage Manager's going potty. He wants to know if you'll step into the breach.'

There was a startled silence. Then: 'Could you just repeat that?' croaked Scott.

He couldn't believe he had heard properly. Surely it wasn't true! Could it be, could it *really* be that his luck had finally turned?

The call boy took a deep breath.

'It's Miss Lamarre, sir. They still can't find her. The Stage Manager's going po—'

'Not the whole of it, idiot! Just the last bit. About stepping into the breach.'

'The Stage Manager wants you to go on in her place, sir. He's desperate. Every seat is sold for this evening's performance, and the star's missing. Will you do it, Mr Sinister? Will you save the show?'

Well. What would anyone say to a request like that?

372

For the first time for simply ages, a great smile spread across Scott's face. He stood, swept his cloak about him and pulled open the door with a flourish.

'Prepare the main dressing room,' he said grandly. 'I am on my way.'

CHAPTER TWENTY-THREE
The Mystery Tour

The Wizards were gathered in the foyer of the Magician's Retreat, waiting for the coach that was to take them on the Mystery Tour. They were all muffled up in case of draughts, and greedily eyeing the enormous hamper containing the light snack which was to fortify them during the excursion. All except the Venerable Harold, who had evidently found the excitement of a Mystery Tour too much to bear and had gone to sleep on a nearby sofa.

'Are we all here?' cried Dave the Druid, bustling

about with a clipboard. Having organised the trip, he had taken it upon himself to be leader.

They were. All except Alf the Invisible, who couldn't strictly be described as *here*, although some floating crumbs and a smear of airborne cream indicated that he was present.

And Ronald, of course. (*We* know where he is, don't we? But they didn't.)

'I'm still not sure about this,' moaned Fred the Flameraiser.

'Well, it's too late to change your mind now,' said Dave firmly. 'Here comes the coach.'

'Looks like young Ronald's going to miss all the excitement,' remarked Frank the Foreteller sadly. 'Shame, really.'

'No one bothered to check his room, I suppose?' enquired Dave the Druid. 'No? Oh well, too late now. Right, someone pass Harold to the front. We'll stick him in the back seat, along with the hamper.'

Down on the promenade, a large crowd of Witches and their Familiars were assembled by a sign that said THE MYSTERY TOUR, QUEUE HERE. The entire Coven was present, apart from Pongwiffy,

Hugo, Sharkadder and Dudley. Even Bonidle and her Sloth had turned out of bed for this. Gaga was there too, all decked out in snorkel and flippers, carrying a large oil painting entitled 'The Minstrel Boy's Revenge', which she claimed to have won in a paragliding competition.

There was a great deal of excitement and much wild speculation about their possible destination.

'Ah hope it's Scotland,' said Macabre dreamily. 'Ah'll pop in for a decent bowl o' porridge wi' mah Uncle Fergus. Ah've brought mah bagpipes, just in case. He likes a wee tune.'

'I rather hope it's somewhere with a decent reference library,' groaned Greymatter, still doing battle with One Across. So far, she had worn out six pencils and thirteen dictionaries – but still the correct answer eluded her.

'Somewhere you could get a decent hot meal would be a fine thing, wouldn't it, Ag?' remarked Bagaggle longingly.

'It would, Bag. Old Molotoff's starvation diet is getting on my nerves.'

This brought a chorus of heartfelt agreement from everybody.

'Hear hear!'

'Down with Old Molotoff and her rotten breakfasts, I say!'

'I sneaked a look over her shoulder into the larder this morning!' Bendyshanks informed everyone. 'Stuffed with pies and jelly and cake and stuff, it is. And all we get is eggs. Eggs, eggs, eggs.'

'Eggsactly!'

'What I can't understand is why Sourmuddle's taking it all in her stride,' remarked Ratsnappy. 'She's always had a good appetite, has Sourmuddle. You'd think she'd be the first to complain.'

'What's that? Did I hear my name mentioned?' demanded Sourmuddle.

'We were just saying about the breakfasts,' explained Bendyshanks. 'We want to complain. We're all starving.'

'Really?' asked Sourmuddle. 'Snoop and I aren't. Are we, Snoop?'

'Ah,' said Snoop, 'but that's because . . .'

He caught Sourmuddle's eye and stopped abruptly in mid-sentence.

'That's because we're not greedy,' Sourmuddle finished off for him. 'I've told you before, it's not Done to complain about food. We're in a strange place with strange customs. When in Rome, do as

377

the Romans do.'

'I bet the Romans got more to eat than boiled eggs,' complained Sludgegooey. 'In fact,' she went on, 'in fact, they got *loads* to eat. I heard that they got so much they couldn't eat it all, so they'd stick their fingers . . .'

Luckily, more information about the Romans' famous eating habits was prevented by the timely arrival of the coach.

'Hey!' shouted Bendyshanks, jumping up and down. 'It's here! Look! It says Mystery Tour on the front!'

'It's the same one that brought us! It's George, look! Bags I the back seat!'

'Wait a minute,' said Ratsnappy. 'I hate to put a damper on things – but aren't those *Wizards* I see?'

She was right. They were. A mass of bearded faces, incredulous with horror and topped with pointy hats, were pressed against the glass.

There was immediate consternation.

'Well, if anyone thinks I'm sharing a coach with a load of *Wizards* . . .'

'Look! They've got the best seats and all!'

'What a cheek. How come they got picked up first?'

'They've got a hamper too! Lucky so-and-sos.'

Sourmuddle, as befitted her role of Grandwitch, reacted with dignity. It took more than a coachload of Wizards to unsettle her. Calmly, she picked up her skirts.

'Come along, girls, best foot forward. We're not going to let a few Wizards spoil our outing, are we? Open the door, George, we're coming in!'

The Wizards had indeed taken the best seats. The best seats were towards the back, away from the engine and the draughty door. They muttered and rumbled under their breath as the Witches and Familiars filed in and took their seats in sniffy silence.

'Pshaw! You see? Riff-raff! I told you!'

'If I'd known a load of *Witches* were coming on this trip . . .'

'They're bringing *animals* on, for goodness' sake. Is that a *haggis* they've got there? And are those *bats*, do you think?'

'Whatever is the world coming to?'

'There should be a law . . .'

Bendyshanks, who was the last one in, treated them all to a stony glare and plumped down heavily on Alf the Invisible's lap. They both howled with fright and Alf hastily fled to another seat.

'The air was all bony there for a moment,' explained Bendyshanks lamely in answer to the quizzical stares, and tentatively sat down again, looking quite shaken.

'Everyone in?' growled George. 'Right then. We're off.'

And with a shrill blast of the horn and an almighty grinding of gears, the coach lurched away.

There was a tense silence from both parties as they drove along the prom. It wasn't often that Wizards and Witches shared such a confined space. In the normal course of events, they avoided each other. If a Witch and a Wizard should pass each other on the street, they would stick their noses in the air and look the other way. They despised each other's Magical methods, for a start. With the Wizards, it was all lightning and colourful explosions, which the Witches considered flashy. They preferred cackling over cauldrons, a practice which the Wizards thought of as common.

For a while, nobody spoke. Then, suddenly, Sourmuddle spoke up.

'Is somebody eating smelly cheese at the back there?' she demanded primly. 'If so, you can throw it out of the window.'

Fred the Flameraiser gave a guilty start and looked around wildly, unsure of what to do.

'Don't you do it, Fred,' advised Frank the Foreteller. 'You eat as much cheese as you like.'

That really set the cat among the pigeons.

'Boo! Throw it out!' bellowed the Witches. 'Stop the coach! Make him throw it out.'

'Don't do it, Fred! You stand firm!' countered the Wizards. 'Keep going, driver, if you know what's good for you!'

'Throw it out! Stop the coach!'

George sighed. It looked like it was going to be another of Those Days.

CHAPTER TWENTY-FOUR
The Main Attraction

Meanwhile, back in Gobboworld a long, excited queue had formed for the popular Main Attraction. The Bobble Hat of Doom, the Roller Coaster, the Bungee Jump and the Helter-Skelter lay idle. The various sideshows and stalls had all been abandoned in favour of this, the latest amusement, which was proving to be an absolute winner.

The Main Attraction had been hastily set up on a roped-off platform rather like a boxing ring. This was where the Goblins normally conducted their celebrated Wet Bobble Hat competitions – jolly occasions when particularly daft volunteers would stand grinning vacantly while eager crowds armed with long hoses attempted to squirt their hats off. That was a lot of fun, of course – but in terms of pure pleasure, it had nothing on this, the latest diversion, an absolute corker which really had them rolling in the aisles.

It was a Main Attraction that couldn't fail.

It was called Get Your Own Back, and consisted of *five* highly enjoyable, fun-filled activities. Hoop the Hag, Splodge the Wizard, Singalonga Superstar, Poke the Pet – and, for the grand finale – Wash the Witch!

Sharkadder, Ronald, Lulu, Hugo, Dudley and Pongwiffy, bound hand and foot, stood in a grim-faced line while hordes of enthusiastic Goblins fought for the pleasure of throwing hoops at Sharkadder's nose (Hoop the Hag), hurling tomatoes at the hapless Ronald (Splodge the Wizard), singing interminable tuneless duets with Lulu (Singalonga Superstar), tickling Hugo and Dudley with feathers tied on the end of long poles until they begged for mercy (Poke the Pet), and last – and best of all – setting upon Pongwiffy armed with a bucket of warm water, a large sponge and a huge bar of pink soap! (Wash the Witch. What else?)

Warm water! Soap! Pongwiffy! Can you imagine?

'Roll up, roll up!' shouted Plugugly through a megaphone, banging on a bucket containing an unpleasant mess of overripe tomatoes. Below him, Eyesore, Lardo, Slopbucket, Stinkwart, Hog and Sproggit moved among the crowds, distributing hoops, tickling sticks, sponges, and buckets of warm, soapy water. 'Dis way fer de Main Attraction! Step right up! Chance of a lifetime! Get Yer Own Back fer a change!'

Nobody needed any coaxing.

'I suppose they think this is funny,' ground out Sharkadder between clenched teeth. Cheers rang out as a fourth hoop rattled on to her nose, neatly lining up with three others which had already met their mark. 'Hoop the Hag indeed! I've never been so insulted in my life. Some holiday this is turning out to be. Ouch! That hurt!'

'Grooo,' said Ronald through a mouth full of tomatoes. He had always hated tomatoes. They were in his hair too. Pulpy juice trickled into his ears and dripped on to his thin shoulders. Even his nice yellow shorts were getting stained. It was a high price to pay for a paddle.

Next along, Lulu was singing. Singalonga Superstar was proving to be an inspired idea. Goblins enjoy a good sing-song, and it wasn't often they got the chance to warble along with someone as famous as Luscious Lulu Lamarre. One by one, grinning sheepishly, they filed on to the platform and whispered their requests into her ear. Once Lulu had kicked off, they mumbled along tunelessly while their friends cheered and whistled and took photographs. 'Oh I Do Like to be Beside the Seaside' was a popular one.

'I'm not singing any more,' Lulu had complained at one point, stamping her foot petulantly. 'My throat hurts.'

'Fair enough. You can give out kisses instead if you like,' offered Slopbucket with a hopeful giggle and going all pink.

Lulu burst quickly back into song.

Compared with the other victims, Hugo and Dudley had it easy. After all, they were only being tickled. But, as Hugo said later, it's no fun being tickled by your sworn enemies.

Of all of them, though, Pongwiffy suffered the most. Coming into contact with soap was her worst ever nightmare and the Goblins knew it. My, how

they applied themselves! How they rubbed and scrubbed and lathered and mopped! There was lather in her eyes and up her nose. She could hardly be seen for foam. The sea had been bad enough, but this! This was without doubt the greatest indignity she had ever suffered.

'You'll be sorry!' she spluttered through a mouthful of froth. 'I'll get you for this, you see if I don't! Oi! Plugugly! Sproggit! You wait till we get back to Witchway Wood! I'll pulverise you! I'll turn you all into creepy-crawlies and make you live under my stove! I'll turn you into bedbugs and make you live under my mattress. I'll . . .'

But another grinning Goblin was approaching with the foaming sponge, and the rest of her threats were drowned out.

'There's only one good thing about this,' remarked Sharkadder as another hoop landed on her beringed nose with a clang.

'What's that, Auntie?' choked Ronald, by now as near to a bottle of ketchup as it is possible for a human to be.

'At least none of the others is here to see this,' groaned Sharkadder. 'We'd never live it down!'

'I beg your pardon, driver?' said Sourmuddle. 'Could you just repeat that? For a moment I thought you said we were here.'

'We are,' said George, switching off his engine and pulling open the door. 'This is it. End o' the Mystery Tour.'

'Do correct me if I'm wrong,' said Sourmuddle politely, 'but I believe that sign over those big gates says Gobboworld.'

'That's right,' said George. 'In you go. You got one hour to enjoy yourselves. Then I'm leavin'.'

There was a shocked silence from both Witches and Wizards alike. Nobody moved.

'Go on, then,' urged George. 'Out you get. You can't stop in the coach. Safety regulations.'

'You mean this is *it*?' demanded Fred the Flameraiser from the back. 'You stuck us in with a coachload of common Witches who won't even let a man *eat cheese* and brought us all that way for *this*?'

This brought mutters of protest from the Witches, along the lines of 'Hear that? Who's he calling common?' and so on.

'Why, what's wrong with it?' argued George

defensively. 'Thought yer'd like to visit Gobboworld. Somethin' a bit different, innit?'

There was an instant outcry.

'Well I never!' said Bendyshanks, disgusted. 'What a swiz!'

'And tae think Ah thought it was Scotland!' wailed Macabre as her vision of a hot bowl of porridge poured itself away. Rory laid a sympathetic hoof on her lap.

'Disgraceful!' huffed and puffed the Wizards, equally put out.

'Outrageous! Shouldn't be allowed!'

'Some Mystery Tour! The only mystery is why we ever came on it!'

'Well, I for one will certainly be demanding a refund,' said Sourmuddle crossly. With a sigh, she stood up and reached for her handbag. 'Oh well. Come on, girls. Now we're here, we might as well take a look, I suppose. There's nothing else to do. Unless, of course, our esteemed fellow passengers would like to share the contents of that yummy-looking hamper with us.'

'Dream on!' shouted the Wizards. 'The hamper's ours!'

The Wizards were smarting. To their

eternal shame, they had lost the battle of the cheese. Ratsnappy had simply marched up the aisle to where Fred the Flameraiser sat, snatched away his sandwich and thrown it out of the window.

It had been an embarrassing defeat. It had made the Wizards all the more determined to defend their hamper against all comers.

'So are we getting out or what?' enquired Dave the Druid.

'I think we'd better,' agreed Gerald the Just. 'We might as well get our money's worth. Besides, I'm sure our driver could do with a break,' he added fairly.

'You're tellin' me,' said George.

'But what about the hamper?' came the anxious chorus. 'Will it be safe?'

'I'll lock it in the coach,' promised George. 'Out you get, then, gents. Only an hour, mind, then back 'ere sharp. I got a schedule to keep.'

With a great deal of sighing and complaining and creaking and casting about for scarves and woolly mufflers and suchlike, the Wizards filed from the coach and shuffled off to catch up with the Witches, who were marching in a determined crocodile towards the ticket booth.

CHAPTER TWENTY-FIVE
The Rescue

The Arm saw them coming and quailed. One minute everything was nice and quiet, the next its cosy world was turned upside down, along with the cup of tea it was currently enjoying.

Witches!?

Wizards!!??

Together???!!!

Ulp!

Whatever were they doing here? Could it be – horrors! – could it be that this was a properly organised rescue party who had somehow found out about the new Main Attraction and was coming

391

to take revenge? The sight of so many pointy hats was truly frightening and it gave the Arm a real turn.

Lesser arms would have immediately retreated in alarm and reappeared holding a white flag. Not this Arm. This Arm was a pro. It set down its empty teacup, then stuck out again, effectively blocking the entrance. Granted it was shaking a little and its thick black hairs stood up on end – but to its credit, it held firm. Its mudder would have been proud.

'Open the gates, if you please,' demanded Sourmuddle briskly. 'I've got a party of Witches here on a Mystery Tour. We've come to look at Gobboworld. Not our choice, you understand, but now we're here we might as well.'

'Oh, you don't want to go in *there*,' gibbered the Arm. 'You wouldn't like it. Not your sort of thing at all.'

'How do you know?' snapped Sourmuddle. 'You haven't a clue about what Witches like. Now open up before I get annoyed.'

'Anyway,' added the Arm hopefully, 'anyway, we're closed.'

'Oh yes? What's all that cheering I can hear coming from inside, then?'

'I meant full,' amended the Arm. 'That's it. We're

full. An' anyway, it's private. Only Goblins allowed.'

'Enough of this nonsense!'

Dave the Druid bustled impatiently to the front. 'Stand aside, Sourmuddle, I'll deal with this. Come along, man, come along! We Wizards haven't got all day. We've got a Convention to attend.'

'Hear hear! Quite right. You tell him,' rumbled the Wizards supportively.

'I need ter see yer tickets,' pleaded the Arm.

'Tickets schmickets,' snapped Sourmuddle. 'Since when have Witches needed tickets? Now hurry up and open those gates. You don't keep Witches waiting.'

'Or Wizards,' poked in Dave the Druid.

'Well, I dunno . . .' muttered the Arm. 'I got my instructions, see. Nobody's allowed to enter without a tick— *ow*!'

It broke off with a sharp cry of pain as Sourmuddle smacked it. Hard, right on the back of the wrist. Hastily it withdrew into the booth.

'Something wrong with your ears?' enquired Sourmuddle. 'When a Witch tells you to do something, you do it. Naughty boys who don't listen to Witches get smacks. Now. Open those gates this minute. Or do you want another?'

The Arm didn't want another. Without any more argument, it pressed the button that opened the gates.

Inside, Get Your Own Back was still doing record business. There was no doubt about it. It was proving to be the high spot of Gobboworld. There wasn't a Goblin there who didn't want to have a go.

The queuing system had long since broken down. A baying rabble now clustered thickly around the platform, pushing and shoving and howling with impatience. Some of the bigger ones had already had two turns, to the annoyance of some of the smaller ones who had been waiting for ages.

One such Goblin was right at the back of the milling crowd. His name was Squit. And it was because he was right at the back that he was the only one who heard the main gates rumble open behind him. Squit glanced back over his shoulder – and saw a sight that made him do a double take, then go weak at the knees.

'Oooer,' said Squit. 'Er – boys? *Boys!* I think we got visitors.'

And indeed they had.

Just inside the gates, the coach party stood in a

tableau of frozen disbelief. Their mouths hung open and their eyes boggled at the scene before them.

'Witches!' squawked Squit, beating frantically on the wall of backs. 'Witches and Wizards, *'undreds* of 'em! Look to yer rear! Emergency, emergency! We bin rumbled!'

The word went round like wildfire. Well, actually, it didn't. Goblins are slow to cotton on, and it was more like a damp squib on a slow fuse. Eventually, though, the message filtered through. *The Witches* were here! *With the Wizards!*

Slowly, the cheers and catcalls died away. Hoops were guiltily lowered. Tomatoes were hastily stuffed into pockets. Tickling sticks were hidden. Soapy sponges were abandoned. The crowd parted, peeling back on two sides and providing a clear pathway that led from the platform back to where the unexpected visitors stood in shocked disbelief.

'Uh-oh,' said Plugugly sadly. 'Dat's us done for, den. Caught in de act. Goo'bye, cruel world.'

Up on the platform, aware of the sudden silence that had fallen, the six wretched captives raised abject eyes and stared at their rescuers with a mixture of relief and shame. Relief that their ordeal was over. Shame that they should be discovered in such embarrassing circumstances.

'I'm not seeing things, am I? That *is* Pongwiffy up there, under all that soap?' asked Sourmuddle, finally finding her voice. She sounded doubtful. It was hard to recognise Pongwiffy without her customary layers of grime.

'It certainly looks like it, Sourmuddle,' agreed Macabre grimly. 'What a turn-up, eh?'

'What's Sharkadder doing with all those rings on her nose, do you think, Ag?' asked Bagaggle, sounding puzzled. 'Is she doing an impression of a curtain rail, or what?'

'Possibly, Bag. And isn't that Lulu Lamarre the Superstar? What's *she* doing?'

Consternation was also running through the ranks of the Wizards.

'Are my eyes deceiving me, or is that young Ronald up on that platform?' quavered Harold the Hoodwinker, sounding puzzled. 'All covered in tomatoes, isn't he? And where are his trousers? Not very dignified, is it?'

'I'm afraid you're right, Harold,' confirmed Frank the Foreteller gleefully. 'Dearie dearie me. Looks like the lad's made a bit of a laughing stock of himself, don't you think? Got himself in another

396

pickle. Or should I say chutney, ha ha? *Tomato* chutney, I meant. Get it?'

'Letting the side down, I call it,' tutted Alf the Invisible. 'A very poor show indeed.'

'Of course, it's probably all the Goblins' fault,' said Gerald the Just fairly.

'True,' chorused all the Witches and Wizards together, then looked at each other in surprise. It wasn't often they found themselves in agreement.

'How long did the driver say we've got?' Sourmuddle asked Dave the Druid, beginning to roll up her sleeves.

'One hour,' Dave told her.

'Excellent. That should be plenty of time. I think this calls for a bit of united action, don't you? A temporary truce. All for one and one for all. Agreed?'

'Agreed,' nodded Dave. 'Just this once, mind.'

'Right. Let's teach these Goblins a lesson they won't forget. Ready, everyone?'

'Ready!' came the chorus from Witches and Wizards alike.

'*Then let's get 'em!*'

And the Goblins scattered, screaming, in all directions, as the rescue party charged.

CHAPTER TWENTY-SIX
A Triumphant Return

What a different atmosphere there was in the coach as it wended its way back towards Sludgehaven that evening. Instead of argument, there was laughter and singing. Instead of bickering, there was hearty backslapping and self-congratulation, particularly among the Wizards, who weren't used to physical exercise. Reducing Gobboworld to a pile of smoking rubble had proved to be a lot more strenuous than shuffling between bed and dinner table — but my word, it had been fun! In fact, it had been a real tonic. Even the

398

Venerable Harold the Hoodwinker looked ten years younger. Well, five, maybe.

'We showed 'em, didn't we?' shouted Fred the Flameraiser. 'We knocked the spots off those Goblins! They won't mess with Wizards again in a hurry. Did you see my karate jabs? Aaiiiiii – ha!'

'What about me, then?' piped up Harold the Hoodwinker in his quavering little voice. 'Did you shee me wallop that big one? Thwack, right on his nose! Didn't think I still had it in me.'

'But did you see *me* when I took over the hose?' crowed Frank the Foreteller, flushed with triumph. 'I made 'em run all right!'

'Ah, but you should have seen when I chased a great gang of 'em into the mud pool! Terrified, they were!'

'Terrified? You want to see terrified, you should have seen the one I chased up the Roller Coaster – white as a sheet he was. You see, the way it happened was like this . . .'

'And it was fair too,' Gerald the Just was saying. 'That's what I like about it. We didn't use the unfair advantage of Magic. We beat them fair and square, and that's all there is to it.'

'What a day, eh?' sighed Dave the Druid. 'Almost

worth young Ronald getting captured for. What d'you say, young Ronald? Feeling any better yet?'

Ronald, wrapped in a blanket, stared out of the window and said nothing.

'I say we break open the hamper,' suggested Frank the Foreteller. 'I reckon young Ronald here would like a bite to eat. What about it, lad? Fancy a nice *tomato* sandwich, ha ha ha?'

Ronald picked pips from his hair and continued to say nothing.

'There, there,' Gerald the Just consoled him. 'Don't take it to heart. I'm sure we all made fools of ourselves in our youth. Tell you what. We'll take you back to the hotel and clean you up, then order a whacking great six-course celebratory dinner. Then tomorrow we'll all come and hear you read out your paper at the Convention. Now I can't say fairer than that, can I?'

Ronald cheered up a bit.

The Witches too were all in excellent humour. There was nothing like wiping the floor with Goblins to put them in a good mood. All, that is, except Pongwiffy and Sharkadder. They weren't in a good mood at all. Bedraggled, bruised and humiliated, they sat slumped soggily together in the front seat with Dudley and Hugo on their laps, stonily ignoring various jibes along the lines of 'Who got caught by Goblins, then?' and 'Been starring in a *soap*, Pongwiffy?' and other such staggeringly witty comments.

It was no fun, being the butt of everyone's jokes.

'Hear that?' muttered Pongwiffy to Sharkadder as yet another chorus of 'I'm Forever Throwing Goblins' started up. 'It's all very well for them. They haven't suffered like I have. Look at me! I'm all *pink*! It'll take weeks to get back to normal. Yuck!'

'You? *You?* What about me? Have you seen my *hair*? I've never been so embarrassed in all my life. I've become a complete laughing-stock, and it's all your fault, Pongwiffy, and I'll never forgive you. You've completely ruined my holiday.'

'Well, I like that!' said Pongwiffy, hurt. 'I was only trying to help Scott. At least that part of the plan worked. We got *her* out of the way, didn't we?'

She fired off a look of dislike at Lulu, who was sitting in tight-lipped silence next to George at the very front. She was being given a lift back to Sludgehaven at the Wizards' gallant insistence. The Witches were in far too frisky a mood to care one way or the other.

401

'At least Scott got his chance,' Pongwiffy went on. 'The show should be ending round about now. Oh, how I wish we'd been there to see it. I just *know* he'll have been a success. Just imagine it, Sharky. Our very own Scott's name back up in lights and all thanks to me. It'll make all our suffering worthwhile, won't it?'

'No,' said Sharkadder bitterly. 'Nothing could make up for what Dudley and I have been through today. Except perhaps a huge, greedy supper. But we won't get that at old Molotoff's.'

Outside, evening had fallen. The coach wheezed its way to the top of the last hill. A pale moon floated in the dark sky, lighting up the big welcoming sign that read: YOU ARE APPROACHING SLUDGEHAVEN. MAGIC STRICTLY FORBIDDEN. The lights of Sludgehaven glimmered below. From here, the distant pier looked like fairyland.

Cheers broke out, accompanied by the unmistakable sound of corks popping from bottles of celebratory fizzy lemonade. The Wizards had broken open the hamper, and were busily passing around chicken legs and sausage rolls.

'Well, come on then,' shouted Sludgegooey.

'Pass a few down to the front. Don't keep 'em all to yourselves. There's a lot of hungry Witches down here. Give us a sandwich, you greedy lot.'

'Not jolly likely,' crowed the Wizards. 'Get your own sandwiches.'

'I thought we had a truce,' Sourmuddle reminded them. 'One for all and all for one. United we stand, united we fall, remember?'

'That was Goblins. This is food,' explained Dave the Druid through a mouthful of chocolate cake. 'With food, it's Every Wizard for Himself. Sorry.'

'Well I'm jiggered!' grumbled Sourmuddle, disgusted. 'There's Wizards for you.'

Down in Sludgehaven, crowds of excitedly chattering theatregoers streamed back along the pier, away from the Pavilion, where they had just been enjoying what had been, by common consensus, *the best show they had seen in a very long time*!

For Scott, it had been a charmed night. The sort of night of which every actor dreams. One of those wonderful, enchanted evenings when everything for once had gone right.

His make-up had gone on like a dream, and when

403

he changed into his stage gear of top hat and tails, the tea lady slipped him a chocolate biscuit at no extra charge and told him he looked quite the toff.

The coffee machine in the proper dressing room worked. The stage hands addressed him politely, patting him on the back and saying 'Good luck, Mr Sinister, we know you can do it' and 'We're all behind you, Mr Sinister', and encouraging things like that. When he stood waiting in the wings, listening to the warm murmuring of the audience out front, he felt ready for anything. His luck had turned. He could feel it in his bones. He couldn't wait to get out there and do his stuff!

The lights had dimmed on cue. The overture had started on time. The curtains hadn't stuck. When he had come running gaily on stage, he hadn't tripped over. His joke about the haddock was greeted with uproarious laughter. He had remembered the words of the songs and managed to stay almost in tune. When he sat on a stool in the spotlight and sang a particularly drippy love song, several female Trolls and an entire clutch of Banshees wept so much they were politely asked to leave.

His tap-dancing routine had gone down a treat – never had his feet skipped so lightly or his

404

legs kicked so high. He had even managed to do the splits without rupturing either himself or his trousers, which takes real talent, as anyone in show business will tell you.

Throughout his entire performance, the audience had been on the edge of their seats, hanging on his every word, laughing, clapping, joining in with the songs, roaring for more. At the end, they had given him a standing ovation and made him come back on to take bow after bow after bow.

Backstage, after the show, his dressing room had bulged with flowers, chocolates and messages of congratulation. The Stage Manager had pumped his hand up and down and trebled his salary on the spot. Well-wishers filed in and out, telling him he was the tops and how they had always secretly preferred him to Lulu Lamarre and asking him when his next film was coming out.

And now, with the sound of clapping still ringing in his ears, he stood on the top step of the theatre with the night breeze cooling the sweat on his brow, shaking hands, signing autographs for fans and posing for pictures, murmuring 'Thank you, luvvies' and 'You're too kind, darlings', just like he always used to before his slide into oblivion. Mmm. The

405

sweet smell of success. How he had missed it.

He didn't notice the scruffy coach that squealed to a sudden halt at the end of the pier. He didn't notice the wild-eyed creature with tangled locks and a torn pink gown and one gold shoe who threw herself down the steps and came stumbling towards him along the pier. He didn't notice until she hurled herself into his arms with a shrill squawk.

'Scott! Oh, Scott, it's me! Am I too late? Have I missed the show?'

He staggered backwards and almost missed his footing — but didn't. Tonight was his night and nothing could go wrong.

'Lulu!' he cried, recovering his balance. 'Whatever can have happened to you? You look simply dreadful.'

'It was those old Witches again,' sobbed Lulu. 'They tricked me, Scott! They pretended to be rich producers and old boatmen and then the dead fish came alive but it wasn't really, it was them and there was a horrible cat and a sick hamster and they put me in a boat and made me sit next to a wet Wizard in shorts and then the boat capsized and I had to swim to shore and then some horrid Goblins came along and tied us all up and made me sing and then –'

'Darling,' said Scott gently. 'My poor, hysterical darling, get a hold of yourself. This sounds like the far-fetched plot of some very silly book. You've been working too hard, precious. None of this happened, sweetheart. It's all been a terrible dream. You need a nice rest away from the public eye for a while.'

'But . . .'

'No buts, angel. It's tough at the top. It takes grit as well as talent. It's obvious you can't take the pace. Besides,' he added, trying not to sound too pleased, 'besides, you've been fired.'

Lulu burst into loud sobs.

'There there,' Scott soothed her, patting her back. 'Never fear. Scotty will take care of you. And in a couple of years, when you're back on your feet again, you never know – maybe I'll offer you a bit part in my next movie.'

'Oh, Scott! Scott! Boohoo! I've missed you, Scott.'

'And I've missed you too, Lulu, darling.'

Back in the coach, Pongwiffy, Hugo, Sharkadder and Dudley surveyed the tender scene with disgusted eyes.

407

'Well, there's gratitude!' said Pongwiffy. 'Look at 'em! All lovey-dovey. It's enough to make you sick. That's the last time I save *his* career.'

CHAPTER TWENTY-SEVEN
No Feast For The Wicked

'And what time of night do you call *this*?' demanded Mrs Molotoff. She was standing in the doorway in dressing gown and slippers and with her hair in paper curlers, having been roused from bed by a thunderous knocking at the door, accompanied by rowdy singing.

'Supper time,' Sourmuddle told her briskly.

'*Supper?* At this time of night? How dare you!' squawked Mrs Molotoff, bristling with fury. 'I told you, this is a respectable guest house. You have to obey the rules.'

'Well, that's just where you're wrong,' said Sourmuddle stoutly, to everyone's surprise. 'I'm

409

Grandwitch and I do what I like.'

The Witches murmured excitedly among themselves as their noble leader marched up the steps, took a firm handful of dressing gown, and placed her nose close to Mrs Molotoff's.

Could this be a showdown?

'Listen here, you old skinflint, and listen good,' hissed Sourmuddle. 'I've pretty much had enough of you. I've got a party of ravenous Witches here. We've just returned from a highly successful rescue mission, and we're in a party mood, see? And what we'd like right now is some proper food. I'm not talking eggs, mind. I'm talking cold turkey and raspberry jelly and sherry trifle and chocolate biscuits and little-sausages-on-sticks. And some of that nice fruit cake you keep in the tin on the top shelf. In fact, I'm talking a major *feast*, understand? So why don't you just toddle on into the kitchen and make a start, eh? Else I just might lose my temper and do something nasty. I'm going to count to three. One . . .'

'This is intolerable!' spluttered Mrs Molotoff. 'The House Rules clearly say No Feasts.'

'Bother the House Rules,' said Sourmuddle. 'Two.' Little sparks were beginning to fizz at her fingertips. Mrs Molotoff went pale.

'You're not allowed to do that! There's a No Magic law in Sludgehaven . . .'

'Bother the law. Three.'

She muttered briefly under her breath, twiddled her fingers and, with a blinding flash, Mrs Molotoff disappeared! Her dressing gown and slippers were still there, and a neat little pile of screwed-up papers – but she had gone.

In her place squatted a small, surprised-looking chicken. It blinked once or twice at the shocked company and gave a couple of angry clucks. Then, suddenly, its spindly legs crossed, a desperate expression came over its face and it headed for the nearest bush at a run.

'Ooooh,' gasped the Witches. 'Now you've done it, Sourmuddle! You used Magic! You turned Mrs Molotoff into a chicken!'

'That's right,' said Sourmuddle cheerfully. 'I rather think she's gone to lay an egg.'

'Hooray!' yelled the Witches. 'Good old Sourmuddle!'

'Actually,' added Sourmuddle, with a little chuckle, 'actually, girls, I've got a confession to make.'

She rummaged deep in her handbag, and brought out something that everyone instantly recognised.

'It's the larder key,' confessed Sourmuddle. 'Or, rather, a copy. I pinched the real one when old Molotoff wasn't looking and had a duplicate made. Snoop and I have been sneaking down at night and helping ourselves. We've enjoyed quite a few midnight feasts, haven't we, Snoop?'

'Well I never!' gasped the Witches, torn between disgust and admiration. 'You old dark horse, you!'

'You mean we've been going hungry all this time and you and Snoop have been busily stuffing yourselves behind our backs?' cried Ratsnappy. 'Well, if that doesn't take the cake!'

'Tee hee hee,' tittered Sourmuddle, obviously delighted with herself. 'I took the cake all right. Sneaky, aren't I? Sneaky and crafty and underhand. Which is why I'm Grandwitch and you lot are still milling about in the ranks. Am I right?'

Ruefully, the Witches nodded. She was right.

'Anyway, enough of all this chat,' cried Sourmuddle. 'Come on, girls, in we go. Someone wake Cyril up and stick him in the kitchen with an apron on. It's party time!'

CHAPTER TWENTY-EIGHT
Loose ends

Like all good holidays, the last few days flashed by at the speed of light. Most of the time was taken up with the traditional holiday pursuits of sunbathing, eating, paddling, fishing, eating, sleeping, eating and clock golf. Of course, quite a few interesting things happened too.

There was a visit from the man from the Council, who had somehow got to hear that a certain Coven of Witches had been using Magic, which of course was strictly against the law.

Sourmuddle remarked that, while of course

she saw his point, she would remind him that her girls had been mainly responsible for the total decimation of Gobboworld, for which the residents of Sludgehaven should be eternally grateful. She followed this up by asking him mildly whether he'd spent much time as a slug recently? The man from the Council saw her point too, and agreed to drop charges.

There was the highly successful Coven outing to see the rediscovered superstar Scott Sinister starring in the Summer Spektacular, which Pongwiffy and her fellow hostages sniffily refused to attend on principle. After all, as Hugo was heard to remark, 'Zere is such a sink as pride.'

There was the time when Gaga went snorkelling in her pointy hat and got mistaken for a shark, causing the entire beach to be evacuated.

There was the memorable occasion when Sharkadder visited the Hall of Mirrors for the first time and fell in a dead faint at the sight of her greatly magnified peeling nose.

There was the wonderful moment when Greymatter finally saw the light and answered One Across. *Words spoken by backward giant (3,2,2,3).* Answer: Eef If Of Muf.

Then, of course, there was the time the Brooms, bored silly with hanging around in a shed, broke out and went skinny-dipping at midnight. And the night when Sharkadder's hedgehog hair rollers got loose and ended up in Bonidle's bed. Then there was the occasion when Macabre got into a row with two Mummies about sunbeds and . . .

Well, you get the picture. Suffice it to say that the Witches had a whale of a time. Pongwiffy did too, as her many talents include a wonderful ability to bounce back. In no time at all, she got over the business with Scott Sinister and Lulu and was able to put the horrible experience of being washed by Goblins behind her. Much to her delight, her customary dirt soon began to build up. In fact, it must be said that, by the end of the celebratory feast, she was a good way towards being her old self again.

The Wizards had their moments too. Such as the one when Alf the Invisible fell over the balcony and nobody noticed. And that terrible time when the hotel ran out of greasy sausages. And Black Wednesday, when they realised they had posted their postcards without putting any stamps on and would have to do them all over again.

And what of Ronald? Well, depending on what you think of him, you will be either pleased or disappointed to hear that (at Gerald the Just's insistence) he finally got the chance to read out his paper. His four-hour-long address on the subject of pointy hats went down in Convention history as the only speech ever to empty the hall. After the first ten minutes, even the hardened Convention-goers, the ones with the briefcases and the serious beards, were begging to be allowed to go for a drink of water and were not coming back.

It won a prize, of course, and got published in an obscure Wizardly journal. And that cheered Ronald up enormously. From that moment on, he decided never to go paddling again, but to concentrate on his studies instead. Sadly, it didn't do him any good. Among his fellow Wizards, he was never taken seriously and was always referred to disparagingly as 'Ronald the Paddler' instead of Ronald the Magnificent, which is what he would have liked to be called. And to this day he hasn't got a chair. Or a locker.

But for four long hours, it did his ego a bit of good.

Mrs Molotoff remained a chicken for the duration of the holiday. When the spell wore off and she finally returned to normal, conditions improved at Ocean View. She wasn't so inclined to henpeck Cyril. She'd had enough henpecking to last her a lifetime.

Also, she found she had gone right off eggs. She wouldn't have an egg in the house. At the very mention of the word, she would give a little wince and have to go and lie down in a darkened room.

But that was later, after the Witches had left.

On the night of departure, they assembled sadly in the front garden with their Familiars, their luggage and their Brooms. They had decided to fly back to Witchway Wood – mainly because George had put his foot down and refused to drive them, but also because they fancied the idea. The weather conditions were perfect, with a big yellow moon hanging in the sky. The Brooms champed at their bits, eager to be off.

From inside Ocean View, there came the sound of a vacuum cleaner as Cyril began the big clear-up.

There was a lot of fussing about with string and rope and elastic bands as people attempted to strap metre-wide trunks on to thin pieces of stick. And

418

that was without all the extra bits and pieces they had collected! The shells, the interesting pebbles, the dried seaweed, Minnie and Manfred, the straw hats, Sourmuddle's goldfish, the sticks of rock, Gaga's oil painting, Mr Punch's nose, the towel from the bathroom, the . . . Well. You know the sort of thing.

'Are we all ready then?' said Sourmuddle. 'Did anyone remember to give a tip to Cyril? Those were pretty good breakfasts he cooked.'

'Aye,' said Macabre. 'Ah gave him a tip. Ah told him to put more salt in the porridge.'

'That's all right then. Right, everyone, this is it. End of holiday. Back to Witchway Wood and the humdrum round of cackling over cauldrons and trudging around wet fields looking for spotty toadstools in the fog.'

'And trying to buy non-existent ingredients in Malpractiss Magic Ltd,' said Sludgegooey.

'And the Friday night Coven Meetings,' Macabre reminded them. 'Don't forget them.'

'And the brews,' chipped in Bendyshanks.

'And writing seriously good poetry,' added Greymatter.

'And playing our violins,' chorused Agglebag and Bagaggle.

'And washing my hair,' supplied Scrofula.

'And sleeping in my own little bed,' yawned Bonidle.

'And watching Gaga loop the loop over a full moon,' said Ratsnappy.

'And getting made up nicely,' said Sharkadder. 'With a decent mirror.'

'And sitting down in my own little hovel in front of a nice cosy fire with a hot cup of bogwater, squabbling with Hugo and listening to the rain,' said Pongwiffy.

They all looked at each other.

'Yeah!' they shouted with one accord. 'Let's go home!'

And with wild whoops, they mounted their skittish Brooms and took off into the night sky.

From the bush in the garden came the sound of straining, followed by a plop.

Mrs Molotoff had laid another egg.

FINAL GOBLIN NEWSFLASH

A report has just come in that, somewhere high in the Misty Mountains, a Gaggle of heavily bandaged Goblins are trudging home. Many miles of hardship and suffering and torment lie before them - the usual sort of stuff, but in reverse. Storm clouds are gathering, abysses are looming, packs of wolves are closing in, Abominable Snowmen lie in wait. When they get back home they won't be able to relax, for a certain Witch will come looking for them, you can bet on it.

But all this lies before them. Right now they are in good spirits. The night is balmy. The moon is full. No one has fallen down a precipice - yet. For sustenance, they have with them a rare treat - a lovely bucketful of overripe tomatoes. And, as they keep telling each other, they did it! They have been to Gobboworld. In fact, for a few enchanted hours, they were the heroes of Gobboworld.

Oh yes. They have had their moment of glory. For the moment, anyway, they are content.